Passionate Secrets

BOOK 2 OF THE SECRETS TRILOGY

LANA WILLIAMS

Cover Design and Interior format by The Killion Group
http://thekilliongroupinc.com

DEDICATION

Mom, this one is for you.
Thank you for all of your love, support, and
those amazing bits of wisdom you've shared.
I was listening.
I love you!

CHAPTER ONE

London, June 1882

Michael Drury, Viscount Weston, had to stop himself from whistling as he entered his townhome on Park Lane. What would the neighbors say at such ungentlemanly behavior? Still, his good mood couldn't be repressed. His meeting with Adolphus Vandimer had gone swimmingly. Soon, not only would he have a significant interest in Vandimer's lucrative shipping venture, his family's country estate would be returned to its rightful ownership.

Oh—he'd nearly forgotten—he'd have a wife as well. A brilliant business arrangement all around, if he did say so himself. He ignored the tug of regret at releasing his boyhood dream of marrying for love and having a real family. Such things were best left discarded on the schoolroom floor. His parents' relationship had certainly convinced him of that.

"Good day to you, my lord." His ever efficient, if dour, butler greeted him.

"And to you, Jeffries."

"There's a young lady to see you."

"With a worthy charitable endeavor?" That had become a regular occurrence of late. Some were commendable. Most were not. While requests were normally handled by his man of business, the more passionate believers often found their way to his home. Jeffries had become adept at sorting through those who called on Michael directly. These days, there was no end to the people who came to plea for one project or another. Everyone wanted something from him now that he had money.

"She says her business is personal in nature. Her name is Miss Emma Grisby."

Michael froze, astonished at this turn of events. Emotions rolled through him, one at a time, until he was no longer certain how he felt. Never mind that the first one had been pleasure.

"Shall I send her away?" Jeffries asked. "She appears to be in rather desperate circumstances."

"I'm sure she does." Michael bit back disappointment. Not her, too. Or was she here as part of some scheme her beloved uncle had plotted...if he truly lived? "I'll see her."

He gave a grim smile and tried to tell himself he welcomed this meeting. At last he could put away his idyllic reminiscences and see her for what she'd become. Yet the idea of listening to some lie she'd concocted caused a knot to form in the pit of his stomach.

Unwelcome, memories of her as a young girl drifted through his mind, pulling at him. She'd been only fifteen or sixteen when he'd known her ten years ago. Her uncle, Professor Grisby, had lived with her family and served as a father to her and her siblings. While they'd lived modestly, they always seemed to have such fun with each other. That was something with which he had no experience.

The contrast between his last two visits had been startling. At the earlier one, her mother had been teaching her to dance.

Emma's big brown eyes had been lit with

innocent delight, her face filled with joy as her mother whirled her about the room, humming a waltz. Emma had laughed. Oh, how she'd laughed. The sound struck Michael, reverberating through him and filling him with longing. Never had he shared an experience like that with his mother or father.

Then he'd taken a turn with her. It had been a night he'd never forgotten. One that changed his view of families forever, especially his own.

The next time he'd seen her—at Professor Grisby's funeral two months later—couldn't have been more different. The devastation carved into Emma's expression had twisted his heart. All that delight snuffed out. Those brown eyes dark with the weight of her shattered world. Her family sobbing around her as she alone held a fragile shell of composure.

He'd attempted to visit them soon after, to offer his assistance though he'd had no money to give them then. But he'd been too late. They'd moved and left no forward address. Then his own life had forever changed, and he'd had no time to search further for them.

He pushed away the memories to deal with the present, bracing himself as he entered the drawing room. He'd grown weary of being disappointed by people. Distant relatives and supposed friends had come out of the woodwork since he'd rebuilt his wealth. It was now easier to expect nothing of anyone.

A drab form perched on the edge of the armchair nearest the door. Did she plan to flee if he didn't give her what she wanted? At his entrance, she bolted upright, betraying her nervousness. She was dressed in grey from head to toe, the muted color giving her a mousy appearance. Her cheeks were thin, her brown eyes difficult to see behind her spectacles. Her hair was pulled back ruthlessly into a tight chignon and, if he wasn't mistaken, held a hint of grey which matched her complexion.

Odd. He remembered her much prettier as a girl.

Before he had a chance to offer a greeting, she dipped low into a curtsy.

"My lord." The huskiness of her voice took him by surprise.

"Miss Grisby," he said. "It's been some time since we last met."

"Indeed it has. I apologize for my sudden arrival, but I've come to call in a small debt you owe my family."

Michael's hackles rose.

Of all things she could've said to him, that was the one certain to put him in a foul mood. He'd spent the past nine years paying off his family's debts, removing the line of creditors that had seemed never ending. He no longer owed anyone and intended to keep it that way.

"Well, now that we're done with the pleasantries, allow us to discuss business."

Her cheeks pinkened at his sarcastic tone. At least that brought a sign of life to her dull appearance. Despite her thin face, it seemed as though she ate well enough based on the thickness of her figure. Surprising, considering how slim she'd been in her youth.

He mentally shook himself. None of that mattered. "I confess I don't remember owing money to your family."

Her chin lifted and a spark shone in those brown eyes. "I'm not interested in your money, my lord. My uncle provided tutoring to you on several occasions without payment."

"Yes, he was one of my professors at Cambridge at the time. I believe that was part of his position." He didn't bother to keep the bite out of his tone.

She swallowed visibly and he thought he caught a glimmer of shame in her expression. Here it comes, he thought, bracing himself. The tragic story of their dire circumstances.

"Correct. However, he provided assistance to you far beyond that of a normal teacher. In exchange, we would ask you to provide a letter of reference. I am presently seeking a governess position with the Marchioness of Warkshire. It's my understanding she's a cousin of yours?"

"Indeed."

"A letter from you would go a long way toward helping me obtain the position she has available."

Michael folded his arms across his broad chest as he studied her. At times like this, he was almost grateful for his ability to read auras. The damned skill had been bestowed on him ten years ago at university when her uncle, Professor Grisby, had conducted an electromagnetic experiment that went terribly wrong. Michael and two of his friends had been injured, but her uncle had paid the ultimate price—death.

Or so they believed.

Two weeks ago, evidence had come to light suggesting that either the professor truly had survived, or someone was playing a nasty joke. But Michael wasn't about to introduce that subject. He'd wait for her to do so.

The dark glow hovering an inch or two above Emma's head and shoulders told him her intent to find a governess position would not succeed. That was all he could see—success or failure of the endeavor a person was about to embark upon.

Even if he provided her with an outstanding reference, she wouldn't obtain the position.

"Have you served as a governess before?" His curiosity over the reason for her upcoming failure demanded an answer.

"Yes. For the past eight years in fact."

He frowned as he did the math. "That would've made you—"

"Quite young when I obtained my first position." Her brow rose as though daring him to state a number aloud.

A vision of her reprimanding one of her charges for misbehaving filled his mind. She was certainly no one with whom to be trifled. Her no-nonsense attitude combined with that husky voice made her an authority figure.

"Why not obtain a letter of reference from your previous employer?" he asked, unable to let it go.

"I have letters from several of my previous employers."

The odd way she phrased it gave him pause. "And the most recent one?"

Her lips tightened as pink flooded her pale complexion again—something he was starting to look forward to. "That was not an option."

He waited to see if she'd explain.

With a deep breath, she added, "I left under less than ideal circumstances."

The evasive answer only left him more curious. "Who was your previous—"

"Will you make good on your debt or not?" Again, those brown eyes flashed.

Ire pulsed through him. "Do *not* use that word. We both know there is no debt. I don't appreciate you implying otherwise."

She opened her mouth to protest but he held up his hand to stop her. "However, I am willing to provide you with a letter of reference."

Her eyes closed for the briefest moment, and she tipped her chin down as though saying a quick prayer. He could see her brows arched nicely now that the frame of her glasses was out of the way. Ridiculously long dark lashes closed over her eyes. Her slim nose tipped up the tiniest bit at the end.

He'd forgotten that about her.

Those eyes opened and held his gaze for the space of a heartbeat. If he didn't know better, he would've sworn memories of better times danced through her mind as well. "Thank you."

The simple statement of gratitude made him feel petty for considering denying her request. But there were other matters of concern here. He mustn't forget that.

He needed to know if the little evidence he'd seen was true and her uncle still lived, if she'd been in contact with him. Michael had no intention of allowing Emma to disappear again without gaining some answers. Not after events of late.

He moved to his desk and, with as much casualness as he could muster, asked, "How is your family?"

Her pleasure at his agreement to write the letter fell away.

"Fine. Thank you."

He studied her a long moment, wondering what the truth of the matter was. "Your mother is well?"

"Yes."

As he withdrew a sheet of paper from his desk drawer, he continued, "Your sister and brother?"

Emma bit back the bitterness that stole her breath. The poor health of her younger sister was what had driven her here under false pretenses to collect a nonexistent debt. Yet what else could she do?

She'd lost her governess position due to her employer's wandering hands. Tessa's illness had worsened. They owed the doctor money but needed to pay rent. She had no choice. "Forgive me for being rude, but we both know you don't care so I won't bother answering."

He frowned and she leveled him a look that

dared him to disagree.

As he opened his mouth—whether to protest or agree—she found she couldn't bear to hear either. "If you have a need to make polite conversation, allow us to discuss the weather instead. June has been quite pleasant, wouldn't you agree?"

She glanced down to check the cuff of her sleeve, hoping the patch wasn't showing. She well knew she didn't look the part of a successful governess but every penny she earned went to the doctor or medicine.

Her fingers bore traces of white ash and she realized she must've touched her face or hair. She could only hope her disguise was still in place. Long ago, she'd learned beauty was not an asset when applying for governess positions and she hid hers with as many tricks as she could.

Michael—rather Viscount Weston—hadn't bothered to reply to her comment about the weather. She could no longer think of him as Michael. That was something that belonged in the past along with the fleeting friendship she'd mistakenly thought they shared.

As he bent his head to scrawl on the paper, she studied him. Age had only increased his attractiveness, adding strength to his appearance. His hair was black as a raven's wing, his eyes as blue as the morning sky. The strength of his jaw balanced with high cheekbones and a narrow nose with just a hint of a bump near the bridge.

She bit her lip as she reminded herself it didn't matter. Viscount Weston had cut off their association immediately after her uncle's death. Therefore she had to conclude he had no interest in her or her family, and that meant she had no interest in him.

Still, she couldn't help but watch him while she had the chance. He'd certainly looked her over thoroughly. The way he'd studied not just her face but all around her head and shoulders had been disconcerting, as though he was trying to discover her very essence. For a long moment, she'd held her breath, worried that he would see beneath her disguise.

Sometimes, in the dark of the night, in her cold bed, she permitted herself to remember the evening she'd danced with him. Her heart still fluttered at the memory. She couldn't allow herself to think on it too often, else a deep longing coursed through her for things that could never be, filling her with melancholy.

She continued to watch him, determined to memorize every detail of his appearance so she could retrieve it later. A stab of regret filled her at the suspicious way he'd greeted her, as though he'd known she'd wanted something from him. She straightened, reminding herself that asking for a letter of reference was of little consequence. It took only a few moments of his time, nothing more. By the look of his elegant home, he could afford much more than that.

Desperate times had forced her to take drastic action. As far as she was concerned, being unemployed with an ill sister and near-to starving family excused her forward behavior. But she had no intention of sharing that with him.

After her uncle's funeral, he'd never bothered to speak with them. She'd wondered if he felt guilt for her uncle's death and that was why he'd severed communication with her family.

Whatever the cause for his behavior, it had hurt.

Deeply.

He sealed the letter, then rose and walked over to her. "I fear it will do no good, but here it is."

"What do you mean?"

His expression froze. "Only that I have little sway with my cousin." He held out the letter to her.

As she reached for it, their fingers brushed. She paused at the unexpected contact before reminding herself that his touch meant nothing.

"Thank you. I truly appreciate it." At last she met his gaze, only to find him looking all about her again. "Why do you do that?"

"Do what?" He looked nonplussed at her question.

She stopped herself mid-air from touching her hair, not wanting more ash to come off. "Never mind. It doesn't matter."

And it didn't. She wouldn't see him again. The despair the thought caused had to go away along with the lump in her throat. Anger was much easier.

"I'll bid you good day." She curtsied and turned away, not daring to look at him.

"You've nothing more to say?"

She swung back, confused at his words. "I said thank you."

His eyes narrowed as a scowl twisted his lips. The expression was one she'd seen many times when her uncle had tried to explain some complicated concept on the occasions when Michael had visited their home. The memory nearly made her smile.

But not quite.

"What else would you have me say?" she asked.

"There's no news you'd like to mention?"

Heat crept up her cheeks at the idea of not being completely honest. Had he somehow heard of Tessa's illness? "No."

It was the truth after all. She didn't have news that she *wanted* to tell him.

When he only continued to stare at her, she added, "I must be going. Thank you again."

"Might I have my carriage take you to your destination?"

Pride once more reared its head despite the long walk ahead of her. "No, thank you."

"I insist."

"No, thank you," she said with more firmness then hurried to the door, anxious to escape, unable to remain in his company any longer without asking why.

Why had he abandoned them upon her uncle's death?

After all, she reminded herself, it didn't matter any longer.

Michael watched Emma go, torn between forcing her to accept a ride and allowing her to leave on her own, which was what she so obviously wanted.

"Jeffries?" he called when he heard the front door close.

"Yes, my lord?"

"Please have Miss Grisby followed. Discreetly, of course. I must know her address."

Jeffries nodded, quite used to receiving such odd requests, and hurried away to fetch a footman for the task.

Unsettled at the strange turn of events, he went to his study only to stare out the window, wondering where Emma was going and who awaited her there. Could it be her uncle?

Emma clenched her lips tight, determined not to cry as she began the walk home. She'd gotten what she wanted—what she needed. She had no reason to be upset.

But seeing Michael—rather, Viscount Weston, she reminded herself—again had stirred more memories, more longing than she'd expected. She drew a deep breath. By now she should be used to wanting what she couldn't have, what would never be. What she needed to do was focus on the task at hand.

Tomorrow she had an appointment to see the Marchioness of Warkshire, the viscount's cousin. With luck and the reference letter she held, the marchioness would hire her to teach her three young children. Emma's wages would be substantial enough to obtain the medical care Tessa so desperately needed.

Her sister's image formed in her mind and helped to settle her emotions. Tessa's pale, thin face and weak smile as she lay in bed made Emma's heart squeeze. She shook her head.

That picture would never do.

Instead, Emma pictured her healthy and whole, no longer ravaged by the disease that had stolen her youth the last two years. The doctor said the best hope to treat her consumption was a sanatorium where she could have plenty of rest, fresh air, and a nutritious diet. At the moment, they could provide her with none of that.

The long walk gave her the time she needed to calm down, to regain her equilibrium before seeing her family. Tessa seemed especially sensitive to people's moods and would notice Emma's distress immediately. Emma straightened her shoulders and forced her lips to curve into the semblance of a smile.

The neat street of Park Lane gave way to Knightsbridge, then to the busier area of Piccadilly. Each neighborhood seemed to have its own personality. Her stomach grumbled as the scent of freshly baked bread drifted from a bakery but she hurried past. She briefly paused before the window of a department store, scanning the clever displays so she could describe them in detail to her sister.

Out of the corner of her eye, she caught sight of a young man watching her. She turned to face him, but he walked away without looking back. Ignoring the sensation, she continued on her way, keeping a watchful eye on the clouds. With luck she'd arrive home dry and in time for a cup of tea.

Though the loss of her position had come at a terrible time, she appreciated the opportunity to spend more time with her family. Being away so much made her thankful for every moment they spent together, made more precious by Tessa's illness.

Shuddering, she pushed away the unpleasant memories of her previous employer's wandering hands. His wife wouldn't have allowed her to remain even if Emma had wanted to, not after catching her husband acting so inappropriately.

She turned her focus to the present, hoping she'd start her new position with the marchioness in three days.

At last she arrived at their small flat on Trenary Lane. She climbed the two flights of stairs and retrieved her key from her pocket to let herself in.

"Miss Grisby?"

Emma turned to see their neighbor from down the hall approaching and gave an internal sigh. The woman's rounded shoulders were draped in a faded yellow shawl, her expression grim.

"Mrs. Dobbs. How are you today?" Emma forced a smile.

"Better than you, I'd guess. Trouble is brewing." The stout old woman shook her head, loosening coarse gray strands from her chignon. She claimed to have some gypsy ancestors, and Emma thought it probably true with her dark eyes and hawkish nose. However, Emma didn't care for the way the woman tossed about fortunes whether asked or not.

"Oh? You might have something wrong today, Mrs. Dobbs. All is well." She tried to stave off whatever dour premonition the woman wanted to share with her. She already had a difficult enough time hiding her worry from her family.

"I fear it won't be for long. Tomorrow will bring misfortune."

Emma's heart sank. "Well, I'll have to hope for the best, won't I?" Of all the things the woman could've said, why had she chosen those particular words? "I must be going. Take care, Mrs. Dobbs."

Anxious to escape before the woman told her anything more, she unlocked the door of their flat.

"Hello," she said as she smiled at her mother, hoping she hadn't overheard Mrs. Dobbs.

"Welcome back, dear." Her mother sat in the small sitting room area. The window behind her sparkled, the clean panes cast a warm glow over her. The sight brought a genuine smile to Emma for the first time since she'd left that morning.

Jane Grisby had a perpetual positive attitude that surrounded a core of strength Emma could only hope to emulate. Her mother's determination had seen her family through hard times, including the death of her husband, then his brother. How could Emma possibly complain about her lot in life when compared to her mother's?

Emma's memories of her father had faded over the years. He'd never been around much and had died when she was thirteen. Uncle Grisby had moved in soon after and had been a huge influence in her life. She owed much of her knowledge and skills to him. He'd taken the time to teach her things most boys her age didn't know, let alone girls. Despite these modern times, most men felt educating girls, who spent their lives caring for a home and family, was a waste of time and money.

Not Uncle Grisby. He'd told her that since women were the center of the family, they needed to be educated. She'd never have guessed she'd make a living by teaching others the things he'd taught her. To this day, she was grateful for his foresight. Without her ability to serve as governess, they might very well be living in a workhouse.

"How did things go? Did the viscount remember you? He was such a nice young man." Her mother's nimble fingers continued stitching the hem of a shirt as she spoke. Her skill with a needle was wasted on mending, but it helped earn some money and allowed her to stay home and tend Tessa.

"Yes," Emma answered. "I was able to obtain the reference letter." She withdrew it from her pocket and waved it in the air, forcing a smile. "With luck, I'll have a new position by this time tomorrow."

"Excellent." Her brown eyes, so like Emma's, were warm and friendly. Though just past fifty, her face was lined, an outward indication of the internal worry she rarely revealed.

Emma had only told her the basics of why she'd lost her previous post, not all of it. The last thing her mother needed was another reason to worry. Emma wanted her to save all her energy for Tessa.

Remembering the details of that night made Emma nauseous—and impossible to share with her mother. The reek of brandy on the lord's breath. The feel of his absurdly soft hands groping her body. The unexpected strength of him. The terror that had nearly frozen her in place.

She shook her head, determined to push away the memory. Besides nothing had happened, thanks to his wife. In reality, Emma would've quit if she hadn't lost her position. She couldn't have stayed at their home when she didn't feel safe. She didn't miss the lord or the lady or their constant bickering but did miss the two children she'd taught.

"Please wash off that awful ash, dear," her mother requested with a frown. Though she understood the reason Emma wore her disguise, she didn't like it and frequently mentioned it. "Then we'll have tea with Tessa and Patrick."

"Where is Patrick?"

"Running an errand for someone, but he promised to be back."

"He's had many errands of late." She couldn't help but be suspicious. Young boys often found trouble, and while she loved her brother dearly, she wasn't naive enough to believe his behavior was perfect.

"A friend introduced him to someone who hires boys for a variety of tasks, including errands. He pays well enough and Patrick seems to enjoy the work."

Emma merely nodded, determined to speak with him when she had the chance. Since her little brother had no man in his life, she tried to keep extra watch over him when she was home. Yet she was there so infrequently that she wasn't sure how much good it did.

The small flat they rented made Emma feel stifled. No wonder Patrick escaped as often as he could. It consisted of two rooms with one serving as a kitchen and sitting room and the other as a bedroom. Tessa slept in the bed and their mother slept on a cot beside her. Patrick slept on the floor of the sitting room. When Emma was here, she joined Patrick on the floor.

Her mother kept the flat tidy. Curtains hung from the windows, helping to give a cozy feel. The small space always smelled clean despite the unpleasant odors that lingered in the hall. Coal dust seeped into every nook and cranny, but her mother battled it each day. Rugs were beat and all possible surfaces wiped down.

Emma washed her face and hands and dabbed most of the ash from her hair before putting on the kettle for tea. She went to the bedroom to check on Tessa. Her sister slept on her side, her pale, thin face looking ill even in sleep. She'd lost so much weight and her frame hardly left an impression under the cover. As Emma watched, she coughed, her body convulsing with the effort.

Emma's chest tightened. She wished things were different—that they had decent food to fill their bellies and give them strength, that they had medicine to help heal Tessa and ease her symptoms, and that the doctor bills were paid so they could send for him without the shame and guilt of knowing they owed him money. The man had his own family to feed.

Shoving her worry aside, she changed her gown, anxious to be rid of the ugly, patched grey one she wore and even more eager to be free of the bindings around her middle. She untied the knot at her side which held the strip of cloth that served to flatten her breasts and thicken her middle.

Left in her chemise, she rubbed her stomach, all too aware of the red marks that crisscrossed her body. She drew a deep breath, relieved to be free of the band. It was silly as the bindings were no worse than a corset, but somehow the restriction bound her very spirit. With a shake of her head, she admonished herself. The bindings had protected her, slowing the lord who'd tried to accost her. She had the freedom and the strength to rise each day, to venture into the world whereas Tessa was trapped—bound to the bed by the illness that had claimed her body.

Emma closed her eyes, praying for a miracle.

Praying for her sister to be whole and healthy, for her family to be in a warm, cozy home where once again, they could share laughter and fun and food.

With a sigh, she opened her eyes and reached for her other gown. Though her faith was strong, she had a difficult time understanding why her prayers went unanswered. God helped those who helped themselves, but she didn't see what more she could do.

As Emma finished fastening her gown, Tessa coughed, waking as the spasm wracked her slim body. Emma sat on the edge of the bed and lifted a cup of water to her sister. Tessa coughed again, covering her mouth with her hand. She reached for a handkerchief from the bedside table and wiped her mouth.

Emma stared at the crimson stain on the cloth in dismay. "You're bleeding," she whispered to her sister.

Tessa's eyes went wide as she looked down at the handkerchief. "Oh, dear."

"I'll send for the doctor."

"No!" Tessa grabbed Emma's arm. "No. I'm fine. I just need a sip of water."

"Tessa, I'm sending for Dr. Barnes," Emma insisted as she handed Tessa the water. "You're getting worse, not better."

"We'll wait until tomorrow. After you obtain the new position. Then we can send for him."

"Tessa—"

"No, Emma. You know we can't afford it. I'm not taking away our supper by calling the doctor. Some of mother's nice hot soup will do more good than anything Dr. Barnes would give me."

Emma   nodded   reluctantly,   even   more

determined to gain the position and the money
that came with it.

CHAPTER TWO

Emma sat on the edge of the ornate chair in the formal drawing room as the Marchioness of Warkshire reviewed her letter of application and references. Emma made certain her posture was perfect. Her hands were folded neatly on her lap, her feet tucked under her chair, and a calm and composed expression was on her face. These were the very qualities she'd be expected to teach the Marchioness's three young daughters, to act as a lady at all times.

On the inside, matters were quite the opposite—her heart pounded rapidly, her palms were sweating, and she had to remind herself to breathe. It was all she could do not to go down on her knees and beg for the position. Her entire family's livelihood depended on this interview, but she knew sounding desperate would not help.

The marchioness was striking, her dark hair drawn back in an artful chignon, her alabaster skin flawless, her elaborate gown the color of the Caribbean Sea. At least what Emma guessed it to be from a painting she'd seen.

Emma's insecurities surfaced, making her feel undeserving of sharing a room with the marchioness let alone speaking with the beautiful lady or her children.

With a stern reprimand to her doubts, she reminded herself that she had all the necessary qualifications and then some. She could play the piano, draw adequately, speak French and a smattering of Italian, conjugate Latin, and was skilled in geography, arithmetic, and knowledgeable about a variety of literature. All thanks to her deceased uncle. The education he'd given her was priceless and made her an excellent governess, as she'd been told on numerous occasions.

It was only the part where she had to take orders from parents who knew nothing of how to teach young children with which she had problems. Well, that, along with any lord who thought an unattached woman living in his home was fair game.

"You mentioned you had another letter of reference?" The marchioness raised a delicate brow with her inquiry.

"Yes, from Viscount Weston."

The lady frowned and managed to look even more beautiful. "My cousin? How are you acquainted with him?"

"My uncle was his professor at Cambridge." Emma had rehearsed her answer, hoping it implied she came from a long line of educators. She handed over the envelope.

"I see." The marchioness broke the seal and withdrew the letter. "Hmm," she said as she read it, then folded it and tucked it back in the envelope.

Emma wondered what that meant. Perhaps she should've read the letter. Surely the viscount hadn't written anything that would strike against her.

"We received letters of application from several qualified candidates," the marchioness said, avoiding eye contact.

Emma's heart sank.

"I wanted to meet each of them personally before deciding which governess would best suit our family. The education of my children is of the utmost importance to me."

"Of course," Emma agreed, trying to quell her panic.

"I'm afraid I've decided on one of the other candidates. I hope you understand." The marchioness offered a small smile with the devastating news.

"May I ask why?" Emma knew her question was impolite, but she had to know.

The lady appeared affronted at Emma's inquiry. "I don't owe an explanation to you, Miss Grisby. However, I will tell you the other candidate is well qualified and her letters of reference were outstanding."

Emma could hardly believe it. Obviously, whatever Viscount Weston had written had been less than flattering. She caught herself from saying anything further. No purpose could be served from angering the marchioness. The person who deserved Emma's wrath was the viscount and she intended to give him a piece of her mind.

Michael drummed his fingers on his desk, impatient with himself. His lack of concentration today was ridiculous not to mention annoying. The financial report before him on his latest venture in a Latin American railroad required his complete attention but, instead, he picked up a small piece of paper that held a single line of information.

102 Trenary Lane

Surely the only reason it captured his interest was because Miss Grisby might provide him with clues regarding her possibly resurrected uncle. Michael thought it too much of a coincidence that she'd contacted him now, so soon after he'd become suspicious about whether her uncle had truly been killed in the accident.

Michael didn't believe in coincidences.

He'd tried to determine what ulterior motive Miss Grisby might have to seek him out. But she'd asked only for the letter of reference. She'd made no other comments, no other inquiries. Nor had she asked for money—something everyone else did, strangers and acquaintances alike. Despite that, he still felt her visit had to be tied to recent events. He withdrew the list he'd started of recent events, adding a new one: *Emma involved?*

Michael wished he'd made more of an effort to find Miss Grisby and her family after the funeral ten years ago. At the time, he, Stephen, and Lucas had still been recovering from their own injuries and grappling with their newfound aura-reading abilities. When he'd attempted to visit the Grisby's home a week later, they'd already moved. The neighbors didn't know where they'd gone. In a city the size of London, it was difficult to find anyone.

He'd tried Cambridge as well, but the only thing they'd reluctantly revealed was that the Senate had decided to pay the professor's pension to his heirs according to his wishes. Knowing Miss Grisby and her family would be taken care of had given Michael some peace. With careful management, the pension should've lasted them for quite some time. Obviously, those funds were gone now if she was serving as a governess. Or perhaps she felt a calling for the work.

He'd intended to continue his search for her family, but within days, his mother and father had been killed. His life had been turned upside down in the aftermath, and he'd had no time to worry about anyone else's family.

He shook his head. He had no desire to relive those terrible days when grief and guilt had warred within him all while he'd been adjusting to the lasting effects of the accident. When he'd had to endure the gossip surrounding the events of his parents' deaths at their country estate. When he'd realized how deeply in debt his father had cast them. When the creditors had come calling before the funeral had been held.

With a deep breath, he shook off the dark memories to focus on the issue. Evidence had begun to surface three weeks past indicating Professor Grisby hadn't died in the electromagnetic lab experiment ten years ago at Cambridge. This, despite the fact that Michael and his two friends had seen the professor's terribly damaged body, attended his funeral and grieved for his loss along with his family—Miss Grisby included.

The clues had started when one of those friends, Stephen Davenport, Viscount Ashbury, had been attempting to protect the woman who was now his fiancé, Abigail Bradford, from the man who'd murdered her father.

That man, Vincent Simmons, had attempted to force Abigail to give him a lunar meteorite which had belonged to her father—a stone said to enhance the conduction of electromagnetism. Professor Grisby had been searching for that very stone before his death.

Then Simmons had captured Abigail and her sisters in an attempt to obtain the meteorite. Michael and Ashbury had succeeded in freeing them and detaining Simmons who they'd turned over to the police. While they were sorting it all out, they'd received a note addressed to 'Michael,

Stephen and Lucas' that appeared to be from Professor Grisby.

It seemed impossible that the professor could be alive, that Simmons could somehow be working for him, but evidence was mounting. Unfortunately, Simmons, who now resided in prison, wasn't speaking.

In the midst of all this, Ashbury had discovered an article in the paper about a reclusive scientist who claimed to be conducting experiments similar to what Professor Grisby had done. When all the pieces of information were gathered together, it seemed an odd twist of fate—one that Michael could not overlook.

On top of all that came the visit from Emma. Surely the purpose of her visit hadn't been merely for a reference letter. She had to know or want something. Perhaps a consultation with Ashbury on this matter would shed some light.

Being reunited with Ashbury these past few weeks had made Michael realize how much he'd missed his friend. The accident had caused a rift between them that was difficult to explain. Michael knew he was to blame. Between his injuries, the strange phenomena of aura reading, and the awful death of his parents, his world had been turned upside down. He'd placed the fault on everyone else, refusing to accept the part he'd played in the accident.

As the amount of debt his father had accumulated came to light, Michael had been devastated. It had taken him nine long years to rebuild his life. He hadn't made any effort to form friendships, only business associates and casual acquaintances. Keeping his distance from Ashbury had made it easier to pretend he was still normal, unburdened by the ability to see auras.

When his old friend had re-entered his life, he'd realized how stupid that had been.

Michael couldn't help but smile at the thought of Ashbury and Abigail, who were now planning a wedding. The two were perfect for each other. Her lightness countered Ashbury's darkness, and they made each other whole. While on the surface, their match was a good arrangement, they had much more than that. Their obvious love for each other made him reconsider his reason for marrying—but no—he knew he carried the same destructive seeds his father had, making marrying for love impossible.

Ashbury had been the farthest from the blast the night of the experiment. He saw auras of good and evil, which had nearly driven him crazed. Michael's ability to read success and failure was bad enough, but to know someone intended to do harm of some sort made Ashbury determined to do whatever he could to stop them. No wonder he suffered from severe headaches and melancholy. Lucky for him, Abigail had come along, for she had truly saved him.

Lucas remained in Brazil where he'd fled as soon as his injuries had healed. As he was the 'spare' heir, his presence in England wasn't required. They'd heard nothing from him since his departure.

Angry voices coming from the foyer interrupted his musings. He rose from his desk to find out what the devil was going on.

"Either open the door or move aside."

The feminine tone puzzled him. He couldn't envision his fiancé, Catherine, speaking in such a manner.

"I'm sorry, miss. The viscount is not receiving." Jeffries sounded equally determined to stop the visitor.

"He'll see me. Have no doubt," the angry voice insisted.

The door flew open to reveal a disheveled Miss

Grisby. She glared at him, one hand still on the doorknob. Jeffries stood directly behind her, eyebrows raised, waiting to see if he should bodily remove her.

Michael eyed her appearance, taking in her crooked hat to the same grey gown as the previous day to the strands of hair dangling along her flushed face. Even her spectacles sat askew. Had she run all the way here?

"You are a scoundrel of the worst sort," she proclaimed as she adjusted her spectacles.

"Normally, it takes ladies much longer to realize that." He nodded to Jeffries and the butler backed away and closed the door.

The heated glare she sent him would've reduced a lesser man to ashes. "How dare you provide a letter of reference that would prevent me from obtaining the position with your cousin."

"Whatever are you speaking about?"

She folded her arms over her middle, disapproval in every line of her rigid stance. "I've just come from my interview and things were going well."

"I'm pleased to hear that."

"Until she read your letter."

Puzzled, he could only frown at her. "I assure you, there was nothing in the letter that could've caused her to change her mind."

Her eyes narrowed. "I don't believe you. You told me when you handed it to me that you thought it would do no good."

He hesitated, remembering her dim aura and his certainty that she wouldn't win the post.

"Only because she holds little regard for me." He latched on to the explanation with relief. At her obvious disbelief, he explained further. "I fear I teased her relentlessly when we were young. She's never forgiven me for it."

When she continued to glare at him, he added,

"My letter described you in the highest regard. I promise."

Miss Grisby seemed to deflate at his words. Her shoulders slumped as she dropped his gaze. The fiery woman before him returned to a grey mouse. Though he didn't care to be the target of her ire, he preferred her anger to this. Surely those weren't tears glistening in her eyes.

Her silence made him even more uncomfortable. "I'm sorry you didn't receive the position. Did she say why?"

She shook her head.

"Should I ask her?" He could see how important the post was to her and felt responsible. "Perhaps I could speak with her in person," he found himself offering, much to his dismay.

"No." Miss Grisby shook her head. "Never mind. I'm just...disappointed." She met his gaze, her chin held high. "My apologies for barging in on you. Thank you again for the letter." She bobbed a curtsy and turned to go.

"Do you have other...prospects?" Despite his suspicion of her, he couldn't allow her to leave like this. Not when she was so obviously distraught. Not when memories of better days floated in the back of his mind.

She turned back reluctantly. "Not yet. I'm certain I'll be able to find something soon."

He might've believed her if she'd said it with more confidence. Apparently she had no additional openings to apply for as her aura showed him nothing. He could only see auras when a person had an immediate intent.

"This position was very important to you, wasn't it?"

She sighed and gave a small shake of her head, making him feel as if she thought he couldn't possibly understand what it had meant to her. "It was a promising opportunity with generous compensation."

Michael hesitated, considering the meager information he'd been provided along with her address. Based on the location of her family's flat, it seemed they were in dire need of income. The neighborhood was rough, many of the residents one step away from a workhouse.

"If it's money you need—"

Her pale cheeks flushed as the spark returned to her eyes. "I did not come here to beg for money."

He held up his hand, amazed at her prickliness. "I'm well aware of that. You came here to call in a nonexistent debt." He couldn't help but remind her of the small deceit.

Her gaze dropped at his rebuke. "I only—"

"May I make some inquiries to see if any of my acquaintances are in need of a governess?" This was the perfect excuse for him to keep an eye on her and contact her again. He told himself he needed to remain in touch for no other reason than to see exactly what she and her uncle were up to.

"That is kind of you. Thank you." Her expression held little hope that he'd come through with his offer.

Had so many let her down that she no longer took people at their word? It seemed he'd struck upon one thing they had in common.

"I'm sorry to have bothered you," she said.

For one brief moment, those large brown eyes looked up at him, holding him with their intensity. Everything else fell away as he held her gaze. His breath caught as awareness sizzled through him like an electric current.

Her lips parted as she gave a tiny gasp before dropping his gaze, the glare of spectacles preventing him from seeing her eyes. "I must be on my way," she mumbled and spun away.

"Wait!" He had the strangest urge to keep her

with him, to see where that sizzle might lead.

She paused in the doorway but didn't look at him. "Yes?"

He gave himself a mental shake. What on earth was wrong with him? He was allowing memories of better times to affect his thinking. She might be concocting some scheme with her uncle at this very moment.

"How will I reach you if I find a suitable position?" he asked, wondering if she'd tell him the truth.

Still, she didn't look at him. "I'll leave my address with your butler." Then she closed the door behind her.

He stood there until he heard the front door shut then walked to the window where he watched her hurry away as though hounds snapped at her heels.

Surely it was only simple curiosity that caught his interest.

Emma stabbed at the broadcloth with her needle, wishing she had a better outlet for her frustration.

"Dear, perhaps you should allow me to finish that." Her mother's soft words made her feel even worse.

She closed her eyes, attempting to calm her roiling emotions. What she really wanted to do was throw herself on her bed and have a good cry. But with no bed to call her own, she couldn't even have that small indulgence. Instead, she sat in the meager light of the window, trying to assist her mother with the pile of mending she'd taken in. Every pence they gained was precious right now.

"I'm sorry. I suppose I'm more disappointed

that I didn't obtain the position than I realized," she murmured. Swallowing the lump in her throat, she ripped out the uneven stitches in the seam of the jacket determined to try again.

"Well, of course you are," her mother said in a no-nonsense voice. "Who wouldn't be? The trick is to cast your thoughts toward your next endeavor."

Emma knew she treaded a fine line between being truthful to both herself and her family about their situation and hopeful that everything would work out. She studied her mother's calm countenance. Did she know Tessa was coughing up blood? Emma knew Tessa would make every effort to hide it from their mother. Even as she opened her mouth to ask, a soft moan from the bedroom caught her attention.

Her mother's worried gaze slid to hers. Emma ventured to guess that at the very least, she knew Tessa's condition was worsening.

Emma set aside her mending and rushed into the bedroom. "Tessa?"

Her sister lay on her side and opened weary eyes to look at her. Her breathing sounded raspy, her face pale.

"Is it bad?" she whispered. But Emma saw Tessa's answer in her frightened eyes.

Tessa didn't respond. Her attention seemed completely taken by drawing her next breath.

Emma swallowed hard. She ran her hand along Tessa's brow, wishing she could take this burden from her, that she was the one ill.

"I'm fetching the doctor, Tess," she told her and pressed a kiss upon her cheek.

Tessa shook her head, but Emma hushed her. "It will be fine."

Emma would convince him to come, no matter the cost.

Michael paused in the doorway of the drawing room at Ashbury's home on Park Lane, a short carriage ride from his own residence. He studied the flushed faces of its two occupants with amusement. "If I didn't know better, I'd think you were dallying."

Ashbury's slow grin was all the confirmation he needed.

Abigail shook her head at her fiancé's smile. "How are you, Weston?"

"Not as well as you, I'd venture to guess." He couldn't help but tease her. She made it far too easy. Her embarrassed smile was his reward.

"What brings you here?" Ashbury asked.

"You'll never guess who paid me a visit."

Ashbury arched a brow. "If I'll never guess then I suppose you must tell me."

"Emma Grisby."

Shock froze Ashbury for a moment followed quickly by anger. "What did she say? That her uncle is alive and well? That he fooled us all?"

"Nothing of the sort." Michael sat in the chair opposite them. "She requested a reference letter as she was interviewing for a governess post with my cousin."

"Oh, please." Ashbury rose to pace the room. "Surely you didn't believe that flimsy excuse?"

"Not at first—"

Ashbury spun to face him, his green eyes accusatory. "You helped her?"

"Yes. I paid a visit to my cousin and learned that Miss Grisby truly did interview for the position. However, my cousin had another applicant who'd served as governess for an earl, so she chose her over Miss Grisby."

"We need to speak with her. No, we'll follow

her until we find out—"

Michael held up his hand to stave the tide of Ashbury's plan. "I'm having her followed. I have her address."

"Who is she?" Abigail asked curiously.

Ashbury returned to his seat. "Professor Grisby's niece. It's a shame to think he's using her."

"We don't yet know that," Michael argued. Why he felt the need to defend her eluded him. Hadn't he had the same suspicions?

The bland look Ashbury gave him made him feel as though he'd been taken in by her. Perhaps he had. At the very least, he had to admit she'd caught his sympathies.

"So you have a plan to keep her under watch?" Ashbury asked.

"Not exactly. I have one of the runners following her."

As part of his effort to prevent harm coming from those he saw with criminal intentions, Ashbury employed people to assist him in gathering information, running errands or even following someone. Their nondescript attire and knowledge of the seedier parts of London often came in handy. Michael had joined him in his efforts. Few people noticed a street urchin lingering about, including Miss Grisby.

"How does she seem?" Ashbury asked.

"Rather desperate to be honest. I'm still trying to determine what's going on, but their flat is in one of the poorest areas. Her clothing had been mended several times over." He shook his head as he pictured the mended cuff she'd continually tried to hide. "It seems she genuinely needs a position of some sort. I told her I'd ask my acquaintances if they knew of anything."

Ashbury's eyes narrowed. "You *have* been taken in by her. You always had a soft spot for her."

Michael scoffed even as a vision of a younger, happier Emma danced through his mind. "I hardly think trying to help her find a position means I've been duped."

"If she's so desperate for funds, a governess post won't fulfill her needs," Abigail added.

Ashbury turned to his fiancé. "Few other options are available to her. Other than making a good match." Ashbury turned to Michael. "That's it!"

Abigail blinked, obviously as confused as Michael. "What is?"

"She needs to find a husband. And, if Weston assisted her in finding one, he'd have an excuse to stay near her."

"Have you gone mad?" Michael asked.

"We've already discussed that possibility, remember?"

Michael shook his head, exasperated with his friend. "Might I remind you that I'm engaged?"

"I'm still not certain you're making a wise decision, but what does that have to do with anything?"

Michael chose to ignore Ashbury's comment. "I can hardly escort Miss Grisby about while planning my own wedding. My fiancé will not approve."

"But it's the perfect solution." Ashbury's excitement at the idea set Michael's teeth on edge.

"Stephen's suggestion does have merit," Abigail suggested.

Ashbury smiled at his fiancé, obviously pleased she'd taken his side. "This will work brilliantly. You can launch her into society. Give her a season. Help her find a husband. And the entire time, she'll be right under your nose."

"I couldn't possibly do all that." The idea of spending so much time with her made his mouth go dry as he remembered that sizzle. Not to mention that Catherine would be less than pleased by such an arrangement.

"You *can* with your grandmother's assistance," Ashbury insisted.

Michael's mind searched for an excuse to stem Ashbury's enthusiasm. "You haven't seen Miss Grisby of late. I don't know that she'd attract a husband."

"Oh, please." Ashbury waved his hand in the air. "Your grandmother can transform her into an adequate catch. Sweeten the deal with a small dowry."

Michael sputtered as he remembered Miss Grisby's reaction to him offering her money. He couldn't imagine proposing this crazed plan to her. "I hardly think—"

"You have more money than you know what to do with. This is the perfect arrangement. Admit it." Ashbury slapped him on the back. "Miss Grisby will gain the financial stability she needs, and we'll be able to watch her every move. It solves everyone's problems."

"Except for mine," Michael muttered. Reluctance filled him at the thought of spending so much time with Emma. That was certainly not part of the plan he'd set for his well-ordered life.

"Please, Dr. Barnes," Emma pleaded from the doctor's front step. "She's coughing up blood. I don't know what to do." She tried to keep her tears at bay, but her worry for Tessa was overwhelming.

The tall, grey-haired man rubbed his forehead from the doorway of his modest red brick home on Villiers Street. "Miss Grisby, you haven't paid your account for nearly six months. I can't help you anymore."

"I know and I'm terribly sorry for the delay in your payment. I'm searching for a position and expect to find something very soon." Emma hoped her tone sounded positive rather than desperate.

"You couldn't pay me properly when you did have a position." He shook his head. "I'm sorry. But I have to care for my family too."

Dr. Barnes had been their physician for as long as she could remember. His shoulders were stooped, whether from age or the burden of trying to help families like hers, she couldn't say. He'd been her rock through Tessa's illness, and she didn't know what she'd do without him. The idea of him not helping them anymore wasn't acceptable.

"Perhaps we could find some sort of trade. Does your wife need assistance cleaning your home? Is there mending we could do? We'd be pleased to do anything you need." She dug her nails into her palm, hoping against hope he'd agree. "Mother is an excellent cook."

His tired blue eyes looked at her as though he didn't know what to do with her. "Do you imagine that other families haven't offered the same thing? That our house isn't full of things we don't want or need from people unable to make good on their account?"

Emma's heart sank. She bit her lip to keep her tears at bay. "Is there anything you could simply tell me to do? Something to help her cough at least?"

He stared across the street as though pondering her question. "How long has she been coughing up the blood?"

"It started yesterday."

"You do realize it's common for the symptoms of consumption to grow progressively worse."

"No! No, it's not worsening." Emma refused to consider that possibility. "This is just a temporary setback. There has to be something I can give her to help."

Still he hesitated. Emma wanted to grab his arm and shake him, to somehow force him to aid them. Instead, she tried to think, to use her intellect—the one skill she had—to solve this problem as she had so many others.

"Perhaps you need help with your files. Or some research? I'm excellent at research. You might remember that my uncle was a professor at Cambridge, and I often assisted him in organizing his notes and documents and helped him write up his findings."

Dr. Barnes tilted his head to the side and she drew a hopeful breath, wondering if she'd somehow caught his interest.

"Organize them? How so?"

A few minutes later a deal had been struck, and Emma hurried away, a tin of pastilles in her hand. Dr. Barnes said they contained compressed herbs that would release as they dissolved in Tessa's mouth almost like candy. Emma was certain they wouldn't taste like a sweet, but if they helped, she knew Tessa would gladly take them. Emma planned to return on the morrow to assist Dr. Barnes with compiling some research and noting various sources for a paper he was writing for publication. She was thrilled to have found something to offer in trade. Though her services would only be temporary, Dr. Barnes had agreed to pay Tessa another visit in addition to giving her the pastilles.

She slowed her pace, suddenly aware that someone watched her. Dusk was falling and though this was a quiet neighborhood, a woman walking alone was never wise. A quick glance over her shoulder revealed only a street urchin kicking a rock in the road behind her. He glanced up and studied her under the bill of his cap. Not much older than Patrick, he looked out of place in this neighborhood. With a cheeky grin, he ran past her and on down the street.

She frowned, trying to think of where she'd seen him before. A memory niggled at the back of her mind, but she couldn't place him. With another look over her shoulder, she quickened her pace, anxious to reach home before dark fell.

CHAPTER THREE

Professor Joseph Grisby slowly made his way toward the gate of Pentonville Prison, a walking stick in one hand, a doctor's bag in the other. He hid his limp as best he could, but the pain on his left side made walking difficult even with the aid of a cane. Though no longer recognizable to family or friends, he wore a dark brown wig with matching mutton chops to hide his scarred face in addition to his hat. The glue that adhered the whiskers to his face itched terribly. The shaded spectacles he wore hid the damage to his eye from the casual observer.

A physician visiting the prison wasn't an unusual occurrence. The contents of his bag, if searched, would look quite normal. The small bottles with mysterious, foul-smelling liquids along with some basic tools were what a doctor would carry. Plus they might be needed to ensure Vincent Simmons' cooperation.

The fool had gotten himself caught. Again. Quite annoying and terribly inconvenient. His nephew had proven useful ten years ago but of late, Joseph was having doubts. Yet Vincent's resourcefulness and willingness to justify the means with the end result was difficult to find in an employee. The fact that he was family held little weight with Joseph. But, until he found a more suitable replacement, he had to make do with Vincent.

Joseph admitted he'd underestimated both Abigail Bradford and Stephen, Lord Ashbury. They still had what he needed—the lunar meteorite—but he could only deal with one problem at a time. Besides, he held high hopes he could soon persuade them to bring the stone to him.

It took patience on his part to convince the warder to let him in, but he finally approached the cell where Vincent was being held.

"Simmons, the doctor's here to visit you." The guard who escorted him rattled the cell door.

Vincent turned and stared for a long moment before recognizing Joseph and drawing near. "Good day to you, *Doctor*. Didn't expect to see ye here."

"I came to inquire how you're faring," Joseph said.

Vincent scowled as he watched the guard walk away. "I'm in prison. How well do ye think?"

He'd been there only two weeks but already the affects could be seen. His frame appeared thinner. A bruise discolored his cheek.

"Yer limpin' worse than usual. Is the pain bad today?" Vincent asked.

"It is always dreadful." Joseph's left side had taken the brunt of the electromagnetic blast. Between the broken bones from the debris and the burns, his body had never truly healed. It was a miracle he'd survived. In fact, the men who'd been assisting him—Stephen, Michael and Lucas—hadn't found a pulse and presumed him dead. But they were wrong. His heart had slowed significantly for a time, a side effect of the electromagnetic jolt he supposed.

Now he found relief from the endless pain

where he could. His preference was absinthe, an anise-flavored spirit that contained alcohol and medicinal herbs, which colored it green. Vincent disliked the drink, but Joseph found it quite palatable.

"Them two blokes, the viscounts, have already been here askin' about ye." The slyness of Vincent's tone set Joseph's teeth on edge. While he'd admired the trait previously, he found he didn't care for it when it was directed at him.

"Oh?" He'd known Stephen and Michael would try to obtain information from Vincent. He would've done the same in their shoes. "What did you tell them?"

"Nothin'," he said with a smirk, "despite their offer of money."

The greed in Vincent's tone concerned Joseph. That was always the problem with hired help, even if they were related. Keeping their loyalty required constant payment. Yet Vincent had been with him a long time. Joseph hated for their association to end.

"'Tis most unfortunate that you're in prison again. How am I to continue my work with you in here?"

"I'm sure ye can fix that just like ye did last time," Vincent said. "Mayhap this time, it won't take so bloody long."

Joseph sighed, still undecided if he should bother.

Vincent drew closer and lowered his voice. "Were ye able to save the devices from the warehouse?"

"Two of the three." He cleared his throat, noting how the raspy sound made Vincent flinch. "I had some men dressed in police uniforms remove them."

"Snuck them out right under their noses! Damn me, but that was clever of ye. I look forward to hearin' yer plan to free me."

"I'm in the midst of forming one." He set the case down and retrieved a small silver flask from the dark interior. "Care for a drink?"

Vincent eyed the flask warily. "Is it that green stuff you're so fond of?"

"No. This is something much more special. Have a sip while I advise you of my plan."

Vincent took the flask and sniffed the contents. Joseph had made sure he'd only smell the faint apple scent of fine brandy. With a smack of his lips, Vincent took a long sip, then another. "Nothing like that heat slidin' down yer throat into yer belly." He sighed with satisfaction as he passed the flask back to Joseph through the cell bars. "Now then, how are ye goin' to free me?"

"In a coffin."

"How's that?" Vincent's eyes shifted, losing focus, a sign of the drug's quick affect. Fear etched his face. He blinked rapidly but was unable to prevent his eyes from closing as his knees buckled and he crumpled to the ground.

Joseph lifted the case, adjusted his cane and walked away, pleased the problem had been solved so easily.

Michael paced his grandmother's drawing room, awaiting her arrival. The room, decorated in a warm, golden yellow, was at odds with his dark thoughts. He was very uncomfortable about broaching the idea of giving Emma a season with his grandmother. It seemed too much to ask of her when she'd never even met Emma.

If she approved, which he doubted, then he'd have the task of speaking to Emma about it. Somehow he was certain that would not go well.

She wouldn't even consent to a ride in his carriage. How could he possibly convince her to accept help to attract a husband?

He still hadn't determined how he'd gotten talked into this whole scheme. Passing Emma off as an eligible lady seemed an impossible task. While she was intelligent, her drab appearance would make it a challenge to catch a man's eye. The addition of a small dowry was unlikely to be enough to lure in a husband.

The entire scheme made him question why he'd decided to rekindle his friendship with Ashbury. Blast the man for his crazed notions.

"Good afternoon, Michael." Viscountess Weston glided into the room, still attractive in her seventy plus years.

Her solid support and understanding during his parents' tumultuous relationship had kept him sane. He'd felt jerked to and fro when his parents alternately used him and ignored him, depending on the status of their own relationship. His grandmother's steady love had been the rudder on his ship, keeping him on course through his childhood.

With a smile, he stepped forward to clasp her outstretched hands and press a kiss upon her soft, papery cheek. Her lilac scent engulfed him in warm memories.

"You look beautiful," he told her, still holding her hands as he admired her appearance.

Her sparkling blue eyes, so like his own, lit at his compliment. "You are a scoundrel, but I'll accept your kind words anyway."

"You should know I only speak with sincerity."

She laughed. "What brings you by to visit an old woman?"

With a wave of her hand befitting the queen, she directed him to a pair of chairs. A maid appeared with a tea tray and Michael's stomach grumbled at the clever sandwiches and biscuits she set before them, his favorites among them.

"First of all, you are not old, and second, do I need an excuse to visit my grandmother?" Guilt pecked at him as he took a seat. He dropped by to see her on a regular basis but still not as often as he'd like.

"No, but I can tell by your expression that something is on your mind." With elegant, efficient movements she served the tea and plated an assortment of delicacies for him.

"You know me too well. Before we discuss that, how are you?" he asked.

She lived alone in a townhouse he'd acquired for her, one of his first purchases after he'd paid off his parents' debts. She'd moved in with a distant cousin when his father—her son—had gambled away her home. Head held high, she'd never grumbled at the awkward situation in which she'd found herself, all due to his father's recklessness.

Michael had insisted she decorate her new home as she wished, not according to a budget. But practical woman that she was, the bills he'd paid had been quite modest. He'd been concerned that her home would be less than comfortable because of it. He needn't have worried. Her taste was impeccable. This room in particular was warm yet elegant, modern yet traditional. The chairs were comfortable enough for a man. He felt quite at home here and for that reason alone, he could've hugged her.

"I'm doing very well," she answered as she sipped her tea. "I'm attending a musical this evening. Would you care to join me?"

"Perhaps. I shall see if Catherine is interested."

"That would be lovely." Did he imagine it or was her smile forced? Surely not.

"As you so cleverly guessed, there is something I want to discuss," Michael said, deciding he wanted it over with.

She looked up from her tea. "Does it have anything to do with Miss Vandimer?"

"Not at all." For a brief moment, he thought he detected disappointment but when he looked closer at her expression, he saw only her usual serenity. He must've been mistaken. He hoped she approved of his engagement to Catherine, although in truth, he'd never asked.

His grandmother was the reason he'd offered marriage to Catherine—to gain back the five hundred year-old sprawling country estate that had been in the Weston family since the first Viscount Weston had built it. It was his grandmother's birth place, and Catherine's father now owned it. He knew it had appalled his grandmother when Michael's father had gambled it away along with most of their possessions.

But that conversation was for another day. He needed to resolve this issue first.

"This involves an old acquaintance of mine. Do you remember my professor at Cambridge? The one who was killed?" He bit into a smoked salmon sandwich, one of his favorites, as he awaited her answer.

"Yes, of course. That was terrible. You still bear scars from that night, do you not?"

He nodded and forced himself to keep from rubbing his stomach where a scar left a jagged reminder of that night. He'd told no one of the full events that had occurred, nor had he ever spoken of the auras he saw as a result of it except to Ashbury. In the beginning, he'd held hope the ability would go away. Now, he didn't see how he could explain it without sounding like a blundering fool. Or worse, insane.

"Professor Grisby's niece stopped by to see me."

"Oh?" Her eyes lit with curiosity.

How much did he tell her? Surely less was better until he knew if there was any chance of something coming of the situation.

"She's twenty-six, I believe. Of marriageable age at any rate." He thought of her dark brown eyes looking up at him and felt his chest tighten.

"You've decided to offer marriage to her instead of Miss Vandimer?" The hopeful note of her voice took him by surprise.

"No. No, of course not." He shifted in his chair at the very idea, almost spilling his tea in the process. "It seems she's in a rather desperate situation financially, or rather her family is, and I thought perhaps we could assist her in finding a husband."

"You're playing matchmaker?" She looked astounded at the idea.

"Nothing of the sort. I merely thought we could introduce her to a few men at one or two balls and see if anything comes of it." When he said it like that, it didn't sound very difficult. In fact, it sounded rather easy.

"Is she attractive?"

He thought again of those brown eyes, her tilted nose and flushed cheeks. "In her own way, I suppose. If you can convince her to remove her spectacles." He tried to picture her without them. Her eyes held gold in their depths, her lashes were long and dark, and without her glasses, he thought she'd look quite...different.

"Michael?"

"I'm sorry." He berated himself to keep his mind on the task before him. "You were saying?"

"I suppose I could meet the girl to see whether I'm able to help her." Her frown revealed her doubt.

"I can arrange that." At least he hoped he could. In truth, he would be surprised if Emma agreed to it or anything else he suggested.

"You want to find this girl a husband out of the goodness of your heart?"

He scowled, feeling much like a schoolboy caught with a frog in his pocket. "Is that so difficult to believe?"

She raised a brow. "Let's just say it's rather out of character."

He held his ground, unwilling to tell her more despite her suspicions. Not yet. Whether or not Professor Grisby had somehow survived the accident was something he didn't want to discuss until proof had surfaced.

"Her family has not fared well since the professor's death. They live in a tiny flat on Trenary Lane. Miss Grisby appears to be the main supporter of her family, but she is currently without a governess position and has no prospects for one."

"Oh dear. It sounds as if she's in rather desperate circumstances."

"Indeed."

"But she's willing to entertain this idea rather than find another governess post?"

"That remains to be seen." It occurred to him that it would be far easier to simply give Emma money but he knew she'd never accept that. It wasn't an option if there was any chance her uncle lived and could take the money. Instead, he'd have to concoct some excuse to make this whole scheme sound logical and appealing. How on earth was he to manage that?

"I'll leave her in your capable hands." She sipped her tea. "I assume she's intelligent if she's held the position of governess."

"Knowing her uncle, yes. From my brief conversation with her, she seemed so." He finished a biscuit in one bite and helped himself to another. "I realize this is a lot to ask of you."

"We shall see if she's worthy of the time and effort required, not to mention the cost." His grandmother continued to study him as though he were an oddity at a museum.

"I'll take care of that part. It's your time I'm worried about. If you're willing to consider this, I'll make arrangements to introduce her to you." He just had to determine how to make that happen.

Emma scanned the advertisements in the paper, hoping to find a suitable position for which to apply. She'd spent the morning at Dr. Barnes' office, assisting him with his notes and intended to return on the morrow to finish up the project. Unfortunately, he wouldn't need her for much more than that.

"Anything?" Tessa asked from where she sat propped up against the pillows on the bed. She seemed to feel better today although she was still far too pale to suit Emma.

"Still looking," Emma replied, her finger skimming along the lines of newsprint.

"Read them to me," Tessa demanded. She rarely had the energy to read herself but enjoyed hearing news of the outside world.

"Hmm... What do you think of this one? 'Wanted, a superior resident governess to twin boys and a little girl in South Wales'."

"That would never do. It's too far away. We'd never see you."

"True." Nor did it pay enough to make the distance worthwhile. "Here's another: 'Wanted, a thoroughly respectable governess for a family of six young children. Must be experienced, really fond of children, and a good needlewoman'."

"How could you possibly have time for needlework with six children to look after?" Tessa dismissed it with a wave of her hand. "The parents would expect you to fill every spare moment with work."

Emma sighed. "You're probably right. What of this one? 'Wanted, a superior young lady experienced in the management of children, able to teach them, attend to toilettes and wardrobes and assist with domestic duties. Some knowledge of cooking desirable. Good health and energetic disposition essential'."

Silence greeted her words. She looked up to find Tessa staring at her in disbelief.

"You're joking," she accused.

Emma frowned and looked back at the advertisement. "It seems a legitimate situation."

"You'd be nanny, maid, governess, and cook. Of course you'd need an energetic disposition. It makes me tired listening to the list of duties. That's ridiculous." Tessa drew a shallow breath, the slight rattle in her chest worrying Emma, but she knew better than to voice it.

"Tessa, I can't be too selective," Emma reminded her sister. "I must find a post immediately."

"No. I refuse to see you miserable again. You must find one you'd enjoy," Tessa insisted. "Do you realize how many hours each day you're there?"

"Of course I do. But it's called 'work' for a reason." Emma bit her lip and told herself to calm down. Just because she was frustrated at the lack of positions noted in the newssheet gave her no reason to take it out on Tessa. The poor dear had no idea what it was like to work in a stranger's home. To be at the beck and call of demanding employers.

While teaching children was a task Emma

enjoyed, the position of governess was awkward at best. She wasn't part of the family, yet she wasn't considered a servant, at least not by the other servants. In truth it was a lonely position as she didn't fit in with any of the other residents of the house.

Tessa's shoulders wilted. "This is all my fault. If I weren't sick, I could work too."

"No, you must never think that." Emma reached out and squeezed her sister's hand. "I'm happy to work. I'd be working even if you were healthier."

Tessa watched her for a long moment. "That may be true, but I am well aware of the extra burden my illness puts on you and everyone in the family."

"Tessa," Emma said, a lump forming in her throat. "You're never a burden. You must know I'd do anything for you."

"I'm tired of not being able to help." Her big brown eyes welled with tears. "I can't even help Mother clean. I feel so worthless. Even Patrick does more than I."

Emma could only imagine how difficult it must be to remain in bed, never feeling useful. Everyone needed a purpose in life. Even a sick, young girl. "You're helping me now."

The look Tessa gave her clearly stated her opinion on that. "Perhaps I could try mending again." She pushed herself higher up against the pillows. "I feel a bit better today. I think I could manage a piece or two."

Emma examined her closely. She did seem better today, thanks to the pastilles the doctor had given her. Yet any extra activity could exhaust her, causing another setback.

The doctor had also advised them not to worry her. Stress of any sort could worsen her condition. Emma was torn between wanting her to rest and allowing her to feel like she was contributing to the family. What an impossible choice when either could end badly.

"If you're certain you feel up to it?"

Tessa nodded, determination in the set of her mouth.

Emma heard a key in the door then Patrick greeted their mother.

Her little brother grew taller and lankier each month. She mightn't have noticed except for the shortness of his knee breeches. He shared the same brown eyes as she and Tessa, the same cheerful disposition as their mother.

He strolled into the bedroom. "Watcha lookin' fer?"

Emma narrowed her eyes. "If you'd like to phrase that question in proper English, you'd receive an answer."

He rolled his eyes. "No point in puttin' on airs. Won't take me nowhere."

"Patrick Leon Grisby." Their mother's stern tone from the other room brooked no argument.

"Yes, ma'am." He scowled at Emma. "What are you looking for?" he asked again, enunciating each word with care.

"A new home to let," Tessa answered.

"Truly?" His eyes went wide at the thought.

"No, of course not, silly. We're trying to find a position for Emma."

Emma shook her head. Tessa might be ill, but she never missed an opportunity to tease her brother.

Patrick scowled at Tessa before returning to their mother's side. "Is there anything to eat, Mother?"

Before their mother had a chance to answer, a knock sounded at the door.

Emma shared a worried look with Tessa then rose to join her mother at the door. Dr. Barnes wouldn't arrive until early evening. The only other person to pay a visit of late was the landlord, demanding rent. Surely he wasn't here to try to collect again.

Her mother wiped her hands on a rag then squared her shoulders. She put a polite smile on her face and opened the door with Emma directly behind her.

A footman, attired in a deep blue uniform with yellow trim, bowed and said, "A message for Miss Emma Grisby."

Unease trickled down Emma's spine. "I'm Emma Grisby."

"Good day, miss. Viscount Weston requests a meeting with you."

"Oh?" A tiny flicker of hope flamed to life deep inside her. She hadn't thought he'd remember his offer to inquire among his friends for a governess post. Perhaps she needed to reconsider her opinion of him. Mayhap he wasn't the cold-hearted lord she'd envisioned.

Her mother gave her a questioning look.

"He mentioned he'd ask his acquaintances if they knew of anyone with a possible position. Perhaps he's found someone," Emma offered.

"Oh, that's so kind of him." Her mother's brown eyes warmed.

"That remains to be seen," Emma felt obligated to caution her.

"Now, dear," her mother started.

Emma patted her hand to ward off what she knew was coming next. Her mother insisted Emma should hold a more optimistic view of life, yet how could she with everything that had happened? How many times had a man disappointed them? Her father, her uncle, even Viscount Weston, not to mention a few of her employers. All had made promises they'd failed to keep. Emma had learned the only person she could trust was herself.

"I'll hear what he has to say," she told her mother. That was as much as she could offer.

"If you're ready, miss, Viscount Weston would like to speak with you now. I'm to bring you in the carriage," the young footman informed her.

She glanced down at her gown. "I'll need a few minutes to prepare."

"You look fine," her mother said.

"But I'm not dressed appropriately," Emma said, hoping her mother understood that she needed to change into her governess attire, including the binding around her middle and the ash on her skin and hair.

Emma didn't miss her mother's frown of displeasure as she turned to the footman. "Would you prefer to wait or return later?"

"I'll wait with the carriage, if it's all right with you, miss." He bowed again and moved down the hall.

"I'm going to see the horses," Patrick said with a smile and hurried after him.

"Stay out of the way, Patrick," Emma called out.

"Who was it?" Tessa called out from the bedroom as soon as the door closed. The girl had ears like a rabbit.

Emma hurried into the bedroom to change and update Tessa, anxious to hear what the viscount had to say. Dare she hope he might truly care enough to aid her?

CHAPTER FOUR

Michael rose as Emma entered his study. He'd considered holding this meeting in the drawing room and offering her tea but decided that would set the wrong tone. If they managed to come to an agreement, it would be a business transaction. Nothing more. No need to bring social niceties into it.

"Good afternoon," he greeted her, surprised at the pleasure he felt at her arrival.

She curtsied with no smile in sight. "You wished to see me?"

He frowned. They would definitely have to work on her social skills if she wanted to attempt to catch a husband.

"Yes. Please take a seat." He gestured to the chair in front of his desk before taking his own.

She wore the same gown as the previous two times he'd seen her. He recognized it from the mended spot on the cuff. He'd be pleased when she was properly attired and he'd seen the last of the drab grey garment. If he could convince her to accept his plan, that was. He couldn't help but study her critically, wondering if it was even possible to find a man who'd take interest in her.

"Has no one told you it's rude to stare?" An arched brow became visible over the frame of her glasses.

He tapped a finger on the polished surface of his desk, annoyed that he'd managed to irritate her already. That was no way to gain what he wanted. He'd best remember the purpose of this endeavor—to keep watch over her. His intent was to hold a friendly meeting, but if she didn't agree to his terms he was prepared to use leverage to gain her cooperation. Markus, one of the runners, had found out that Emma's sister was ill. Though he didn't yet know the details, surely paying for medical care was of concern.

One of the other runners who'd followed her yesterday had reported that she'd made a visit to a home on Villiers Street and come away with a package in her hand. Another runner was watching that house now to see if it might have anything to do with Professor Grisby.

"I have a business proposition for you."

"A governess post?" The hopeful note in her voice brought forth his guilt, but he reminded himself he was trying to help her as well as observe her activities.

He leaned back in his chair, still unsure how to best suggest Ashbury's plan. "I did mention your need for a position to a few friends of mine but to no avail. Unfortunately, few of my acquaintances are in need of governesses." That much was true. "However, I can't help but wonder if that would truly solve your problems."

Her back stiffened. "What problems?"

Really? She'd pretend she had no financial woes? Is that how she made it through each day, by pretending all was well?

"It appears your family is in need of funds," he said, keeping his tone gentle.

"As are many families these days. What is your point?"

"An ordinary governess post would provide

only a modest income at best."

"Do you think I'm unaware of the wages I would earn as a governess? I'd remind you that I've held the position for many years. Why do you think I was so interested in the post with your cousin? That's the sort I need and exactly what I'm qualified for."

Her confidence was admirable, he'd give her that much, but it was time for the cold, hard truth.

"How many of those quality positions have you applied for?"

Her jaw tightened. "What business is that of yours?"

"I'm not criticizing you. I'm trying to help."

"By questioning my method of finding a post?"

He stifled a sigh of frustration. Lord, but the woman was prickly. "Allow me to state this more clearly. I can't help but wonder whether finding a governess post will be sufficient for your financial needs. There aren't many out there that would pay well enough to truly make a difference."

"What else would you have me to do? Positions for women are rather limited."

He paused a moment before deciding it would be best to be blunt. "Find a husband."

Silence greeted his statement. He could see shock ripple through her at his words. Obviously, she'd never considered the notion.

"How could a husband take the place of a well paying job?" Emma stared at Viscount Weston, wondering if the man was mentally unstable. He made no sense.

"The right husband could provide for you and your family."

Emma rose as anger filled her. The viscount had no idea of what he spoke. She'd had enough of this conversation. "The way my father did? The way my uncle did? Men are not the answer to our problems." She was tempted to add him to her list. Hadn't he abandoned them as well?

He held up his hand. "Please, hear me out."

The only concession she gave was not to walk out the door. She remained standing, trembling with anger and hurt. That small flicker of hope she'd held had extinguished. How stupid and naïve of her to think the viscount could assist her in any way.

"I'm not speaking of some clerk at a warehouse as a husband. I'm suggesting a wealthy one, perhaps even a lord or at the very least, a wealthy merchant."

"Oh, certainly," she said. Could he be any more insulting? How dare he make fun of her situation. "They're lined up outside my door. I need only pick one."

A spark of anger lit his blue eyes. He rose and moved around his desk to stand before her. It was all she could do not to step back. "If you'd listen for a moment, perhaps I could explain in full what I'm suggesting."

Her mouth went dry as she held his gaze, reminding her that she didn't know this man at all. She couldn't have spoken if she'd wanted to, not with him so close. The scent of his cologne swirled through her, muddling her thoughts. Her gaze caught on his chin, the strong length of his jaw, the sculpted lines of his lips. She forced herself to look up into his eyes but that riveting blue sucked the breath from her lungs.

"No ordinary man would do," he said.

No, she thought. He wouldn't. However, a man like Michael— She stopped the thought before it could take hold. The idea of marrying hadn't crossed her mind. The hopes and dreams she'd held as a young girl had long since passed. Placing the welfare of her entire family in the hands of a man held no interest for her.

"Marriage is a business arrangement for many people," he continued.

She scoffed. "How would I meet this extraordinary man who'd consider marrying me? I have no dowry, no title."

"I'd like to introduce you to my grandmother, Viscountess Weston. If you're both in agreement, she'd assist in launching you into society."

Fear speared through Emma at the images that created. Of her standing against a wall in her plain governess attire while beautiful people danced around her. Of, once again, watching, but not belonging.

"No, thank you," she blurted out, unable to bear the idea of enduring such a thing.

Silence greeted her refusal until at last she made herself meet his gaze. But rather than the pity she'd feared to see there, only understanding was visible.

"Marriage to the right man would solve many of your problems. It could provide you with security for your future."

"No." She backed up a step only to bump into the chair she'd recently vacated. Remaining standing seemed impossible so she dropped into it.

He narrowed his eyes, looking at her curiously. "Why?"

"What I need is a position. A husband is of no help to me."

"I disagree."

"How would you know? You've never had a husband, nor do you know anything about what my family needs."

He folded his arms over his chest as he propped a hip against the desk. "Do you refer to the overdue rent? Or perhaps to the money owed to the doctor?"

Outrage made Emma's hands shake and her heart pound. She allowed that to push back her embarrassment. "Have you been spying on us?"

"What of your sister? Is she recovering from her illness?"

Emma stood again, anger lending her strength. "How dare you!" She leaned forward to put her face in his, wanting to grab the lapels of his jacket and shake him. "Who do you think you are?"

He leaned forward as well until his nose was a mere breath from hers. "I believe I'm the one person trying to help you."

"By spying on us?"

He unfolded his arms, and she startled when she felt his finger trail on the underside of her chin. His touch unsettled her nearly as much as what he'd done. "I want to help you," he whispered.

She did her best to ignore his touch. "Why?"

His finger stilled at her simple question. "Does it matter?"

She jerked back. Wasn't that what she'd told herself the first time she'd come here? That it didn't matter? Then why did it? Because this man mattered. She couldn't say why, but Michael mattered far more than she should've allowed him to.

Michael stared at Emma, realizing he couldn't answer her question. He wasn't completely sure why he was helping her. Of course it was because he needed to keep an eye on her to see if Professor Grisby contacted her. But there was more to it than that. What exactly, he couldn't say. Perhaps it was their shared past. Perhaps it was because he felt sorry for her. Yet none of that seemed quite true.

Something in the golden depths of her brown eyes pulled at him. When he was this close to her—

He drew back, unwilling to complete that thought. This was a business arrangement and his job was to gain her agreement to the plan. If that required him to create a reason she'd believe, so be it.

As Ashbury had pointed out, discovering any sign of Professor Grisby would be much easier if they had his niece under close surveillance. The rest of her family had proven fairly easy to watch as they moved about very little. If Michael had to guess, the professor would contact Emma rather than her other family members. She'd been their anchor since Michael had first met them.

"I'd merely like to help an old friend." When she looked unconvinced, he added, "You and your family need assistance and I am in the position to do so. It's not so different than when your uncle was kind enough to aid me."

That excuse seemed to take hold. The crease in her brow eased but then returned before he could draw a breath of relief.

"I don't see how this could possibly work. I don't even want a husband."

"Financial security for the rest of your life seems a fair trade for you to serve as companion for a man of your choosing."

"My choosing?" Her shock would've been amusing under other circumstances.

"Of course. You don't think I'd select him, do you? That's up to you."

"What if I don't...find a man who I think is appropriate?"

"You can leave at any time and return to your search for a governess post." Within a few weeks, he and Ashbury should've determined whether her uncle lived and if so, what he was doing. After that, she could return to her life and continue serving as a governess as far as he was concerned. This was a temporary business arrangement. No matter that a tightness filled his chest at the thought of her walking away.

Her gaze flitted around the room, much like a butterfly that couldn't decide where to land. "I would have nothing to wear."

He couldn't help but smile for he hadn't expected to hear such a normal female complaint pass her lips. "My grandmother will assist you in selecting the proper attire, and I'll see to the cost."

"No. I couldn't possibly accept such generosity." Her lips formed into the stubborn line with which he was becoming annoyingly familiar. "I have no way to repay it."

An idea took hold, one he felt certain would end her argument and give him what he wanted as well. "I offer you a trade. My grandmother is quite lonely and in need of companionship as well as a project. Assisting you in this endeavor would solve both of those issues."

He could see that she weighed the validity of his comments, and he pushed harder. "Having an intelligent, educated person spend time with my grandmother would bring her much joy and bring me peace of mind. I couldn't put a price on that."

She shook her head, but he could see that she seriously considered his idea. Her aura remained clear, however, giving him no hint as to her intent. "I would have to think on it further."

Michael waited a few moments before offering a few more details, hoping to make her more comfortable. He believed in full disclosure in his business dealings, at least when it benefited him. "It would be more convenient if you stayed with my grandmother. In addition to assisting you in selecting the appropriate gowns and necessities, she has connections with those in the *ton* who host balls and other events. She could garner the proper invitations for you."

She bit the fullness of her bottom lip. The gesture woke an awareness inside him that he didn't welcome.

"As I said, I need to think about it and consider what's best for my family."

"Of course." He didn't want her to think about it too long. He needed her somewhere he could watch her as quickly as possible. "May I suggest you meet my grandmother on the morrow to aid you in your decision?"

She blinked as though surprised but nodded, giving him a small victory. However, he had a feeling the battle was far from over.

Emma drew a deep breath, oddly nervous to broach the subject Viscount Weston had proposed with her family. Now was the perfect opportunity. They all sat in the bedroom so they could eat with Tessa. The soup they shared was more like hot water than soup. No meat in sight, only a bit of onion and cabbage to give it some flavor. That was a good reminder of why she needed to seriously consider his suggestion.

She set down her bowl on the small table beside the bed. "As all of you know, I met with Viscount Weston today. He had an interesting proposal."

"What would that be?" Her mother tilted her head to the side. Emma felt as though her mother looked directly into her heart. Not for the first time, she wondered what she saw.

"Yes, please tell us." Tessa asked as her spoon clattered into her empty bowl.

Without thinking twice, Emma rose and poured half of her soup into Tessa's bowl despite Tessa's protest then the remainder into Patrick's. "I'm not hungry. I had tea at the viscount's." She lied with a smile.

Patrick nodded and quickly ate, but Tessa

watched her with narrowed eyes.

"As I was saying," Emma continued, "the viscount advised me that his grandmother is in need of a companion." Her throat clutched at the half lie, yet she couldn't bring herself to tell them the full truth.

"That could be interesting, assuming she's nice. Do you know her?" Tessa asked.

"I meet her tomorrow." Her stomach tightened at the thought, and she was glad she hadn't finished her soup.

"What would your duties be?" her mother asked.

"She lives alone, so I would keep her company, read to her and the like. The interesting thing is she'd like someone to attend balls and other social events with her." She dropped her gaze, berating herself for twisting the truth. Why didn't she just tell them the viscount had offered to help her find a husband? Was it because she feared the mission would be a failure? How could she possibly attract a man, especially one who was a member of the *ton*?

"Oh, that's marvelous," Tessa exclaimed. "But what will you wear?"

"The proper attire would come with the position. The viscountess would assist me in selecting a few gowns and the viscount would take care of the cost."

"That's very generous," her mother said. But Emma could tell by her tone she hadn't yet determined if this was a good idea or not.

Emma felt the same way.

"Would you have to stay with her?" Patrick asked with a frown.

"Yes." When his lips twisted in a scowl, she added, "It's no different than if I were to find a governess post."

"True, but we miss you terribly when you're

gone," Tessa said as she shared a disappointed look with Patrick.

"I know, and I miss all of you as well. But she doesn't live too far away, so I should be able to visit often."

"Does the position pay well?" her mother asked.

Emma hesitated. It wouldn't pay much of anything unless she got a husband. How could she possibly explain that? "I believe so, but I'll know more after I speak with the viscountess directly."

"It don't seem like a good idea to me," Patrick grumbled.

"It doesn't," Emma corrected him. "Why not?"

"You'll be livin' in some fancy place, wearin' fancy clothes. You don't belong in a place like that."

The tightening of her stomach turned to full blown panic. Patrick was right. She didn't belong there. She'd be trading her governess disguise for a different one. How was that improving anything? In truth, this was a gamble. Would she be better off continuing her search for a governess position so she could earn wages sooner?

Her gaze traveled around the small room, catching on Tessa. Her sister's eyes were far too big in her pale, thin face. The prominent bones of her wrist were visible because her night gown was too small. Emma looked at Patrick who wore clothes that not only had been mended and patched too many times but that he'd outgrown. Already, she and her mother worked their fingers to the bone.

The truth was, they couldn't continue like this. The viscount was right—her governess post barely paid the rent, let alone adequate food or the doctor's bill.

Resolve formed inside her, pushing away her doubt.

"I'd remind you that we don't belong here either, Patrick."

His eyes widened at her tone.

"We belong in a good home with plenty of food. If this helps us move to that, then I will gladly do it."

Patrick dropped her gaze and nodded but still didn't look pleased at the idea.

"Can you imagine what it will be like attending a ball?" Tessa sighed. Emma could've hugged her for shifting the conversation. "The music, the gowns, the decorations. You must describe it all to me."

"I don't think—"

"Oh!" Tessa cried out. "What if you meet a man at a ball? He might fall in love with you and—"

"I hardly think that's possible," Emma interrupted her. She spoke the truth. She didn't see how she could manage to draw a man's interest in that way. It would be a challenge, especially considering how long she'd been perfecting the art of not attracting them.

"It could happen," Tessa said, refusing to give up on the idea.

"Emma, you shouldn't do anything you're not comfortable with," her mother reminded her.

"Of course not," Emma agreed. Yet already she felt uncomfortable. But hadn't her uncle always told her that growth in one's character came from such situations?

Her mother picked up the mending on her lap, her hands never still. "I suppose it won't hurt to meet the viscountess." Her gaze met Emma's. "You've always been a good judge of character. Meeting her will help you make your decision."

"We'll know more tomorrow then." Her stomach fluttered at the thought.

Michael scanned the crowded ballroom that evening, looking for his fiancé, Miss Catherine Vandimer. With everything going on of late, he'd neglected her and was certain she'd remind him of it.

At last he spotted her speaking with several acquaintances, most of whom were men. Her popularity with the male species had not diminished despite their engagement. He knew her behavior was rather flirtatious, and he realized he'd have to speak to her about it if it continued. Never would he allow her to make a fool of him as his parents had done to each other.

As he watched her, doubt reared its ugly head once again. For some reason, he still couldn't imagine spending the rest of his life with Catherine.

He reminded himself that she was an attractive woman who would suit him well. Her blonde hair was artfully woven into a chignon. The deep blue satin gown reflected candlelight which was echoed by the diamond and sapphire necklace she wore, one of the many generous gifts from her wealthy father. Her beauty carried an edge, and he well knew her blue eyes could turn to frost at the slightest provocation. She was no timid wallflower.

As she leaned toward one of the men much too closely, he realized he didn't feel even the slightest pang of jealousy. Perhaps the seeds of destructive love that his parents had shown so often had bypassed him. He could only hope so.

His parents' public displays of affection and arguments had been fodder for the gossip in ballrooms for years. That sort of attention was something he had no desire to illicit. He went out of his way to make certain his behavior was above reproach. Catherine would need to learn to do the same.

Michael made his way toward her, nodding at familiar faces as he passed.

Catherine caught sight of him and smiled but didn't move away from the man with whom she spoke, Lord Dalton. As she glanced to the lord again with an even bigger smile, Michael couldn't help but wonder if she hoped to rouse some sort of jealous outburst from him.

"Miss Vandimer." He took the hand she offered and brought it to his lips.

"My lord," she said as she dipped her head in acknowledgement. "You remember Lord Dalton?"

"Good evening," Michael said with a nod. He knew the other man vaguely from his activities at the House of Lords.

"Weston. Good to see you." Dalton flashed a charming smile. Michael didn't miss the heated look Dalton gave Catherine.

"I'd nearly given up on seeing you this week," Catherine continued.

"My apologies. My schedule took an unexpected turn." Her aura was dim, and he wondered what task she'd set for herself that wouldn't come to fruition.

"Nothing bad, I hope." She smiled, her brown eyes holding his.

He shook his head. "Shall we find some refreshments?"

They bid Lord Dalton goodbye and Michael offered her his arm. Catherine glanced up at him from under her lashes as though trying to gauge his mood. "You'll never guess who was here earlier."

"Who?" he asked. Catherine's pleasure at gossiping bothered him. Though he well knew most people here enjoyed talking about each other, that same gossip had kept the memory of the outrageous behavior of his parents alive for far too long.

"The Earl of Berkmond. They say he hasn't been seen since his wife died in childbirth several years ago."

"Interesting," Michael said as his mind churned. The earl was Lucas's older brother. He'd liked to speak with him to see if he had any news of Lucas. Now that Michael had been reunited with Ashbury, memories of the three of them together often came to him. Lucas had fled to Brazil as soon as he healed well enough for the journey and had yet to return to English soil.

"The crowd was quite excited at his appearance. Do you know him?" Catherine asked as they reached an alcove where a servant offered lemonade.

"I attended Cambridge with his brother."

"Oh?" She bit her lower lip, the gesture similar to Emma's from earlier. But he felt nothing—no pang of awareness, no desire to nibble that lip himself.

How very odd.

Michael focused his thoughts on the conversation but refrained from adding more information, knowing full well anything he said would be repeated to her friends on the morrow, much like a well-oiled machine.

Instead, he turned his attention to the men in the room, wondering if Emma would find any of them appropriate. He intended to leave introductions to his grandmother but somehow he couldn't picture the little grey mouse amongst the sparkling occupants of the room.

If both his grandmother and Emma agreed, the next few weeks would prove interesting for all of them. He couldn't quite suppress the smile that thought brought.

Michael eyed the woman who sat across from him in his carriage the next day, wondering what was going through her mind. Emma looked as though she posed for someone as her posture was perfect, her hands folded demurely in her lap. Though her features were even, he detected the sizzle of nerves around her. Her aura showed nothing, but that told him she hadn't yet made up her mind whether or not to pursue this endeavor.

"You're staring again," she said as she turned her head to glare at him.

He frowned. She seemed ridiculously sensitive any time he looked at her. "My grandmother is looking forward to meeting you."

She swallowed hard, another hint to her nervousness. "I look forward to it as well."

He considered reassuring her that his grandmother was quite a pleasant person, but the carriage drew to a stop. He still wasn't sure if the two women would find each other agreeable. No need to add to the lies he'd already told her to lead her this far.

Rather than alighting when the footman opened the carriage door, Emma remained seated, staring out. He shifted to see what she looked at but saw only the marble steps and elegant oak front doors. The townhome looked much like the other houses along this street. Not as formal as his own home but quite different from her family's tiny flat. Perhaps all this was overwhelming to her.

He pushed aside the small niggle of guilt and reminded himself how much easier things would be if she were somewhere he could keep a close eye on her. As he opened his mouth to suggest she alight, she drew a deep breath and stepped out of the carriage.

"She won't bite," he said softly as he offered his arm and they mounted the steps.

"That's such a relief." Her sarcastic rebuttal made him smile. He did admire her spunk.

As they settled into the drawing room, he noted how she perched on the edge of the armchair as though once again prepared to flee. Her gaze scanned the room, but her expression remained unreadable.

"Hello, Michael," his grandmother said as she entered the room. Her day dress was a soft rose, the color just vibrant enough to give color to her cheeks and highlight her grey chignon.

"Grandmother," he said as he kissed her cheek. "How are you?"

"Well, thank you." Her blue eyes met his for a long moment before turning to her guest. "Miss Grisby, what a pleasure to meet you."

Emma had risen when she'd entered the room and now dropped into a graceful curtsy. "The pleasure is mine, my lady."

"Allow me to see you, my dear," his grandmother said.

Michael could see Emma fight with her pride at the request. Yet she stood patiently as his grandmother examined her from head to toe. A pale band of light appeared over his grandmother's head and shoulders and Michael breathed a sigh of relief. His grandmother was obviously willing to take on the project.

Now he had only to convince Emma.

"Spectacles off," his grandmother demanded with a wave of her hand.

Emma paused for a moment before complying. Her brown eyes glanced at him before returning to his grandmother. The gentle arch of her brows over those large eyes was quite pleasant. Her features were even, if pale. Her lips formed a narrow line neither happy nor displeased. That seemed to perfectly describe her entire appearance—neutral.

"Michael, don't you have something else to do? Miss Grisby and I have much to discuss." The look his grandmother sent him brooked no argument.

He glanced toward Emma, wondering if she felt comfortable being left alone with his suddenly demanding grandmother.

Emma seemed to understand his unspoken question and gave him the barest of nods though her aura still showed nothing. At least she was willing to speak with his grandmother and learn more about the plan.

"All right then, I'll leave you two to visit." He glanced between the pair, feeling much like a third wheel. This was not at all how he'd envisioned this meeting.

CHAPTER FIVE

Emma's stomach skipped with nerves as Viscountess Weston circled her once again. The reason for her anxiousness escaped her as she hadn't yet decided if she wanted to proceed with the opportunity. However, being judged by her appearance was nothing she welcomed, not after working so hard to diminish it.

"May I be blunt?" Viscountess Weston's expression was quite pleasant despite her rude question.

"Of course," Emma answered. She had no other choice unless she wanted to leave before the conversation started. Besides, she needed to know if the viscountess thought there was any hope of this project succeeding.

"Is your hair truly that particular shade?"

"Pardon me?"

"And your face." The older woman peered closely at her complexion. "Your skin seems overly pale."

Emma felt her face heat as she struggled with how best to respond.

"Ah, I believe I understand." The viscountess stepped back as she studied her further. "This...ensemble is a costume of sorts."

Emma froze in surprise. No one had ever

questioned that her bland attire was anything other than her normal appearance.

At her first governess post, her employer had made her quite uncomfortable with his heated looks, so she'd started to diminish her appearance. As time passed, she'd added another subtle facet to her disguise and then another, attempting to be as nondescript as possible.

The lady's shrewd blue eyes narrowed ever so slightly. "Did situations arise that made you decide to hide?" Without waiting for a response, she waved her hand in a sweeping gesture from head to toe. "It is quite effective, as I'm sure you know, but I can see it's not the real you."

Emma blinked several times, trying to determine what to say. She could think of nothing but the truth without the unsavory details. "My positions required me to live with families, and I found it much easier to appear as plain as possible."

"That sounds like the decision of an intelligent woman."

"One does what one must in order to survive." She swallowed back her bitterness, hoping it wasn't reflected in her tone.

"And your next endeavor is to find a husband."

Emma hesitated, filled with doubt. It sounded so mercenary and impossible when put that way. "I'm considering that as a viable option."

The viscountess continued to study her, the silence lengthening until Emma wanted to squirm.

"I think the best approach would be to introduce you as the granddaughter of a dear friend. We'll say you're staying with me for a time while she's recovering from an illness. Is that acceptable to you?"

Emma released a breath of relief she hadn't realized she held. Somewhere during the course of the conversation, she'd begun to hope that this plan would be the best course of action for her to help her family. "Yes."

"My grandson says you're willing to serve as my companion while we make the necessary arrangements for this endeavor."

"I would be honored to repay your kindness in any way I can. I am quite good with a needle if you need mending, or—"

"Please." She waved her hand in dismissal. "I'm sure your company will be sufficient payment for what little I do for you."

Emma swallowed at the reminder. Michael was the one whom she needed to repay. Finding the means to do so would be much more difficult.

"It will take several days for Madame Drusell, the dressmaker, to prepare the appropriate gowns for you. Perhaps it would be simpler if we had her bring a selection of fabrics here from which you can choose."

"Whatever you suggest," Emma agreed despite the burn of nerves simmering in the pit of her stomach.

"We'll also need gloves, shoes, hats, and cloaks, of course." She tapped a finger to her lips as she thought on the list. "I'm certain there will be more items, but Madame Drusell will assist us in acquiring those."

Emma cleared her throat. That all sounded ridiculously expensive. "Perhaps just one or two gowns—"

"That will never do."

"The viscount suggested that we could keep this simple with just a few balls..."

"Nonsense. Miss Grisby, if you decide to proceed with this, we must go forth in full. Half measures will never do. You must be certain you're prepared to think, act, and feel like a young lady of the *ton*."

Her stomach dropped. There was no way she could attempt to pull off a deceit of this magnitude. Even as she shook her head to disagree, the viscountess raised her hand.

"Just because you haven't been part of that world doesn't mean you don't belong there. You're an intelligent educated lady with the appropriate pedigree, according to my grandson."

Somehow, her words didn't truly comfort Emma. She'd be trading one disguise for another. Would she ever be able to live life as her true self? At the moment, she had no idea who that was.

"Marriage is a long commitment, as I'm sure you know."

Emma nodded, wondering if the viscountess was trying to talk her out of it.

"Picture the man you select by your side in fifty years and choose carefully." The lady's gaze shifted to the window. "I wish my grandson would."

"I'm sorry?"

"Never mind. There's still hope he'll come to his senses."

Emma had no idea of what the viscountess spoke and decided it best not to ask.

Unbidden, an image of Michael filled her mind. His dark hair, blue eyes, even his confidence drew her. Hastily, she shoved the image away. Comparing any man to Michael would be a terrible mistake.

"You must keep an open mind if you want to find a husband."

Yes, Emma thought. But saying such was so much easier than doing it.

"Do you need the spectacles?"

Emma hesitated as she studied the glasses in her hand. Somehow, letting go of them left her feeling naked and vulnerable. Which was silly. She didn't wear them at home and was always happy to set them aside when she walked in the door. Silly, indeed. This was merely one step in the process. She drew a breath. "No. I don't require them."

"Excellent. You have rather nice eyes." The viscountess smiled as though she understood how difficult this was. "We just need to ease the worry out of them."

"That might take a miracle," Emma murmured.

"Do you believe in miracles, Miss Grisby?"

"Please, call me Emma. And, no, I do not."

"Spoken like someone who's never witnessed one."

"Have you?" Emma had never met anyone who claimed to have done so.

"Once. Long ago." The viscountess's eyes grew soft, her smile full of secrets. "They do happen, Emma. But I also know that God helps those who help themselves. So allow us to begin there."

That was something with which Emma could agree.

"Tell me, Emma. Do you like to read?"

"It's one of my favorite pastimes." Not that she actually had the chance to indulge in it very often.

"Excellent. We are going to be good friends. I can tell already. And I do believe we'll have a little fun during the process. What do you say?"

"That sounds lovely. Thank you." A lump formed in Emma's throat as the older woman squeezed her hand, her gaze holding Emma's. Perhaps there was hope for some sort of miracle after all.

"Viscount Ashbury to see you, my lord."

Michael looked up from reading the newssheet

two days later to see Ashbury striding into the room as Jeffries closed the door behind him. The seriousness of Ashbury's expression cut short Michael's greeting. "What's happened?"

"Simmons is dead."

"What? How?" The death of the one man they believed to have contact with Professor Grisby—or at least, the man they suspected was the professor—was a major blow. Though they hadn't convinced him to talk, without him, they had nothing.

"No one seems to know. He was found dead in his cell yesterday."

"Christ. Now what?"

Ashbury shook his head as he paced before Michael's desk. "We watch Emma Grisby even closer."

"I don't think she knows anything about her uncle's survival."

"Truly?"

Michael remained silent. Somewhere during the last few days, he'd begun to believe she'd been nothing but honest with him. She'd sought him out for the reference. Nothing more, nothing less.

"Don't allow her to fool you, Weston. Lord knows what tricks her uncle has put her up to."

"We shall see soon enough, but based on the hovel they're living in, I have a difficult time accepting that she wants anything other than what she's said."

"Did you convince her to allow you to give her a season?"

"I have no idea." He had yet to hear anything from Emma or his grandmother.

"What is taking so long? Why is she hesitating if she is in such desperate circumstances?" Ashbury paced again. "You must speak with her and insist. Tell her—"

"If I push her, it will only make her suspicious.

And she is already distrustful." The sigh Ashbury released made Michael shake his head. "If the professor contacts her, we'll know. We're watching her home and her movements. With luck, she'll agree to the crazed plan you concocted. Then she'll be under my grandmother's roof."

Ashbury paused to glance at Michael. "I never meant to put your grandmother in danger."

"You'd better hope she's not." While that worry had crossed Michael's mind as well, he had to believe that Grisby would never hurt his niece and therefore, his grandmother would not be in any danger.

"What do you think Grisby wants—that is, if he lives?"

"I can't imagine. Do you think he also has some sort of...ability?" Ashbury stared out the window as though hoping to catch a glimpse of him on the street.

"He came back from the dead. Who knows what ability that gave him?"

"I swear he had no pulse. I checked it myself. One half of his face was damaged beyond repair."

Michael remembered that all too well. When he'd recovered consciousness, he'd stumbled over to where Ashbury had been kneeling beside the professor. The sight was burned in his memory. Later, the doctor had told them that it had been a good thing the professor hadn't lived. His injuries would've made life miserable and he never would've recovered fully.

But some detail of that night tugged at his memory. What was it?

"Who was the man who helped us afterward?" Michael asked.

Ashbury paused, eyes narrowed as he tried to remember. "I'm not certain I knew him. I went to the door, hoping to find someone to aid us. A man was just walking toward the laboratory. I assumed he'd heard the blast and had come to investigate. He asked me what happened then followed me into the laboratory to help me check on the professor."

"Did you know him?"

"Bloody hell." Ashbury spun to face Michael. "Vincent Simmons."

"No!"

"I'm sure of it. I never thought of it until just now. He is the one who fetched the doctor."

"So he was aiding the professor back then." Michael rubbed his hand over his face. "Damn. The professor truly is alive."

"I can hardly believe it. Simmons must've been arrested soon after that for the murder of Abigail's father. The professor had to be the one who arranged for Simmons' release from prison prematurely." Ashbury sank into the chair before Michael's desk.

"Simmons must have been important enough to the professor that he made the arrangements for the switch."

"Can you discover if Miss Grisby knew Vincent Simmons?"

Michael shook his head. "I'm not sure how. Not unless we're willing to rouse her suspicions."

"Surely one question will not do so."

"She is the most prickly, wary, suspicious person you'll ever meet. I'll see what I can do, but I'd rather wait to see if the professor contacts her."

"I still can't believe he hasn't already."

"I'm not certain how she'd react to learn her uncle is alive after all these years. He'd better have a good reason for it as he left his family in dire straits." Michael thought back to what Emma had said earlier—that she had no desire for a husband. Men had not played a stable role in her life thus far.

"Perhaps we could make inquiries with some of his former acquaintances and colleagues. Surely there is someone with whom he remained in touch." Michael tapped his fingers on his desk. "I think it might be useful to find out who that doctor was as well. Where was the professor's body taken?"

"Excellent ideas. I'm not certain if we can still discover the answers, but it's worth trying."

Ashbury's gaze held steady on Michael. "There's something I've wanted to say..."

Michael frowned at the seriousness of his friend's tone. "What is it?"

"I owe you an apology."

"Whatever for?"

Ashbury rubbed his temple, and Michael had to wonder if he had another headache brewing. "I should've stopped the experiment that night."

"Why?"

"I was certain the power was not sustainable. But despite my doubts, I said nothing. If I—"

"If you would've bid us to stop, the professor would've had your head." Michael rose to move closer. "I had the same worry, the same doubt. But I did nothing either. The professor was so insistent that we test it."

"But I—"

Michael put his hand on Ashbury's shoulder. "No. You have nothing to apologize for. None of it was your fault."

"I thought certain you blamed me."

"I only blamed myself. Every aspect of my life was a disaster back then. It was easier to release our friendship, especially with the damned aura reading. Then my parents...died." Michael couldn't bring himself to speak of the details. Not even to Ashbury. "And it was all I could do to make it through each day."

Ashbury shook his head. "I still believe I

should've done more, but I appreciate your words. That eases my mind."

Michael held his gaze for a long moment, pleased they'd had a chance to clear the air. "If only we can determine where the professor is and what he's up to."

"How he managed to have the devices hauled away despite the police watching that warehouse is a mystery as well," Ashbury said.

"Clever bastard. Now we need some new leads."

"Which brings us back to Miss Grisby. Do what you can to convince her of the plan to stay with your grandmother. It would make our lives easier."

"Yours perhaps," Michael muttered. "But not mine." Emma Grisby was one big complication, no matter how he looked at the situation.

Emma stared at the yards of silk, satin, and taffeta that surrounded her. The colors and textures were beautiful. Amazing. And so different from the grey woolen gown she wore. With a tentative finger, she reached out and touched one to find the fabric even softer and smoother than it appeared.

She'd never felt more out of her element. Panic took hold and sent her heart racing. She didn't belong here, and she certainly didn't deserve gowns like the sample the dressmaker held up for her inspection.

Emma bit her lip, realizing she had to put a stop to all this. It would never work. "I don't think—"

"Nonsense. Of course you do." The viscountess studied her as Madame Drusell, the dressmaker, held the sample against Emma. "You're very intelligent. It would never do to pretend otherwise."

"It's just—" Emma tried again, only to be cut off by Madame Drusell who, according to Viscountess Weston, had impeccable taste.

"The blue would be stunning."

"Not this shade." Emma remembered only too well that exact color from the day she'd interviewed with the marchioness. "I couldn't wear this color."

"I believe you're right," the viscountess agreed. "A deeper shade would be better."

"Ah, yes." The dressmaker sorted through the swatches and held up one triumphantly. "Perfect! *Oui!*"

Emma blinked as the two women discussed choices and options as though she weren't even in the room. Not wanting to be rude, she cleared her throat. "Perhaps two gowns would—"

"Remember, my dear, no half measures."

"But—"

"Emma, you must trust me on this." The viscountess reached over and squeezed her arm reassuringly. "All will be well."

"The cost—"

"Is of little consequence. Madame Drusell is quite affordable. Now relax and enjoy. Try to think of this as fun. Most young ladies your age would."

Fun? Emma repeated the word in her mind, trying to process its meaning. She couldn't think of the last time she'd enjoyed herself for the pure pleasure of it, certainly not by spending money. How could she with Tessa so very ill and her mother and Patrick doing all they could to keep a roof over their heads and food in their bellies?

"On the morrow, you'll move in with me. Your fittings will begin in earnest. Our first outing will be in three days."

Emma closed her eyes for a moment as butterflies danced in her stomach. There seemed no possible way she could fool anyone into believing she was a lady. What had she been thinking? Even as she opened her mouth to protest, the viscountess took both her hands in hers, a smile on her lips.

"All will be well, Emma. You shall see." The twinkle of confidence in the old woman's eyes struck Emma. "You will surprise yourself. Have faith. Give yourself and our plan a little time."

Emma nodded, trying to take her advice as Madame Drusell assisted her in stripping down to her chemise so she could take measurements. She hadn't worn the binding around her mid-section as there didn't seem to be a point to it any longer. Odd that she felt naked without it.

"You have a delightful figure, my dear," the viscountess proclaimed as though surprised.

Looking down at her body with a critical eye, Emma could only see her flaws. She was a tad too thin, her breasts could be fuller, and her hips should surely be narrower. But as she could do little about those things, she'd decided long ago there were far more important things to worry over.

Various styles and fabric were discussed until Emma's head spun with the details. The idea of wearing so many different gowns seemed both impracticable and ridiculous.

"What of her hair?" Madame Drusell asked. "A lemon water rinse should give it some shine."

"Perhaps some castor oil on the tips?"

"Excellent idea." The dressmaker took out the pins holding Emma's tight chignon. "She might wear it looser, yes? So it softens the lines of her face?"

"Very nice." The viscountess nodded as she

eyed Emma. "I look forward to seeing all of this come together."

The day passed far too quickly. Before Emma could catch her breath, the viscountess had hustled her into her carriage to return home to pack her belongings for the next day when the carriage would fetch her.

Guilt filled her as she hurried down the hall to their flat. She'd spent the day with what had seemed like frivolous activities while her mother and brother had been working. How could her family not resent the time she'd spent away from them?

Mrs. Dobbs, their neighbor, poked her head out the door, leaving Emma to wonder if she'd been waiting for her. "Quite the going-ons, eh, Miss Grisby?"

"How so?"

"You've had more visitors these past two days than the whole time you've lived here." The old woman raised a bushy grey brow, obviously hoping for details.

Fear filled her. Had Tessa's condition worsened? Had they sent for the doctor in her absence? "Please excuse me. I need to make certain all is well."

Before the woman could comment further, Emma had her key in the lock and opened the door. "Mother?"

"In here, Emma."

A large basket sat upon the little table, a brightly patterned cloth lining it. Ignoring it for the moment, Emma hurried into Tessa's room.

Patrick and their mother were gathered around Tessa. Another cloth that matched the one in the basket was spread on top of the bed. A feast littered the surface with more food than their family had seen in the past year. Fruit, bread, biscuits, and thick slices of ham all scented the air, making Emma's mouth water. A crock sat on the side table and her family all held bowls of steaming soup, but rather than the watery mixture of cabbage and onion, this one contained chunks of meat, potatoes, carrots and other vegetables in a thick brown broth. Her stomach grumbled at the sight.

"Where did all this come from?" she asked.

"Viscount Weston's footman delivered it and said it was courtesy of the viscount to celebrate your new position."

Indignation filled Emma. How dare he assume her family needed—

Before she could finish the thought, her gaze caught on Tessa's smile, the delight in her eyes, and her full mouth.

"Wasn't it nice of him?" Tessa managed after she swallowed. "So delicious," she added as she returned her attention to her bowl.

"The food smelled so good, we couldn't wait for you," Patrick added then stuffed another bite of bread in his mouth.

"Slow down, Patrick," her mother admonished. "Wash for supper, Emma, and join the feast."

Emma looked at the smiling faces of her family, and her heart melted a little. Truly, Michael — rather Viscount Weston— couldn't have chosen a better celebratory gift for her family.

CHAPTER SIX

Michael waited in the carriage, hoping Emma would emerge from her lodging house soon. He felt uncomfortable waiting here for her, certain she'd think him too forward for doing so. She'd most likely be irritated that he'd sent a carriage for her and even more irritated that he'd accompanied it. It seemed everything he did annoyed her, and for some reason, that only made her seem more intriguing to him.

In all honesty, he wanted to be certain she hadn't changed her mind. Now that Simmons was dead, Emma was the most likely person the professor would contact. Michael tried to convince himself that the only reason he didn't want her disappearing from his life again was because he didn't want to lose their chance of catching the professor.

He'd been pleasantly surprised at his grandmother's enthusiasm for the task he'd requested of her. She and Emma had apparently gotten along quite well.

Surprisingly well.

He wished his grandmother spoke of Catherine the way she spoke of Emma.

Emma emerged from the lodging house, a large bag in hand, her customary grey dress covered partially by her cloak. He'd be glad to see the last of that dress. Yet he couldn't quite imagine her dressed in the height of fashion. Lucky for him, his grandmother had excellent taste.

Her gaze immediately caught on his carriage, and he alighted to open the door.

"Good day to you, Miss Grisby. I thought you might need assistance with your things."

She hesitated, eyes narrowing. Already he could see her suspicion, her consideration of refusing his offer. Who had made her so mistrustful of the world and everyone in it? What had changed since he'd known her so long ago?

He stepped aside and gestured toward the carriage's interior as the footman took the bag she held.

"How...kind of you." As she moved forward, she glanced up at him from under her lashes.

He caught a glimpse of something for the briefest moment. Something that spread awareness over him. Then the light caught on her spectacles, reflecting the sky, making it impossible to see her eyes.

Surely he'd been mistaken.

Was it his imagination or did her complexion look better today? In place of the pastiness he'd previously noted was a delicate alabaster with a hint of rose. The curve of her cheek, the length of her neck caught his gaze as she stepped up into the carriage. Her hair even appeared darker, less grey. Quite attractive actually.

What on earth was wrong with him today?

"I must thank you for the generous basket you had delivered to our home."

"Must you?" The spear of resentment he felt surprised him. Why couldn't she simply thank him? It seemed as if she'd only said it because good manners dictated she do so.

She blinked as though puzzled by his words.

"Yes, I must. You were far too generous."

He pushed aside his irritation, determined not to argue with her. His goal was to see her safely to his grandmother's, not to annoy her into backing out of the arrangement. "You're welcome."

A tiny frown appeared for a moment as if she were confused by his curt response.

Before she said anything else to frustrate him, he changed the subject. "I'm pleased to hear that you and my grandmother came to an agreement."

"She is an amazing woman." A small smile graced her lips, lightening her expression. "You're very lucky."

"Indeed I am. My grandmother is a special person. You'll enjoy spending time with her."

"I believe I will." She turned to study him. "You are like her in many ways."

Michael stilled as the warmth of her compliment washed over him. Little else she could've said would have pleased him more. He'd been told so often that he was the image of his father that her words came as a surprise. Over the past few years, he'd done everything he could to reverse what his father had done. Doing so had been no easy task, especially when everyone seemed to expect that he was the same man as his father. "That is one of the nicest things anyone has ever said to me."

Her eyes widened with surprise. "I didn't say it to be nice."

"Which makes it even nicer."

"Well, it's true. Your straightforwardness, your attitude, and something about your eyes are all very like her."

He smiled. "Thank you." For a long moment, their gazes held, and warmth stirred deep within him. Those brown eyes tugged at him. The slight bow in her upper lip beckoned. Desire slid through him, much to his dismay. He was engaged and

had no business feeling anything for this woman
other than sympathy for her unfortunate
circumstances.

Yet there was more to Emma Grisby that he'd
suspected. She was an intelligent person who had
a completely different life experience than he.

Once again, he found himself on the verge of
simply asking her if she'd heard anything from
her uncle, but he held back. She had no reason to
trust him with an honest answer, and he didn't
know her well enough to tell if she was lying.

The only thing he did know was that the days
ahead would be interesting. He had yet to
reconcile the memories he had of her with the
woman before him.

Perhaps he needed to set those aside and allow
events to unfold as they may. Somehow, it seemed
as if that would be easier said than done.

Emma paused at the threshold of the bedroom
to which the maid had shown her in Viscountess
Weston's home. She could only stare at the lovely
blue and cream colored décor. "Are you certain
this is the correct room?"

"If you don't care for it, miss, I'm certain the
viscountess will offer you a different one."

"No, no. It's lovely." The interior beckoned, yet
she hesitated.

The canopied bed sat high and was draped in a
deep blue with a bedspread in a paler shade.
Pillows of various shapes and sizes invited her to
sit back and relax. A cozy sitting area with two
stuffed chairs and a low table sat before the
fireplace. A desk complete with paper and pen
stood near the window with a matching chair
before it.

Sleeping in such a beautiful room would be impossible. She'd be too afraid she'd mess it up.

Worst of all was her ragged bag sitting open on the floor, its meager contents ready to be unpacked. It didn't belong in this room anymore than she did.

From the moment she'd seen Viscount Weston waiting for her this morning, she'd felt as if she'd been walking in a dream. As if she'd stepped through the door into a foreign world. A handsome man conversing with her as though he cared what she thought. A beautiful carriage to take her to her destination. A lovely benefactor who'd invited her into her home and given her this room in which to stay.

Overwhelmed, Emma drew a shaky breath. She and her bag were completely out of place here. Who was she trying to fool?

"I'm afraid I've made a mistake."

"Not giving up already, Emma, are you?" the viscountess asked from behind her.

Emma spun to face her, worried she'd offended her. "I'm terribly sorry but I'm afraid—"

"No need for panic, my dear. You've barely started." She dismissed the maid and drew nearer, her gaze steady on Emma. "I know you have more backbone than that. Don't allow the sight of a bedroom to change your mind."

Emma looked over her shoulder at the room again. How could she explain that this room was the size of her family's entire flat? That the cost of the chair and desk would be enough to feed her family for months? She didn't think she could pretend to be part of this world when she felt so out of place in it.

Could she succeed in this charade? Was it the right thing to do? The best way to aid her family? The stakes seemed so high—a life spent with a man. Did she dare trust someone else with her family's well-being?

"I'm sure all this must be overwhelming but keep your mind on the end goal," the viscountess suggested.

Rather than bringing comfort, her words only made Emma further question her goal. "Do you truly think there is any hope of this plan succeeding?"

"How will we know if we don't try?" The viscountess took Emma's hand. "Besides, I believe it will be quite delightful once you give the proper effort to our plan. If you're not enjoying something, it's not worth doing."

Based on the fluttery feeling in her stomach, she was not enjoying herself. Nor had her life thus far allowed her such an indulgence.

"New experiences can be daunting, but they help us grow, don't you think?" Viscountess Weston smiled warmly. "If nothing else, you'll keep me company for the next few weeks, have some new experiences, and then return home."

Put like that, it sounded so easy. Why was she making it difficult? What could go wrong?

Unbidden, Michael's image came to mind. Those blue eyes of his studying her with an intensity that made it difficult to breathe, as though he was seeing her for the first time.

He was what could go wrong. Or rather, her growing feelings for him could go wrong. Putting her trust in anyone other than herself was the one thing she'd sworn never to do. She reminded herself that Michael had so easily abandoned them before. This time was no different. He was merely a passing light in her life. She had to guard herself from becoming dependent on him, from allowing her past feelings for him to grow into the present or worse, the future.

That was what could go wrong.

"No one will force you to do anything you don't

want to do."

She looked at the viscountess, her warm smile and confident manner easing Emma's worries. "Thank you. I'm sorry to seem so uncertain."

"Nonsense, my dear. It's to be expected when one is thrown into a new situation. Now then, we shall begin. Madame Drusell is here for the final fittings. If one of the gowns can be ready, there's a small ball I'd like to attend tomorrow evening."

Emma ignored her suddenly pounding heart and reminded herself why she was doing this. She might meet a man she could come to care for. He might be able to help her and her family.

"That sounds lovely." She might as well begin this masquerade. The sooner she met someone, the sooner she could aid her family. She need only take this one step at a time.

Vincent Simmons awoke with a gasp. Heart pounding, he blinked as he glanced around the unfamiliar room, uncertain where he was or how he'd come to be here. Was this hell? Or worse, purgatory? Somehow, he thought he'd feel different in the afterlife. Instead, he simply felt as though he'd had too much to drink the night before. His thoughts were sluggish, his body heavy, his mouth full of cotton. A massive pounding beat a steady rhythm in his skull.

"You've decided to rejoin the living at last?" The raspy voice of his uncle sounded all too familiar.

Vincent jerked upright, remembering his last thought—that his uncle had killed him. "I'm not dead?"

"No. You just had a rather long sleep. One of the side effects, I'm afraid." Uncle Joseph drew near the bed, his damaged face clearly visible in the pale light.

Vincent looked away, still uncomfortable with the sight. The last thing he remembered was his uncle visiting him in prison. He put a hand to his aching head. "What happened? What did you do?"

"An experiment really. I gave you a bit of this and a bit of that. Something to slow your heart rate so the prison doctor would declare you dead."

"Dead?" The very idea terrified Vincent.

"Describing it as a deep sleep would be more appropriate. It was enough to fool the guards and the doctor. Your body was released for a family member to pick up and I did so, with a little assistance." He gestured toward his left leg as though to remind Vincent of his disability.

Vincent drew a deep breath, trying to digest the information, only to wince. He touched his hand to his side and found a tender spot. "What happened to me ribs?"

His uncle shrugged. "The plan was not without its share of mishaps. I'm afraid your body was dropped once or twice."

Vincent rubbed his forehead, realizing he didn't want to know the details. A few minor aches and pains seemed a small price to pay for no longer being confined to a cell, not to mention being alive. "The police believe me dead? I don't have to return to prison?"

"As long as you don't draw attention to your existence, our secret should be safe."

Vincent breathed a sigh of relief, grateful to have escaped life in prison a second time. For that, he definitely owed his uncle. Perhaps the time had come for him to become more committed to his uncle's goal. "Where are we?"

"Our new temporary quarters. I had to move once more. Inquiries were being made that caused me to be quite uncomfortable."

"Those lords again, eh? Along with that meddlin' Miss Bradford." Vincent shook his head. He still couldn't believe they'd somehow managed to best him.

"They are intelligent men. Now that they've banded together, their efforts are even more effective." Uncle Joseph stared out the dirty window. His eyes had that far away look in them that made Vincent nervous.

"Are ye still going to meet with 'em? Tell 'em you live?"

"Eventually. But that time has not yet come. First, I need to make sure my plans are in place. I want them to see my vision as I do. The discovery of electromagnetism was a landmark breakthrough in science, Vincent. And we are going to take full advantage of it."

"Perhaps ye could explain the whole thing to me again. If I understood the experiments better, I might be of more help." He was all too aware of what a close call he'd had. His uncle could have just as easily killed him. Vincent knew if he wanted to share in the success his uncle kept promising, he needed to become a bigger part of his plan.

"Electromagnets are magnets that can be easily controlled by the amount of current running through them. The copper wire coiled around the magnet concentrates the magnetic field."

Vincent nodded. At least he understood parts of what his uncle told him, but when he started using scientific terms, comprehension escaped him.

"Humans are electromagnetic beings," his uncle continued. "Are you familiar with the study of electrophysiology?"

"Can't say as I am." Vincent rubbed his hand over his face, no longer certain he'd understand no matter how many times his uncle explained.

"It is the study of the electrical properties of tissue." At Vincent's puzzled look, he added, "Human tissue. If magnets can be used to pull and stretch matter, including tissue, we might be able to find a way to control humans using electromagnetism."

Vincent held his tongue. He thought his uncle a bit crazed. The vision he saw was not one that Vincent shared. Controlling people using some sort of device seemed impossible. The last few weeks had proven to him that he was a man of simple needs. All he wanted was a pint at his elbow, food in his belly, and a warm bed to lay his head. He no longer hoped to reach the stars. He only wanted to stay out of prison.

But he wasn't about to tell his uncle that. Else he might find himself asleep again but not waking up.

"We have much to do, Vincent. First, we must obtain the meteorite Lord Ashbury has in order to maintain an even power source for our electromagnetic device. It's vital for the success of our mission."

Vincent scowled, less than pleased with his assignment. He had no desire to deal with Lord Ashbury or the Bradford woman ever again.

The next evening, Emma stood before the looking glass, staring at the image before her. This woman looked beautiful, confident, as though she belonged in this room.

"You look lovely, miss, if I may say so." The maid adjusted her hair one last time then stepped back. "I'll tell the viscountess that you're ready."

But wait, Emma wanted to cry out. *I'm not ready at all.*

Her green silk gown was simple in design but elegant in its fit. A cream colored underskirt drew the eye to a narrow waist and the hint of cleavage at the neckline. Her hair was artfully drawn back to cascade in loose curls to her shoulders.

Gone were the spectacles, the pasty complexion and grey hair. Without her mask, she felt naked, exposed to the world.

Emma had never been more scared in her life.

She closed her eyes. Hadn't she simply traded one disguise for another? Would she never be able to live life as her true self? She wasn't even certain who she was anymore. What would her family think of her appearance? They'd see through her new disguise, just as everyone else would.

A tap on the door interrupted her racing thoughts.

The maid hurried forward to open the door, revealing the viscountess.

"Oh." She walked slowly forward while staring at Emma.

The stunned look on her face made Emma's heart sink. "What is it? It's the dress, isn't it? It's not right for me. The wrong color perhaps?"

"You look stunning." The viscountess's eyes watered as she took Emma's hand. "Absolutely breathtaking. I knew you were an attractive woman, but..."

The emotion in her face made tears well in Emma's eyes too. "Are you certain I look acceptable?"

"Acceptable? My dear, I doubt there will be a man at the ball who won't beg for a dance with you."

Emma smiled. She well knew the viscountess was merely being kind, but she appreciated her words all the same. "It is all due to you and your good taste."

"You're beautiful, but it's more than that. I think it has to do with the way you carry yourself, with the wary intelligence in your eyes."

With a laugh, Emma tried to draw a deep breath, but her corset wouldn't allow it. "I'm not certain I'm prepared for this."

"Nonsense. Of course you are. This is one of those occasions when you must simply step forward and see what happens. Seize life with both hands."

"I confess that I feel like a fraud. As though I'm pretending to be something I'm not." She turned back to the mirror to study the woman there. "Surely people will realize I don't belong, that I'm only pretending."

The viscountess moved to stand beside her, her gown a vivid shade of burgundy that brought out her eyes which met Emma's in the mirror. "You do belong, Emma. And if you start to doubt that this evening, you must ask yourself if you ever felt like you belonged while you were a governess. Perhaps that was where the deceit was. Not here. Not now. Try on this new persona and see if it fits better."

Startled, Emma could only stare at her as her words sunk in. "I've never thought of that."

The older woman smiled. "Enough of this serious conversation. Your only task this evening is to enjoy yourself. Allow us to prepare to depart. I will be ready as soon as I remember where I put my gloves."

"May I look for them for you?"

"No need. I believe I left them in my room. I'll meet you in the drawing room shortly."

The viscountess led the way out of Emma's room then turned the opposite direction in the hall. "I'll be down directly, my dear. Have a glass of sherry while you wait. That will help calm your nerves."

Emma smiled. Maybe she would. That might

give her the boost of courage she needed to make it through this night. Keeping a hand on the railing, she made her way down the stairs, the unfamiliar weight of the skirt and new shoes threatening her balance. She breathed a sigh of relief when she reached the lower level and entered the drawing room.

To her surprise, Viscount Weston stood in the room, one arm resting against the mantle of the fireplace, the other holding a crystal glass.

She stopped abruptly at the unexpected sight of him. For a moment, she considered backing away before he saw her. She was already off kilter. Seeing him did not help. As she hesitated, he turned to face her.

A range of emotions crossed his face so quickly that she wasn't sure what he thought. He immediately straightened and came forward, leaving his glass on a nearby table as he passed by.

"Emma?" The way he said her name, it seemed as if he wasn't quite sure it was truly her.

She lifted her chin, realizing this was her first test of the evening. Would he declare her an impostor? Advise her this would never work? Tell her she didn't belong? "Good evening, my lord." She curtsied and found him much closer when she rose.

Too close.

From here, she could see the length of his dark lashes that framed his blue eyes. His black hair was smoothed back but held a hint of a curl as it brushed his collar, making her want to touch it. He smelled glorious—an appealing mix of the woods and bay rum.

"Miss Grisby." This time he said her name as though he had realized it truly was her. He drew another step closer to take her hand. The warm feel of his skin against hers made her realize she hadn't yet donned her gloves.

"You look...beautiful."

She studied him, trying to decide what that slight hesitation meant. "Your grandmother has been very helpful." She glanced at his jacket, anything to look away from the intensity of his stare. "She thought the gown would be appropriate for this evening."

Michael frowned, trying to make sense of her words. He could see her mouth moving, but her changed appearance slowed his thoughts. From her shining hair to the delicate rose of her cheeks to the arch of her brow, she bore little resemblance to the woman he'd left here only a few days ago.

His gaze dropped as she gestured toward her vivid green gown and the amazing figure she'd so cleverly hidden in that terrible grey attire. Before he did something he'd regret, he pulled his gaze up only to have that slight bow in her upper lip catch his eye. A spear of desire shot through him that shut off his brain completely. "I had no idea."

"No idea of what?"

"That you were quite so beautiful. This is more how I remember you."

Her lips parted at his words, her eyes wide with surprise. "Why...thank you. That's very kind of you."

He shook his head. "That has nothing to do with it. Rarely am I kind."

A blush crept up her cheeks, drawing him nearer. Her aura was golden, shimmering about her as though to celebrate her success.

"Where are your spectacles?"

"I don't really need them."

Unable to resist, he reached out to touch the silky softness of her hair, amazed at the rich color of it. "It looks so different."

She gave a tiny shrug, almost imperceptible. "I

covered it with ash to dull it."

Unable to resist, he grazed his finger along her cheek. "Here too?"

"Yes."

The deep breath she took drew his attention to her neckline, the fullness of her cleavage giving him pause. The green of the gown contrasted with the alabaster of her skin. Her narrow waist made him want to span it with his hands to see how she fit. Gone was the hint of chubbiness her governess attire had suggested. She looked nothing like the little grey mouse who'd perched on the chair in his library only last week.

"Your transformation is remarkable."

He tried to gather himself and remember to whom he was speaking and why she was here. As he breathed in to calm himself, he caught her scent of lilies and sunshine. Her brown eyes held the same awareness he felt but held no invitation, no fluttering of her lashes, no flirtatious smile.

How could he resist such a challenge?

Again, he touched her cheek, drawing one finger along the smooth silkiness. His gaze dropped from her eyes to those lips which parted the slightest bit. Slowly, deliberately, he bent his head and kissed her, wondering if she'd shove him away.

Her mouth was soft and oh so sweet. Passion crashed through him, surprising him with its strength. He deepened the kiss, unable to resist, drawing her into his arms. Her tentative response fueled him. How could she not feel the same fire that burned within him?

He drew back to look at her, to see her reaction. The shocked heat in her eyes pleased him but the wariness remained. What would it take to remove that caution and leave only passion in its place?

He moved to try again, determined to erase the

barrier she'd placed between them, to make her lose control as he nearly had.

"Viscount Weston." His formal name on her lips halted him. "Your grandmother will be joining us any moment."

The sound of heels clicking on tile echoed from the hall. The combination of that, along with Emma's words, helped cool his ardor, but not completely.

One look at the woman before him was enough to heat his blood again. Her hands clasped together as though she needed to hold on to something. He berated himself. Obviously she was nervous yet all he could think about was kissing her. That was wrong for more reasons than he could count, the first of which was his own engagement. The second one being that he had no intention of involving himself with a woman for whom he felt such passion. It had destroyed his father and mother, and he knew that he had those same destructive seeds in himself.

When one lost control, someone else always paid the price.

Yet he couldn't help but reassure Emma. He could see she was nervous and had reason to be. Navigating the *ton* would be much like swimming in an ocean of sharks. "You will be an amazing success tonight. Have no doubt."

She reached up to touch the top of her head. "Is my hair out of place?"

He glanced up to check. "No."

"Then why do you keep looking at it?"

He was saved from having to answer by his grandmother.

"How nice of you to accompany us, Michael."

"I wouldn't miss the opportunity to escort two beautiful ladies to a ball." He bent to kiss his grandmother on the cheek.

"Nonsense. I'm certain there are a hundred

other things you'd rather do, but we appreciate it all the same, do we not, Emma?"

Emma paused before answering, her gaze on his as though weighing his merit. Why did it matter what she thought of him? "Indeed, we do."

"Let us be off and see what the *ton* has to say about our protégé." She looped her arm through Emma's and looked over her shoulder at him. "Come along. This will be quite the adventure. I expect Emma will be the belle of the ball."

Suddenly, the idea of other men ogling Emma annoyed him. He had no right to such feelings, nor any right to kiss her. He needed to remember that.

CHAPTER SEVEN

Emma stared across the crowded ballroom, unable to catch her breath. Especially after that kiss with Michael. Dare she hope he felt something for her? She closed her eyes for a moment, then opened them to find a myriad of colors interspersed with black, swinging in time to the rhythm of the music. All of it blurred as her heart raced.

Once, several years ago, she'd glimpsed into a ballroom much like this. Her young charges had been put to bed and she'd heard the echo of the music through the halls, beckoning her. She'd been unable to resist peeking in from one of the upper balconies. The beautiful ladies, the elegant men, the richness of the décor had been just as overwhelming as it was this evening.

Now she stood amidst the party but still didn't feel as if she belonged anymore than she had then.

"Don't lose your courage now," Viscount Weston murmured in her ear as he moved past her to offer his elbow to his grandmother. "Whom shall we introduce Miss Grisby to first?"

Viscountess Weston smiled over her shoulder at Emma. "We are not going to introduce her to anyone. They will come to us if they'd like to meet her."

"Excellent idea."

The pair moved forward but Michael continually looked over his shoulder to be certain she followed. Emma soon realized those looks from him would be her undoing, for they made her think of their kiss.

Never in her wildest dreams had she expected he might kiss her. Heat flushed her face as emotions swelled through her once again. What was she to make of it? Hope spiraled through her. Why else would he kiss her unless he held some affection for her? Her heart squeezed painfully. She knew she should not read too much into his actions. Men did not always link passion and true caring. She'd learned that much over the years. But she couldn't completely squelch the flicker of optimism deep inside her. She held it close, allowing it to warm her.

Perhaps she would feel the same if some other man kissed her. No. That was not true. She already knew that, and it would be silly to think otherwise. Of course, her experience was based on unwanted kisses from her employers, not handsome men with blue eyes who made her heart beat faster just by looking at her.

Before they'd moved more than a few steps across the room, someone stepped into their path, halting their progress.

"Hello, darling." The lady who greeted Viscount Weston was beautiful in a brittle way with high cheekbones and a narrow nose. Her carefully arranged blonde hair must've taken hours to complete. She offered her cheek to Michael for a kiss, surprising Emma with her forward behavior. Next she greeted the viscountess but received a rather cool reception. Then the woman's cold blue gaze landed on Emma.

Her head tilted to the side as though she found

Emma's appearance an oddity. "Who do we have here?"

"May I introduce Miss Emma Grisby, the granddaughter of a dear friend of mine. She's staying with me for a time," the viscountess answered. "Miss Grisby, this is Miss Catherine Vandimere, Michael's fiancé."

Emma's heart stopped as she tried to grasp the news. The woman studied her, the calculating look in her eyes making Emma uneasy. "How nice to meet you," Emma managed.

"I'm sure. Michael's told me all about you."

He hasn't told me anything about you, Emma thought, but she held her tongue. Hadn't she just told herself not to make too much of their kiss?

She couldn't help but turn to glare at the viscount. How dare he kiss her when he was engaged to another woman?

Michael—rather Viscount Weston—had the grace to appear uncomfortable, as though he realized his behavior was far from appropriate.

"Where are you from, Miss Grisby?"

Emma's mind filled with the image of their two-room flat at the lodging house. She could hardly share the address on Trenary Lane without raising suspicion. While she and the viscountess had discussed answers to several questions, that had not been one of them.

"She and her dear mother live north of London," the viscountess answered smoothly. "They rarely come to the city, so Miss Grisby's visit is very special to me."

Miss Vandimer's mouth thinned as though displeased with the answer. Emma felt like hugging the older woman, for she'd as much as declared Emma's importance to her. How lovely to have a champion. She was so used to fending for herself that she wasn't quite sure what to do or say other than smile.

"I'm sure you'll enjoy the entertainment London has to offer." Miss Vandimer wrapped her hand around Viscount Weston's arm. "It's too bad that my fiancé will be too busy to accompany you."

"Nonsense." The viscountess dismissed Catherine's words with a wave of her hand. "Michael will be more than pleased to escort us when needed. Won't you, Michael?"

Viscount Weston eyed his grandmother as though surprised at her declaration. Nonetheless, he agreed. "Of course. Anything for you, Grandmother."

Emma couldn't help but wonder if Viscountess Weston cared for Miss Vandimer. Surely she was in favor of her grandson settling down and marrying.

"Your gown is quite...lovely."

"Why thank you," Emma said with a smile. Somehow, the pause made it sound as if the woman had another word in mind but chose a polite one. Emma decided to ignore that. "Viscountess Weston has excellent taste, wouldn't you agree?"

Catherine nearly scowled. She could hardly say anything bad about the gown now. "*Trés belle.*"

"*Merci. Le vôtre robe est belle ainsi.*" Returning the compliment seemed the wisest line of defense.

Viscount Weston turned to her, a brow raised in surprise. "You speak French?"

"Yes," she said, reminding herself not to glare at Miss Vandimer. She well knew the woman had been trying to make her feel uncomfortable, as though she were some country miss who hadn't learned proper French.

"Your accent is impeccable."

"Why, thank you." Her uncle had taught her and insisted she perfect her accent.

Viscountess Weston beamed. "Well done." She

turned to Miss Vandimer. "Perhaps Miss Grisby might assist you with your accent."

Miss Vandimer's mouth popped open at the veiled insult.

Viscount Weston patted his fiancé's hand. "Would you honor me with this dance?"

With a lift of her chin and a glare at Emma, Miss Vandimer stepped away with Viscount Weston.

Emma glanced at the viscountess to see her smile remained. Angering Miss Vandimer did not seem like a wise idea, but she could hardly control Viscountess Weston. In truth, it had been rather entertaining.

"We shall find a spot a little farther from the musicians. We need to be able hear." She led the way and soon they were visiting with the viscountess's friends.

Emma's nerves calmed as the night continued. Several men approached, all asking her to dance, and she began to enjoy herself. She knew the proper steps for dancing and though she had little experience, she thought she'd performed quite well.

While a part of her felt guilty for having a good time, another part reminded her that if she appeared miserable, no man would want to spend time with her. That would defeat the whole purpose of the project.

"Have I introduced Lord Tagart?" the viscountess asked.

Emma turned to find a rather handsome man at her side. "A delight, I'm sure."

"The pleasure is all mine," he said with a smile. He had dark hair that threatened to disappear within a few years. His brown eyes were friendly and held a twinkle that made her smile.

Emma liked him immediately.

"The viscountess tells me you haven't been in London long."

Preferring not to lie, she hesitated before settling on an answer. "All this is certainly new to me." She glanced out across the crowded ballroom, only to realize she was searching for Lord Weston. Immediately she turned back to Lord Tagart, determined to focus on someone who mattered. "I'm sure events such as this are quite routine for you."

"Actually, no." He chuckled. "I rarely come to these functions. My aunt requested my presence, and I find myself very grateful to her." He smiled at her, making her realize that he referred to meeting her.

Flattered, she returned his smile, pleased she'd found someone she actually liked. So many of the people here seemed to pretend to be someone they weren't. But who was she to judge when she was doing the same thing? Her mother always told her one shouldn't judge unless one has walked in that person's shoes. She looked down at her own, just visible beneath the hem of her gown.

"Is something amiss?" Lord Tagart asked.

Emma abruptly looked up, realizing he must think her behavior quite odd. "I'm sorry. I was thinking of how my mother always tells me not to judge people unless I've walked in their shoes."

Lord Tagart looked down at his feet, then back up at her as though truly considering her words. "That is excellent advice."

"She's a very wise woman."

"Then she must have a very wise daughter." He held her gaze for a moment. "May I fetch some lemonade for you?"

"That would be lovely. I'm quite parched."

As he departed in search of refreshments, the viscountess moved closer. "Lord Tagart would be quite the catch."

"He seems like a nice man."

"Is being nice important to you?"

She looked closer at the viscountess in surprise. "Shouldn't it be?"

"That is up to you. Something to think about. You need to determine what requirements you have in a husband."

Somehow, the very idea tightened her stomach. She couldn't imagine making a list of what she wanted, but she understood the point. It was one she needed to consider. Now more than ever, she longed for her family. Tessa would easily be able to make a list. She could imagine her sister beside her, whispering in her ear about the merits of that gentleman or the gown worn by the lady across the room.

If circumstances were different, much different, they would've been here with their mother. Now that would truly have been fun.

Instead, she stood here by herself, trying to determine who was a friend and who was not. In many ways, it was not so different than trying to navigate the servants at the homes where she'd served as governess.

"Miss Grisby, may I introduce you to Lord Calverton? He has a lovely home in the country I've had the privilege of visiting." The viscountess gave Emma a pointed look, as if suggesting this was a man whom she should consider.

Soon, a few other men joined their group. She could hardly keep their names straight. Lord Tagart returned with lemonade for which she was very grateful. The glass gave her something to do with her hands and sipping it helped to fill the awkward silences that came with meeting new people.

"Aren't you a grand success this evening?" The whisper in her ear gave her a jolt followed by shivers, and the return of her anger.

"I'm pleased to have met several *nice* people." She glared at Viscount Weston out of the corner of her eye, not ready to forgive him. Nor did she want to appear rude to the other people with whom she was visiting.

"Tagart." Viscount Weston seemed rather surprised to see him at her side. "Good to see you."

"Weston. Congratulations on your upcoming nuptials."

"Thank you."

"Where is your fiancé?" Emma couldn't help but ask, partly out of curiosity and partly because she'd rather keep her distance from the woman.

"I believe she's dancing." The viscount scanned the dancers but didn't appear to search in earnest for her.

Unable to hold her silence a moment longer, she drew Michael aside to whisper, "How dare you!"

He raised a brow at her heated accusation. "How dare I what?"

She glanced about to find their conversation was already drawing a few stares, but she was determined to confront him about this. "You know very well to what I am referring."

Michael knew but didn't care to explain his behavior. How could he when he wasn't certain what had driven him to kiss her? The best he could do was to play it down, as though it hadn't mattered as much as it had. As if kissing her hadn't seemed as vital as breathing in that moment.

He kept his voice low, not wanting to air their conversation any more than she. "A simple kiss to wish you well on this new endeavor."

"You are engaged." The accusation in her tone was echoed by the flash in her eyes.

He shook his head and glanced away. Dare he tell her that her anger only made him long to kiss her once more? "A kiss between old friends. Nothing more."

"I trust it will not happen again."

He bit his tongue to stop himself from telling her he accepted her challenge. His nod seemed to appease her. He'd watched the crowd of men grow around Emma and with it, his concern. Why wasn't his grandmother keeping a closer eye on her?

Catherine had been less than pleased when he'd advised her that he needed to see what was happening, leaving her in the middle of a conversation. He knew she was most likely fluttering her lashes at some other lord. The time had come for a conversation with her about his expectations of the marriage. He had no intention of being made a fool by her behavior.

He pushed aside his irritation with his fiancé to focus on his irritation with the woman at his side. "Perhaps you're going a bit too far with your attempt to meet a man?"

"How so?" She narrowed her eyes as though she couldn't imagine of what he was speaking.

"I thought you hoped to meet a potential suitor or two." He eyed the ring of men nearby. "Not gather a flock."

"I have not done anything wrong," she whispered.

While he knew her behavior had been circumspect as he hadn't taken his eyes off her since they'd parted, she had to be doing something to attract this many.

His gaze caught on some of this season's hopeful debutantes on the other side of the room. Their pale gowns and youthful faces would attract some, but when compared to Emma's more mature form and the intelligence that radiated from her, he knew with whom he'd prefer to speak. Obviously the men before her felt the same way.

Yet when he scanned the group surrounding them as Emma moved back to stand near then, his irritation returned.

"I understand you haven't yet had the opportunity to partake of London's sights. Perhaps you might enjoy seeing one of the museums," Lord Calverton suggested.

"Oh, that would be—"

"Excellent idea." Michael made an attempt at a smile as he turned to Emma. "Which day shall we go?"

Her eyes widened. "I thought you were...otherwise *engaged* this week."

Guilt pricked him at her choice of words. He wasn't aiding her by escorting her when she could be spending time with a potential suitor. Never mind that he found the idea of her in another man's company intolerable. In truth, he needed to keep a close eye on her. What if the professor attempted to contact her during an outing?

"My plans have changed."

Catherine would be displeased to hear he'd be spending more time in Emma's company, but he told himself he had no choice. With Simmons dead, they had few leads to pursue. In all honesty, he was starting to believe that Emma had no idea her uncle lived. If he hadn't contacted her in these past ten years, why would he bother to do so now?

But Michael couldn't put aside the idea that he would. And when he did, Michael had every intention of being there. They needed to know what the professor was up to and why. Heaven forbid if he was still trying to do some terrible experiment with children. Somehow, they needed to find him—before someone else's life was in danger. Emma had to be the key to that.

Emma followed the viscountess up the stairs of the townhouse, her mind spinning much like it had while dancing at the ball. The evening had far exceeded her expectations. She'd thought she'd be standing by herself while everyone else visited. Instead she'd danced and taken part in many conversations. With a smile, she remembered Lord Tagart's kindness, Lord Calverton's shy smile. They were both nice men, very different from Viscount Weston, but pleasant all the same.

With a sigh, she thought once more of his kiss. Unfortunately, any man she met would be compared against him. It wasn't fair, but what could she do about it?

Disappointment filled her as she pondered his engagement. In truth, it didn't matter that he was engaged. How often had she told herself that he was not for her? Nothing had changed. She'd only changed her clothes and her hair, not the person she was on the inside.

She said it again in her mind, more firmly this time.

Not for me.

It failed to help.

"I wonder if I might ask you to read to me for a few minutes," Viscountess Weston requested as she reached the landing. "I find my mind filled with all the conversation at the ball. Reading seems to allow me to sleep better."

"I'd like that very much," Emma said. She truly thought it a good idea. She couldn't imagine going to sleep right now either.

"Lovely. Why don't you prepare for bed and then join me in my room."

Quickly, the maid removed Emma's gown and corset and loosely braided her hair. By the time

Emma knocked on the door of the viscountess's room, she was sitting up in her bed with a book in her lap.

Emma couldn't help but glance around the spacious room. It was decorated in various shades of cream with a pale green accent. The effect was cool and relaxing. A tufted chair stood beside the bed and the viscountess gestured her toward it.

"This is such a treat." She handed Emma the book with a smile.

"I love to read with my family, so this is a pleasure for me as well." She examined the title, surprised to find it was a popular fiction novel. "I've heard this is an exciting story."

"I hope it's not too exciting or I shall never sleep." The smile she gave Emma was much like that of a young girl's and made Emma smile in return. "Let us try a few pages and see if we care for it."

Emma settled into the chair and opened the book. Several pages later, she was well engrossed in the story. She paused to glance at the viscountess but couldn't tell if she was merely resting her eyes or if she was sleeping. She decided to continue to the end of the chapter just so she had a good stopping place. Unfortunately, the author put a clever hook at the end of it. She paused, debating whether she should turn the page.

"Surely, you're not going to stop reading there?" the viscountess asked, her voice slurred with sleepiness. "Read the next few sentences so we won't be left wondering if he braves the storm to go after her."

With a smile, Emma read a few more sentences before pausing again.

"Thank heavens. A hero who didn't try to protect her would not be worth reading about." The viscountess opened one eye. "Don't you agree?"

"Indeed. Though it's her own fault for running out into the rainy night to begin with."

"Hmm...true enough. Making silly decisions in the height of emotional drama happens more often than you think."

"Have you ever done something like that?" Emma immediately regretted the question as soon as she asked it. "I'm sorry. That was inappropriate of me."

"Nonsense, my dear. If we're to become friends, we need to know these sorts of things about each other. And yes. I have. Terribly silly decisions. As is still true today, love matches were rare in my day, but I thought I'd found one with George. Shortly before we were to marry, I became convinced he didn't love me after all."

"How awful."

"Indeed. I heard rumors that the reasons he wanted to marry me had more to do with financial matters than me. I was devastated. And like the silly heroine in the book, I left his company in inclement weather."

Emma held her breath, hoping the viscountess would finish her tale.

"Lucky for me, he followed and convinced me that he loved me and saved me from frostbite." She chuckled. "That was a night to remember."

Emma tried to imagine what it would be like to have a man love her enough to come after her in the middle of a storm. Would she have a chance to find a man like that? Or did she need to accept any man who showed interest in her? Would it be enough for her to find one with whom she could be friends?

With a quiet sigh, she closed her eyes for a brief moment. She was afraid she'd already found a man whom she could give her heart to, but he didn't want it.

CHAPTER EIGHT

Michael stared at Charles Nulty, surprised this soft spoken, timid man could've once served as chief warder of Pentonville Prison for so many years. When Ashbury had sent a message this morning asking Michael to accompany him on this meeting, Michael had expected they'd be speaking with a man of some presence, an authority figure.

The man before them was nothing of the sort.

Instead, he was merely a bewildered old man. Michael could feel Ashbury's frustration mount as Nulty puttered about his drawing room, showing them the collection of small china dogs his wife had accumulated. One at a time.

"This one is a Saint Bernard. Quite an interesting dog, you know."

"Yes, that's fascinating, but as I mentioned earlier, we'd like to ask you a few questions about your position at Pentonville Prison." Ashbury glanced at Michael as though Michael should somehow assist him.

Michael lifted a brow, uncertain as to how he could help the old man stay on the topic at hand. "You were there for many years." Michael tried a conversational tone, hoping that would relax Nulty.

"Indeed. Many, many years." He set down the

Saint Bernard, adjusted its position, then stared out the window for a long moment.

"We're wondering if you might remember a prisoner there by the name of Vincent Simmons."

Nulty turned to stare at Ashbury in surprise. "Do you have any idea how many men went through that prison? How could you think I would remember any of them?"

Michael sighed. He really hadn't expected the man to recall Simmons.

But Ashbury didn't seem convinced. "There are two men we'd like to learn more about actually. The other man was Edward Smith."

The old man hesitated before picking up another figurine, a flicker of something crossing his face.

Ashbury seemed to have caught it as well, for he moved closer to Nulty. "There have been rumors that someone allowed the two men to change places. Smith hung in Simmons' stead."

"That would never be permitted." He set the figurine down, adjusting it to line up precisely with the others.

"No. But you and I both know these things happen."

Michael feigned interest in another figurine, trailing his finger along the smooth surface. "Smith was said to be dying of consumption anyway."

Nulty frowned as he glanced at the item Michael touched. "That one is a Talbot hound brought to England by William the Conqueror. Excellent scent hound."

Michael took a second look at the dog. "I had no idea. Never seen one like it."

Ashbury glared at him, and Michael cleared his throat, bringing himself back to their inquiry.

"We've been told the individual who requested the switch was a man of science." Michael kept his gaze on Nulty to gauge his reaction.

"Science? What would he want with a prisoner?"

"We're hoping you could help us with that. Along with the identity of the man."

Ashbury shifted to stand directly in front of Nulty. "Sometimes, we're forced to do things we wouldn't consider doing under normal circumstances."

"We're not here to cast blame on anyone," Michael added, hoping to encourage an answer. "We only want to discover the identity of the person who requested the arrangement."

"Why does it matter?" Nulty shook his head as he shifted another of the figurines. "That was a long time ago."

Starting to believe the man remembered more than he was letting on, Michael decided to press him further. "We believe this man has been conducting tests with electromagnetism on children. Lives are at risk."

"That's outlandish. I don't believe you." Nulty tightened his lips, much like a belligerent child who refused to listen as he picked up another figurine.

"We have no reason to deceive you."

"If there's anything you can remember, anything you can tell us, it might save someone's life." Michael wanted to throttle the man for being so stubborn.

"Children, you say?" Nulty asked almost reluctantly.

"Who knows what he'll try next in the name of science," Ashbury added. "Dogs perhaps?"

Nulty turned to glare at Ashbury, obviously horrified at the prospect. "Surely not."

"One never knows," Michael added.

Nulty shook his head and heaved a sigh. "I received a message from someone who called himself 'the professor'. Said Simmons was his nephew and that he needed his assistance with research he was conducting. He promised to make sure Simmons behaved and changed his ways."

"Simmons murdered my fiancé's father, all for the sake of a meteorite." The cold green of Ashbury's eyes showed the intensity of his feelings. "Why would you allow him to escape his due punishment?"

"He threatened me," Nulty protested. "I had no choice."

"How?"

Nulty shifted as he rubbed his brow. "In the first message, he offered money. I refused. In the next, he advised me that he knew where my family and I lived. He knew my daughter's name. He named the shop where she worked. The message said if I didn't do as he asked, he would have her...accosted on the way home one night." Nulty swallowed hard. "Again I refused."

Michael watched as the old man struggled with his lingering guilt, something to which Michael could relate.

"Soon after that, two men stopped her on her way home. They tore her dress, struck her, and scared the bloody hell out of her. Another message came the next day, advising me that the next time would be worse."

"These messages bore the same signature?"

"Aye. All were signed 'the professor'. No name." Nulty looked Ashbury in the eye. "Surely you can see that I had to protect my daughter. He left me no choice. Family comes first."

Ashbury nodded. "Yes. Family comes first."

"My daughter had to quit work. She was too frightened, even after I had a guard accompany her."

"At times, it's difficult to find the line between staying true to your honor and protecting your family." Michael avoided Ashbury's gaze as he spoke, not wanting him to read anything more into what Michael said. Those simple words shared far too much of himself.

Nulty pulled at his collar as though it suddenly felt too tight. "I don't know that I could've done anything different than I did at the time. I've gone over it many times in my mind and found no other solution."

"If you remember anything else, please contact us. We need to find this man before he hurts others."

"A meteorite you said? What of this?" Nulty walked across the room to a table with newssheets on it. He sorted through them until he found what he was looking for and handed it to Michael.

"Murder at the Museum," Michael read aloud. He glanced at Ashbury to see if he'd already seen the article.

Ashbury shook his head.

"A guard was found murdered at the Museum of Scientific Research for Rocks and Minerals. The murderer escaped with a unique lunar meteorite, one of the largest ever found." Michael read through the remainder of the article, but learned little else. Still, he intended to add the information to his list.

"Perhaps a trip to the museum is in order," Ashbury suggested.

Michael nodded. "We'll have to hurry. It says here that tomorrow they're moving the meteorite exhibit to a safer location. It might also be time to discover more about the professor's family tree from Emma. If he had a nephew named Simmons, surely she was aware of him."

Did he dare ask her? Or would it only alert her to their suspicions?

Emma breathed deeply, hoping to calm her nerves. The invitation from Viscount Weston this morning to accompany him to a museum had been surprising despite his mention of an outing the previous night. She had to wonder if his fiancé knew of his invitation. Would she be accompanying them as well?

"I hope you enjoy yourself," Viscountess Weston said as she looked up from the book she was reading as Emma entered the drawing room.

"Are you quite certain you don't want to join us?"

"I'm afraid rocks and minerals do not hold my interest."

Emma smiled. "I confess I find them fascinating. Rather unladylike of me, I'm sure, but my uncle took great pleasure in his own collection. We had many enjoyable strolls searching for unusual rocks." She hesitated to say anything further. Sharing her personal life with others was something she'd stopped doing long ago.

"Your uncle sounds like an interesting man."

"He was. I miss him still." She smoothed the soft yellow fabric of her gown. Wearing such lovely gowns each day would take some getting used to. As she donned her gloves, she glanced at the viscountess. "It was very kind of your grandson to offer to take me."

"Hmm...'kind' is not a word often used to describe him."

"He told me the same thing. I don't think we'll be gone overly long. Is there anything you would like me to acquire for you while I'm out?"

"No thank you, dear. You enjoy yourself."

"Good day to you, ladies," Michael said as he entered the room. He bent to kiss his grandmother's cheek.

Something about the sweetness of the gesture and the sincerity of his smile warmed Emma's heart. He adored his grandmother and didn't seem to care who knew it.

"How are you today, Miss Grisby?" He turned to her and smiled, but there was a shadow in his eyes she didn't care for.

"Fine, thank you. And you?"

"Well, thank you. I do think there's something you should know before we depart for the museum."

"Oh?"

"There was a guard murdered there two nights ago."

A shiver seeped down Emma's spine, partly because of the intense stare Michael gave her as he delivered the unsettling news.

"Is it safe, Michael? I wouldn't want either of you to be in any danger," the viscountess said.

"I'm sure the danger has passed. I'd postpone our visit, but the meteorite collection I'm particularly interested in will be removed after today. However, I'll understand if you'd prefer not to accompany me."

"Emma, are you certain you feel comfortable?" the viscountess asked.

Viscount Weston looked at her again for a long moment, as if trying to gauge her reaction to the news. Emma raised her brow in response. Did he expect her to faint? To protest their visit?

Yet as he continued to stare, she had to wonder if he somehow thought she was involved in the crime.

Convinced she must be mistaken, she asked, "The murderer has not yet been apprehended?"

"Not thus far."

"That's terrible," the viscountess added. "What did he take?"

"A rather rare lunar meteorite."

Ignoring the viscount's odd behavior, Emma pondered the matter. "If it's so rare, wouldn't it be difficult to sell without someone recognizing it?"

Viscount Weston nodded.

"If he can't sell it, what use would he have for it?"

"That's an excellent question," he said, his gaze still on her.

Unable to determine why he studied her so closely, she did the only thing she could—ignore him.

The idea of touring a museum where such a tragedy had taken place bothered her, but she realized she trusted Michael to ensure they remained safe. "If you believe it to be secure then I'm happy to go."

"From what I understand the murderer was after a particular stone and was successful in his quest. I would say he obtained what he wanted and has no need to return."

"Very well, then. Let us be on our way." Emma turned to the viscountess. "Are you sure you won't come with us?"

"I'll leave all the excitement to you young people. I'm certain you'll fill me in on the details."

"Of course," Emma said with a smile.

"Shall we?" Viscount Weston asked.

Soon they were settled in his carriage, a maid on the seat beside Emma to serve as chaperone. There was no sign of Miss Vandimer and Emma decided not to raise the topic.

The viscount said little as they traveled to the museum, leaving Emma to wonder at his mood. Rather than disturb the silence, she let it be.

The museum appeared to be a former residence, albeit a very large one. Marble pillars set on either side of a massive staircase gave the entrance a sense of grandeur. Emma glanced at

Michael, but still he said nothing. She wasn't sure if they'd traipse through the entire building in silence or if he intended to speak to her.

No matter, she told herself. She was more interested in the exhibits than her companion. She nodded at the footman who assisted her from the carriage and proceeded toward the steps that led to the front door, the maid trailing far behind.

"In a hurry?" The viscount's voice was so close that it startled her.

"Oh, are you speaking with me now? I'm not certain why you invited me to accompany you if you aren't going to converse." She berated herself for stating her opinion. Even the maid who suddenly studied the flowers growing along the path must think her anything but a well-behaved lady.

"My apologies. I have much on my mind."

She bit her lip, determined not to admit that she did as well. Nor would she inquire as to what bothered him. They were here to enjoy the museum, not each other's company.

Yet her mother's soft spoken voice whispered in her mind. *Be kind. You haven't walked in his shoes.*

"I hope it's nothing serious." She glanced at the arm he offered her, hesitating before placing her hand on it. Touching him for any reason seemed a poor idea. Her emotions were already tangled enough.

"Unfortunately it is. I just have to hope it will solve itself."

She turned his answer over in her mind, wondering if she should do the same. She'd never been one to live on hope. A course of action seemed a better plan.

"What are you thinking?" he asked.

She looked up in surprise. "Nothing. Why?"

"I can practically see the mechanisms spinning

behind your eyes. You're definitely thinking something."

"I know nothing of your problem, so I have nothing to offer you."

"Yes, you do. Go ahead and say it."

With a sigh, she decided she might as well share her thoughts, meager though they might be. "I've found action a sounder plan than hope. Hope seems destined to be unfulfilled."

He stopped and brought her to a halt next to him, those blue eyes studying her as though trying to discover all her secrets. "While I agree that taking action is important, hope is as well. Without hope, what is there?"

"Reality might taste bitter, but disappointment can choke you." How many times had she held hope that someone would reach out a hand to help her and her family? That Tessa would wake up one day and feel better? That circumstances would change and her family would have adequate food and shelter?

"Miss Grisby—Emma—has life been so difficult since your uncle's...death?"

She swallowed hard. Her given name on his lips made her chest ache. What had she been thinking to share her feelings with him? "I don't want your sympathy." Nor his pity. That was the last thing she wanted. "I'm merely saying that God helps those who help themselves." Though she wasn't even certain she believed that anymore.

"True enough. But without hope, why bother to rise each day and put one foot in front of the other?"

She closed her eyes. She'd wondered the same thing so many mornings, and she told him what she told herself each day. "Because others depend on you. Because it's expected of you. Because there is no alternative."

"Oh, but there is. I'm certain you'll find it."

She opened her eyes to find him close. Too close. The outer blue ring of his eyes was a shade darker than the inside. How had she missed that before? His gaze dropped to her lips and awareness spiraled through her. "It's time you had some fun in your life, Emma. You're overdue for an adventure."

Butterflies fluttered inside her. Surely that was only nervousness. "Adventure?"

Michael smiled. "You say that as if it's a foreign concept. Life is not always easy. That's true. But adding a few light-hearted activities makes it bearable. Interesting at the very least."

"I'm not staying with your grandmother for entertainment purposes."

"No, but what harm can it cause? You're here for a fortnight, perhaps longer. I'm merely suggesting that you enjoy it. Starting now. I'm making it a priority to see that you have a few adventures."

His change of mood made her wonder what had come over him.

Without waiting for her reply or responding to her questioning look, he took her gloved hand and tucked it beneath his elbow. "Shall we see what the museum has to offer in the form of entertainment?" For a long moment, he glanced about as though searching for something.

"What is it?"

He shook his head. "It almost feels as though someone is watching us. Do you feel it?"

She'd been so involved in him—or rather, the situation, she hadn't noticed. But now that he mentioned it, she sensed it too.

"Never mind," he said with a smile. "Let us tour the museum."

They walked up the steps, and a uniformed guard opened the door for them, causing a bell to echo through the house.

"Good day to you."

Michael inquired as to the location of the meteorite exhibit and the guard directed them to the uppermost floor. "Professor Wattle is up there somewhere. He can direct you to the exact location."

Emma advised the maid to wait for them in the chair by the door. Then she and Michael proceeded up the stairs.

From what Emma could discern, the entire place was filled with dusty display cases and boxes with all sorts of specimens of varying sizes. It was difficult to tell in what order, if any, the items were displayed.

"Good day." The gravelly voice floating down from the top of the stairs startled Emma.

Michael patted her hand as he looked up. "Good afternoon."

"Thank you for visiting the museum. Is there anything in particular I can direct you toward?" The attendant looked like a retired professor with gray hair, long sideburns, and a pair of spectacles sitting slightly crooked on his nose.

"I understand you have an interesting collection of meteorites."

"Well, it is not quite as interesting as it was two days past, but yes, we do."

"We're terribly sorry to hear about the unfortunate events that occurred," Emma offered. She hesitated to discuss it in detail, uncertain how much to say.

"Indeed. The death of Mr. Bryant weighs heavy on all of us here at the museum. Quite unexpected." He pointed to the ceiling. "The meteorites are on the upper floor, if you'd care to follow me."

They trailed after the attendant who introduced himself as Professor Wattle. "No other visitors have ventured in today. I suppose the news of the murder has scared them away."

"How many meteorites are in the collection?" Michael asked.

"That number is now seventeen." He heaved a sigh as though saddened to have the number reduced.

"Are there any lunar meteorites here?"

"Not anymore. The only one we had was stolen." Professor Wattle paused on the landing of the upper floor and turned to frown at Michael. "I say, it's rather odd that you are asking about the lunar meteorite the day after it was stolen."

"The article in the paper stated a lunar specimen was taken. I thought perhaps you had others."

"Humph. Haven't seen the article. The press can be a nuisance these days. Some news is better left amongst those it concerns."

Emma thought he had a valid point. While the populace needed to know if their safety was in danger, spreading the details of the rarity of lunar meteorites might raise the interest of more thieves.

The professor crossed the floor to a room on the right. The wood floor creaked under their feet, giving an eerie feel to their tour.

"Not all of our specimens are organized. We are continually working on that, in between giving tours, of course."

"I'm certain it's a never ending task."

"We just received a large donation of stones last week. It takes some time to sort through them, to determine what's worthless and what should be displayed. Many of the new items end up in this room until we have the opportunity to examine and catalog them."

Michael made his way down one of the narrow aisles. Boxes sat on tables and on the floor, some overflowing with rocks, others with only one or two inside. Very few had labels. Emma recognized many from what her uncle had shared with her, but others looked no different than ordinary rocks.

"Was the meteorite taken a new addition or had it been in the collection for some time?"

"We'd had that one several years but didn't realize what it was until recently. We don't even have a sketch of it though I am going to attempt to draw it from memory. Somewhere we have the measurements and weight of the thing."

"I'd be interested in seeing that information. Can you send me a message when you have it?"

Professor Wattle seemed grateful to have someone take an interest in his lost meteorite, as if the rock had been one of his favorite children. Again, Emma looked at Michael, wondering at his acute interest in the topic.

As if aware of her curiosity, one side of his mouth turned up in an attempt at a smile. "I find all this quite fascinating."

Somehow, she didn't believe that was the only reason for his interest. She continued along the aisle as the men spoke, stopping to examine whatever caught her interest.

Professor Wattle left them on their own after giving a rather vague explanation of what they'd find in some of the other rooms on the top floor.

"Quite the collection, isn't it?" Michael asked.

"It would be helpful if they were better organized. Providing an explanation of what the stones are and where they were found would make it more interesting."

"That would certainly draw more visitors. You seem to enjoy looking at the collection." He drew nearer to peer over her shoulder at what had caught her attention.

"As you may remember, my uncle collected and I often assisted him." She looked up to find him far too close, studying her. "He searched for lunar meteorites prior to his death."

"He taught you many things, didn't he?"

"I've learned much more than most women my age. That knowledge is what allowed me to become a governess."

He frowned, as though hesitant how to respond. "You must miss him."

She swallowed hard, unwilling to admit just how much. "If it weren't for Uncle Grisby taking the time to educate me, I'm not certain what would've become of us."

"There is far more to you than your knowledge."

She considered the idea, but dismissed it. "My education has helped me in more ways than I can count."

"I'm certain it has, but it's only one of your qualities. You underestimate yourself." He reached out as though to touch her, only to draw back. "I still haven't gotten used to your new appearance. Your transformation is amazing. How did you manage to hide all this," he allowed his gaze to skim over the length of her, "beneath that grey dress?"

"With great care."

"You're clever. More than you credit yourself."

Her heart skipped a beat as his finger grazed along her cheek. She looked up to find his gaze on her lips. She drew a breath to steady herself only to catch his scent—male, woods, and the outdoors. Something about it made her stomach flutter.

Those blue eyes studied her with a hint of heat in their depths. "You're beautiful."

She felt her face flush at his compliment, the warmth spreading through her whole body. In that moment as he looked at her, she felt beautiful for the first time in a very long while.

"Thank you." The words were difficult to say,

for they meant she accepted his compliment—no easy task for her.

His hand cupped her cheek and she couldn't help but lean into it. Physical contact was rare in her world. She hadn't realized how much she'd missed it until now.

Slowly, he leaned forward, as though afraid he'd startle her. Anticipation filled her as his lips drew near.

"Emma, are you prepared to enjoy what life has to offer?"

She blinked, unable to answer yet unable to step away. She was firmly caught though he'd barely touched her. Dare she accept his challenge? While she knew it was wrong as he was engaged, she desperately wanted to explore this feeling. What if it never came again?

With the smallest breath, she gave him her answer by easing forward, helpless to resist him.

At last, those firm sculpted lips touched hers.

Magic.

That's all she could think. How could two pair of lips pressed together create such magic? The sparks igniting in her body couldn't be described as anything less.

He moved his mouth over hers as though thoroughly enjoying the taste of her. He didn't draw her into his arms, just held her tethered to him with his hand on her cheek and his lips on hers.

Then she understood.

The choice was hers as to how much she was willing to take.

Heart pounding, she reached up to place her hand on his shoulder not quite sure where the best spot was. Then she lifted her other hand to touch the back of his head where his dark hair lay against his jacket. How she wished she didn't wear her gloves.

All thoughts fled as she tilted her head to better fit her mouth to his. With a groan he pulled her tight against him and suddenly all felt right with her world. Her body was pressed along his length, the solid strength of him making her feel things in places that she'd never expected.

Magic indeed.

"I do have one other meteorite you might find of interest." The approaching voice of Professor Wattle brought reality crashing back. Michael pulled away as though coming to his senses.

His blue eyes blazed into hers, the heat there catching her breath.

"I'd be interested in any that you have to show us." He turned to face the professor, blocking Emma from view which gave her a moment to collect herself.

Only, she needed much longer than that. How was she to protect herself when desire betrayed her?

CHAPTER NINE

Michael berated himself for the tenth time as the carriage made its way back to his grandmother's. He was engaged yet he couldn't seem to resist kissing Emma. What was wrong with him, and what made her so different from Catherine?

For one thing, Catherine never would've agreed to spend hours in a dusty old building full of rocks. Emma had seemed to enjoy the outing as much as he. With his fiancé, he felt only the smallest stir, but with Emma, his feelings for her nearly overwhelmed him.

Years ago, he'd sworn never to allow passion to control his behavior. Not after witnessing how it had ruled his parents. Their emotions had ranged from burning passion to raging jealousy to outright disdain, all with him being tugged to and fro in the middle. That was why he'd chosen to view marriage as a business arrangement. He rarely showed Catherine any affection and had convinced himself he preferred it that way.

That was not for him.

He'd thought he'd escaped the seeds of destruction that had ultimately ended his parents' lives. But something about Emma brought forth a response in him of which he hadn't thought himself capable.

Was it the bow of her lips? The curve of her jaw? No, his physical attraction to her was only part of it. He genuinely liked and admired her, he realized as he glanced at her. Her intelligent and thoughtful comments were so different from other ladies her age.

The idea that Emma held no hope for the future bothered him. No. *Bothered* was too light a word. Her resignation touched him somewhere deep inside.

Yet who was he to cast stones? Hadn't he taken a similar action by treating his entire life as a business? After living with his parents' volatile relationship, how could he do anything else? He couldn't—wouldn't—live the way they had.

The entire *ton* had known whether things were good or bad between them. They'd made no attempt to hide their feelings from anyone, including him. While their deaths had been a terrible event, the end of the tug-of-war had been a relief. Guilt filled him at the thought. Not even his grandmother knew the depth of his angst.

Now he found himself in a quandary. Part of him wanted to show Emma the lighter side of life. To get her to smile or even better, laugh— something she rarely seemed to do. He well remembered how delightful her laugh had been, and he was determined to hear it again.

That did *not* mean he needed to touch her. He couldn't risk allowing passion to overcome him. God only knew what terrible consequences would come of that.

Emma cleared her throat, then glanced at the maid beside her. She looked Michael squarely in the eye. "I must request that there is no repetition of the previous incident in the museum."

Her ability to speak her mind was one of those things he admired. "My apologies if I offended you."

"I'm certain your *fiancé* would object."

Her emphasis on the term made her meaning clear.

Michael did not appreciate the reminder but couldn't deny that she was right. "You may trust it won't happen again."

She gave a curt nod, looking very much like a governess who knew she did the right thing by reprimanding her charge. Her superior expression annoyed him to no end.

He dearly wanted to shake her poise. "Although I must say it served its purpose."

She narrowed her eyes in suspicion. "How so?"

Michael glanced at the maid, all too aware he should keep his mouth shut. Yet he couldn't resist teasing Emma. "Enjoyment was had by both parties."

"Oh." Her mouth popped open as that lovely shade of pink that he liked so much flooded her cheeks. "Despite that, a reoccurrence would be most unwise."

He raised a brow, appreciating that she didn't attempt to deny that she'd liked their kiss. "I can only promise to try if you will do so as well."

Her gasp caused him to smile. She glanced at the maid who seemed to be trying her best to hide her amusement.

"You, my lord, are incorrigible." Emma glanced out the window before meeting his gaze once again, a small smile on her lips.

Michael watched her for a long moment, then deliberately dropped his eyes to her lips. Her mouth parted in response, and unless he was mistaken, her chest rose as she drew a quick breath. Surely that meant she was as affected by their mutual attraction as he.

That only made the thought of his engagement even more unwelcome. With a scowl, he turned his attention to the passing scenery.

Emma Grisby did not fit into his carefully laid plans, and he'd best remember that.

"Ye want me to steal paper?" Vincent shook his head, thoroughly confused at his uncle's request. "How does that gain us money?"

"Not any paper, Vincent. Bonds. They're worth a significant sum."

"If they're worth so much, then why doesn't everyone take them?"

"Not everyone is smart enough to know how to make this work. Luckily for you, I am."

"So ye're sayin' I just take the paper from the man who's carryin' them and then these papers are ours for the keepin'?"

"Basically. The advantage of these particular bonds is that they are unregistered as the parties involved prefer to remain anonymous. In this case, a certain Italian gentleman involved in an unsavory business. Whoever carries the bonds is considered the owner. Now if they were a registered bond, we would not be able to collect."

Vincent could only stare at his uncle, hoping the old man didn't expect him to understand any of this nonsense.

His uncle sighed. "All you need to do is watch for a man walking along Clerkenwell Road. My sources have advised that the clerk who will be carrying these bonds lives there. He's to carry the documents to a bank on Tuesday morn, but as I mentioned, we do not know a specific time. You'll arrive on Clerkenwell Road shortly after dawn and watch until you see him. You will relieve the man of the bonds by whatever means necessary and return here where I will verify the documents. Then we'll determine our method of cashing them in at the bank."

"Ye're sure it wouldn't be easier to steal some money from the bank directly?" The whole thing seemed far too complicated to him. What good was paper? You couldn't use it to buy a pint.

"These will provide us with a non-traceable method of obtaining significant funds. We need those funds to obtain the rhodite which will grant us an alternative method of maintaining the power of the electromagnetic devices since you haven't obtained another meteorite."

Vincent shook his head. Of course all this was his fault. "I thought the one I took from the museum would help."

"Help, yes. But we need more, which is why we still need the one Ashbury has." His uncle waved his gloved hand in dismissal. "Now then, please do your best not to be seen, especially not by the man carrying the bonds. We cannot afford any loose ends."

"Should I kill him?"

"Only if he sees you. As I said, we cannot afford any loose ends."

Emma readied for the ball that evening with the grim determination of a soldier preparing for battle.

Her pale pink gown was trimmed in a dark wine piping. The bodice was fitted, and the neckline more daring than anything she'd dreamed of wearing. She could picture her mother's frown as well as Tessa's grin of approval.

If she wanted to catch a man, she needed to throw out the proper bait. Apparently that had something to do with displaying her breasts.

Keeping Tessa in mind, she eyed herself critically in the mirror. "I'd like my hair to look different than last night."

"Excellent idea, miss. Perhaps one curl over your shoulder with the rest swept up in back?" The maid held Emma's hair in place for her approval.

"Yes, that will do nicely."

She had to remember the purpose of her time here. Her goal was to find a wealthy husband who would care for her and her family. He didn't need to be immensely rich, but he did need to be pleasant and kind. Marrying a mean-hearted man would not do. She wouldn't allow such a person near her family. Plus she didn't think he'd be as willing to help pay for her sister's medical bills.

Michael flew to her mind, but she immediately thrust him aside. Spending time with him was a waste. It served no point. His suggestion of learning to enjoy herself was nonsense. How could she while her family was in such dire straits?

The sooner she found a husband, the better. Lord Tagart might be a potential candidate. He seemed quite nice and rather handsome. Perhaps she needed to inquire of the viscountess what she knew of his wealth.

She hadn't cared overmuch for Lord Calverton but wondered if she'd judged him too quickly.

Why did the thought of all this make her feel so tired?

"How does that look, miss?"

Emma hardly recognized the woman in the mirror. She closed her eyes. "Very nice. Thank you, Louise."

Before nerves could catch up with her, she rose, collected her gloves and cloak and made her way to the drawing room.

The viscountess already sat in her favorite chair, sipping a glass of sherry. Her face lit with a smile as she caught sight of Emma. "You look delightful."

"Thank you. May I say you look wonderful as well? That color is very becoming on you."

The viscountess smoothed the fabric of her vivid coral evening gown. "This is one of my favorites." She gestured toward the decanter and glasses. "Have a glass of sherry with me."

Emma poured herself a small measure and sipped, grateful for the false courage it would provide.

"The ball will be an even larger affair than the previous night."

Viscountess Weston's words did nothing to calm Emma's nerves. Some of her worry must've shown on her face, for the viscountess added, "That's nothing to fret over. It simply means you'll have more options from which to choose."

"And that there's a bigger chance of someone realizing that I am pretending to be something I'm not."

"Nonsense. You're Emma Grisby. You're not pretending to be anyone else. Just because you're wearing a different gown than you wore last week doesn't make you a fraud." She set her empty glass on the table and rose. "Besides, you're far too young to have determined exactly who you are. Isn't that part of why you're here?"

Emma pondered the viscountess's words, realizing she was right. The past few years had been spent putting others needs first. She wasn't sure who she was any more. Perhaps the next week or two would allow her to discover more.

The viscountess made no mention of Michael, much to Emma's disappointment. She reminded herself that his absence would make it easier for her to focus on her goal. Odd how she couldn't quite convince herself of that.

Soon they arrived at the Jackson's ball, one of

the most coveted events of the season. The size of the mansion took Emma aback.

"Lord Jackson married an American heiress some years ago. Her father is even wealthier than Adolphus Vandimer," the viscountess whispered in Emma's ear. "He gave the mansion to them upon their marriage. Can you imagine how many servants it takes to maintain the place?"

The practical statement made Emma smile. The viscountess patted her arm. "Let us see who decided to make an appearance."

After greeting their hostess, who seemed to notice nothing unusual about Emma, they entered the spacious ballroom.

"Oh, my." Emma could only gawk at the amazing décor.

The entire expanse was decorated to mimic Egypt. The columns along both sides were covered with stone carved with hieroglyphics. The wall sconces were torches, causing a smoky haze to linger in the air. Two massive pharaohs painted in gold and black stood guard at the end of the ballroom, nearly reaching the ceiling. Gold drapes graced the alcoves and potted ferns were placed strategically to provide privacy.

The viscountess leaned close. "They traveled to Egypt three years ago and fell in love with the place. It might have been easier to move there and enjoy the real thing rather than dragging half of it back here."

"It's quite...impressive." The money it must've taken to complete the ballroom staggered her. "Amazing."

"That's one word for it. I've heard Lady Jackson has grown weary of this theme and wants something new, but her husband refuses to change it after all the money they've spent decorating it."

Emma could only shake her head. The ball

gowns and evening attire seemed almost out of place amidst the Egyptian backdrop.

The viscountess saw an acquaintance, and they eased through the crowd toward her. Emma scanned the guests, then stopped abruptly when she realized for whom she was searching. Her mission would be much easier without him here, she reminded herself again. She planted a smile on her face, determined to make progress toward finding a potential husband.

Within moments, someone asked her to dance and the evening passed in a blur. Her cheeks hurt from smiling so much. She met so many people she couldn't possibly remember each of their names. Some were quite pleasant and treated her with kindness and accepted her presence without question. Others were rude though never within the viscountess's hearing.

Everyone seemed to know and like Viscountess Weston. That came as no surprise to Emma. She was clever, wise, and witty with a core of steel underneath it all. Without her, Emma would never have managed the evening.

"That's a unique shade of rose."

Emma turned to see Catherine, Michael's fiancé, at her side. She couldn't help but look for Michael as well, but he was nowhere to be found. "Why thank you." Though once again, the woman's comment hadn't been a compliment, Emma decided to act as though it was.

"I hope you are well this evening," Catherine said to the viscountess.

"I am. Thank you." The older woman turned away to continue speaking with one of her acquaintances, leaving Emma to wonder whether or not she cared for her grandson's fiancé.

Emma didn't blame her. The woman was rather disagreeable. Why Michael had chosen her remained a mystery. Though her father was wealthy, Michael seemed to have no problem with his finances. Surely he didn't need her for her dowry.

Catherine's eyes narrowed and her lips tightened with her displeasure at the viscountess's rebuff.

Unfortunately, that left Emma searching for a congenial topic. "Wonderful ball, isn't it?"

She glared at Emma then purposely dropped her gaze to Emma's low neckline. "You seem to be enjoying it. Next time, try not to make your search for a husband quite so obvious. They'll see how desperate you are and avoid you at all costs."

Her words stung and heat filled Emma's cheeks. Though she knew her gown was no different than most of the women here, Miss Vandimer included, her comment still struck a nerve.

Before she could think of a retort, Catherine moved away to greet someone else.

Cheeks burning, Emma wanted nothing more than to escape the ball, at least for a few moments. From the crowd, to the ostentatious décor, to the conversation, she'd had enough. With a quick word to the viscountess, she eased through the throng, trying to calm herself. Why had she allowed Catherine's words to bother her so much?

She made her way to the edge of the ballroom, hoping to find a place amid the potted ferns to escape into an empty alcove. Instead, she discovered a corridor that led to a room where guests were playing cards.

Already the sounds of the music and people eased. The smoke from the torches had not reached here. She drew a deep breath, at least as much as her tight corset would allow.

Emma paused at the doorway of the room to view the activity. She'd enjoyed playing Whist but it had been some time since she'd done so. At one of her posts, the lady of the house had often invited her to play in the evenings when her husband was gone and after the children had been abed. She'd become quite adept at several games, but her favorite was Piquet.

Only a few ladies graced the otherwise male-dominated room. Several tables had games, some players more serious than others.

One man looked up from his cards, his piercing gaze holding hers. He was a distinguished looking older man but appeared fit for his age. His blue-grey eyes held amused intelligence with a hint of hardness underneath.

With a comment to the other players at his table, he threw down his cards and rose. Surely, he hadn't stopped playing because of her arrival. Uncertain what his intention was, Emma shifted her gaze to the other players in the room. She was quite certain she'd never met the man, and well knew it would be highly inappropriate for him to introduce himself.

Yet that seemed to be exactly what he intended.

He came to stand before her and bowed. "My apologies for my forward behavior, but I had to meet you."

Emma wasn't certain what to do or say. Speaking with him could very well ruin her reputation, yet it seemed rude to walk away.

A presence at her elbow caught her attention. Lord Tagart cleared his throat. "Good evening, Miss Grisby."

Relief filled her at the lord's presence as she returned his greeting.

He glanced warily at the stranger then said, "May I present Mr. Adolphus Vandimer?"

She looked in surprise at the man as Lord Tagart completed the introduction. Catherine's father? She could see the resemblance in the shape of his eyes as she studied him closer.

Mr. Vandimer took her hand before she'd had a chance to offer it. "You are stunning, if I may say so."

Between his intense stare and the compliment, she was uncomfortable. He could be her father, yet he looked at her as though he wanted to devour her. There could be no denying the heat in his gaze.

Memories of the unwanted attention of her former employer popped into her head. With a polite smile, she took a step back and tugged her hand out of his grasp. "Thank you."

"Do you play?" He gestured toward the tables and at last took his gaze off her.

"On occasion."

"Perhaps you and Lord Tagart would care to join us."

Emma looked back across the room. There were no empty places. She glanced at Lord Tagart to see what he thought of the offer, hoping he might think of an excuse to depart.

"If the lady would like to then, of course, we will join you."

Irritation flickered through her. Yet how could she expect Lord Tagart to read her mind? He barely knew her.

Mr. Vandimer took her hand and tucked it under his elbow. Somehow the gesture felt far too familiar, yet so smooth she didn't have time to protest before he drew her across the room with Lord Tagart in tow.

Her unwanted companion returned to the table where he'd previously sat. "My friends wish to play."

Two of the other players quickly discarded their cards in the middle of a hand and rose, much to Emma's dismay. They disregarded her protests and drew back from the table.

Mr. Vandimer held a chair next to his for Emma and smiled at her.

"There was no need to interrupt the game," she said, holding his gaze. While the others at the table seemed to jump to do his bidding, she had no intention of doing so. He held no power over her.

"Oh, but there was. I needed to play with you."

The way he quietly uttered the words, the underlying meaning could not be ignored. Prepared to leave, she turned only to find Lord Tagart held a chair for her, obviously prepared to play.

"What game do you prefer?" Mr. Vandimer asked.

"Not this one."

He laughed, not the least offended at her response. "Then we will play whatever you'd like."

Lord Tagart held her gaze, an amused smile on his lips. "What do you choose?"

Unbidden, an image of Michael came into mind. He is *who* I choose, she thought. What was wrong with her? He was not an option.

"Shall we play Piquet?" she asked as she took her seat.

Mr. Vandimer gestured for another man to join them, a new deck of cards was delivered, and the game began.

No matter that Emma felt as though she were in over her head. She thought back to what Michael had told her. Why not enjoy the evening? And at the moment, that included a card game far away from the crowded ballroom.

Michael scanned the crush at the ball, searching for Emma and his grandmother. He hadn't intended to arrive so late, but he'd met with Ashbury to review the limited results of their investigation of the warehouses leased to Leon Smith, the name the professor sometimes used.

Nothing. Absolutely nothing.

That was what their efforts had brought them thus far. The whole investigation was maddening. One step forward, two steps back.

He spotted his grandmother amidst the throng along the edge of the dance floor and made his way toward her. But Emma was nowhere in sight. He searched the dancers as he walked but didn't find her there either.

"Good evening." He kissed his grandmother's cheek. "Are you beating off those asking you to dance with a stick?"

His grandmother laughed. "Some refuse to take no for an answer."

"Good thing I arrived when I did. I carry a larger stick than you."

"I'm pleased you're here. Emma stepped away and hasn't yet returned. Perhaps you could search for her?"

"Weston." Catherine said his name as part greeting and part order. She took his elbow before he offered it, causing irritation to trickle through him. "Where have you been?"

The pouty look she gave him caused a tick to form in his jaw. At times, he found her behavior quite annoying. "Business matters." He patted her hand. "I'm here now."

"Just in time to dance with me." She stepped toward the floor, obviously intending that he follow her.

"I would enjoy nothing more than a dance with you, but first I must locate Miss Grisby."

"Whatever for?" Catherine's scowl amused him. At least, he told himself it was amusement.

"My grandmother is in need of her." He lifted

Catherine's fingers off his arm. "I'll be back shortly and then we'll dance."

"If your schedule permits it," she said with a bite to her tone. She turned away to speak with someone nearby.

He knew she'd quickly find another man with whom to dance. Funny how the idea of her in another man's arms didn't bother him in the least. That was one of the reasons he'd thought she'd make the perfect wife.

"I'll see if I can locate Miss Grisby," he told his grandmother, then moved toward the end of the ballroom.

His height allowed him a good view, but still he couldn't see her. Wondering if she'd needed the ladies' dressing room, he moved in that direction.

As he walked past the card playing room, he caught sight of the back of a lady with dark hair and an elegant neck sitting at a table. A familiar neck. She turned her head and brought Michael to a halt.

Not only was he surprised to see Emma in the card room, he was shocked to see with whom she was playing.

Adolphus Vandimer. His soon to be father-in-law. What the hell?

The man was a wolf. There was no other way to describe him. He was relentless and cared little for proper social behavior. Perhaps that was where his daughter had learned her social skills.

Watching Emma in his company made Michael see red. He should've warned Emma about men like Vandimer. They were to be avoided at all costs.

He strode forward, intent on taking Emma as far away as possible.

"Good evening," he greeted the table. He needed to speak with Lord Tagart as well. Why the lord had allowed Emma to play with

Vandimer was beyond him.

"Weston." Vandimer glanced away from Emma to greet Michael. "What has you interrupting our game?"

The question was rude, but so was Michael's interruption. "I'm afraid I must request Miss Grisby's presence. My grandmother is in need of her."

"Of course." Emma set down her cards and rose, her composed expression giving Michael no hint as to her emotions. "Please excuse me, gentlemen."

Vandimer reached out to take her hand, preventing her from stepping away from the table. He glared at Michael. "Surely you can see to whatever it is that your grandmother needs. Or perhaps my daughter can. Miss Grisby was winning, and I quite enjoy watching her."

"Unfortunately, I'm told it's something only Miss Grisby can resolve." Michael took Emma's free hand and placed it on his arm. "If you'll excuse us."

While he had no desire to anger Vandimer, he couldn't allow Emma to remain in his company, even with Lord Tagart nearby. The other lord was no match for Vandimer and could not provide adequate protection for her.

Emma said her goodbyes and accompanied him out of the card room. "Is your grandmother well?"

"She is fine, but you were not."

"Excuse me?"

"You would be wise to keep your distance from Vandimer."

"Need I remind you that you're marrying his daughter?"

"Which is exactly why I can warn you." He pulled her into one of the alcoves that offered some privacy. "I know the man all too well. He is no one to be trifled with."

"I was not trifling with him. He simply invited me to play cards."

"Invited?" He knew Vandimer rarely asked anyone for anything. Instead, he took it. While Michael might admire that in the business world, he did not appreciate it when it came to his personal life. He eased Emma against the wall in the back corner of the alcove, hoping for more privacy.

"Well, perhaps demanded is a better term." Her eyes widened when Michael moved closer.

Once again, he had to appreciate that she no longer wore spectacles. Those brown eyes drew him into their depths but revealed little.

"His wife is dead." He knew his words were blunt, but he wanted her to understand the risk she took by even speaking with him.

"Oh. I'm sorry to hear that."

"He is not. Rumors abound about his exploits with women."

"He's old enough to be my father. I hardly think—"

Michael drew her closer. "He looked at you as if he was trying to decide where to nibble first."

Her eyes widened even more.

Unable to resist, he leaned in, her sweet scent catching him off guard. Christ, no wonder Vandimer wanted her. What man could look at her and not? Especially if they caught her sweet scent.

Unfortunately, that position gave him an excellent vantage of her neckline. The swell of her breasts taunted him, begging him to touch. Spellbound, he could only stare, his mouth going dry at the thought of what lay hidden beneath her gown.

As though realizing where he looked, she drew a deep breath. The movement proved more than he could take. Gently, he traced a finger along her collarbone, then down toward that soft expanse. "I must say, I like your new gown."

His gaze caught hers, tangling in the heat he saw there. No, he berated himself, even as he lowered his head to kiss her. Her lips were hot beneath his. They parted ever so slightly, just enough to invite him in. His tongue danced along the seam of her lips, then dove in.

Desire speared through him, hot and sharp. She went straight to his head like a fine brandy, heating his belly in the process. Again, he allowed his fingers to trail from the softness of her neck down toward the even softer hint of her breasts. More than anything, he wanted to feel the swell of her breasts—needed to just as much as he needed air.

She gasped at his touch but instead of drawing back, she stepped closer. How was he to resist her when she responded like that?

"Emma," he said her name on a moan. What was he going to do with her? He was engaged. He had a plan that made sound business sense. This sort of passion might be in his blood, but that didn't mean he should indulge in it. Emma Grisby was not for him. Not when she ignited him like a torch.

But, Christ, he wanted her so badly he ached.

As though reading his mind, she jerked back, breaking their kiss. Her breasts rose with her breath as she moved his fingers away.

"I thought we agreed this was not wise." Her husky voice only made him want to drag her back into his arms.

Instead, he adjusted her gown then ran his thumb against her lower lip. "Indeed we did. Somehow, I forgot."

"Next time you attempt to rescue me, perhaps you need to determine if the alternative you suggest is truly better."

Those brown eyes of hers held his for a long moment before she left him in the alcove, trying to think of things that would ease the tightness in his trousers.

Thank goodness Catherine didn't have this effect on him. If he could only remember feeling a lack of passion toward her was a good thing.

CHAPTER TEN

"Emma Grisby is the key. I'm certain of it."
Ashbury pushed back his chair from the desk in
his office at The Barbican, the gaming hell he
owned.

"I'm not convinced." Michael could no longer
think of her as having some sort of ulterior plan.
Not after all the time he'd spent with her,
including their kisses. Certainly not after seeing
how she and her family lived. "I don't think she
has any indication that her uncle is alive, nor do I
believe she's involved in any scheme with him."

"We have few other leads. I still think she is
our best hope for finding the professor."

"If he hasn't contacted Emma or her family by
now, I don't think he will. It's been years since he
left them. Why would he do so now?"

Ashbury scowled at him. "Perhaps you're right.
But where does that leave us?"

"Have you noticed anything unusual of late?"

"What do you mean?"

Michael shook his head. "It almost feels as if
I'm being watched at times. I've never caught
anyone doing so, but I've felt as if I'm being
followed. Have you?"

"Now that you mention it, the other day both
Abigail and I noticed a similar sensation."

"We still have the meteorite. Perhaps the professor is considering an attempt to retrieve it. Although if he was somehow behind the theft of the one from the museum, he may no longer need the one you have."

"Does the professor realize his niece is involved with you?"

Michael glared at his friend. "Involved?"

Ashbury chuckled. "You look almost guilty."

"I am only *involved* with her because you insisted on it."

"No need to become defensive."

Michael rose to pace. "Back to the point of your question. I don't know."

"Would he care if she were?"

"I would have to assume he would. Why?" Somehow, he was certain he wouldn't like whatever it was that Ashbury was suggesting.

"I propose you escort Emma to a few places where you can be easily seen."

Michael frowned at his friend. The idea of spending more time in Emma's company seemed like a poor one.

"If you are being followed the professor will soon know Emma is spending time with you," Ashbury continued. "Then give her a day to spend as she pleases. Allow her to go alone. We'll have her followed. Perhaps he'll take the opportunity to make contact with her."

"That seems like long odds."

"Do you have a better idea?"

Michael turned away, frustrated by the whole situation, himself included. "Not at the moment."

"Very well then. I look forward to hearing if you have any results."

"And what will you be doing while I'm escorting Emma?"

"I'm planning a wedding, remember? I am extremely busy."

"I am engaged as well."

"True, but you don't seem to be planning a wedding. Are you?"

Ashbury's words took him aback. It was true. For all he'd done to finalize his engagement, he hadn't taken any steps toward actually getting married.

Somehow the idea held less and less appeal, yet what choice did he have?

That afternoon, with Ashbury's request ringing in his ears, Michael escorted Emma to a bookstore. Abigail and Ashbury were to meet them there. This particular store happened to be one in which Abigail had recently invested. Ashbury was now convinced that all other bookstores were inferior to hers. He thought his fiancé was quite clever in her investments.

In truth, Michael thought she was brilliant with her knack to pick successful financial ventures. When she'd spoken of this one, her aura had glowed. He had no doubt it would bring her much success. He knew Emma and Abigail had a lot in common. Both were intelligent, well-educated women. Michael ignored the pang of longing that filled him as he thought of the closeness Ashbury and Abigail shared. That was not for him.

"Aren't we going in?" Emma asked as he lingered on the sidewalk.

"I don't believe Ashbury and Miss Bradford have yet arrived. I thought we'd wait for them out here."

The curious look Emma sent him had him shifting with guilt. The secrets he kept from her weighed on him more and more. But he wanted to remain where anyone who followed could easily see them.

"It's been a long time since I last browsed in a bookstore." Emma peeked in the window, obviously anxious to explore.

"You'll like this one. Miss Bradbury recently invested in it."

"Truly?" The look of interest on her face made him smile. If he'd told Catherine that, she would've turned up her nose in distaste.

He'd done his best to behave himself thus far on their outing. Though it hadn't been easy.

Today, Emma's gown had a more modest neckline, thank goodness. But the deep green made her skin glow and her hair look like rich mahogany. She turned her head to look down the street, providing him with an enticing view of her neck. He was becoming quite fond of it.

He tore his gaze away to follow hers.

"Is that Lord Ashbury walking toward us now?"

Thank heaven, he thought as he caught sight of Ashbury and Abigail. The longer he stood alone with Emma, the more his defenses weakened. Simply speaking with her was a pleasure he didn't dare risk. They had more in common then he'd thought possible.

Michael made the introductions, watching as Ashbury took in Emma's appearance. Ashbury pulled Michael aside after holding open the door for the ladies.

"I thought you said finding her a husband would be difficult."

"You should've seen her before her transformation. She looks nothing like she did before."

"Hmm. Interesting. She's very attractive."

"I'm surprised you noticed. I thought you were busy planning a wedding."

"I am, but I'm not dead." Ashbury slapped him on the back. "Are you?"

"Unfortunately not," he muttered.

Ashbury laughed. "I'm relieved to hear that."

Michael studied his friend. He appeared so much happier than he had a few weeks ago. "How are the headaches these days?"

"Better. Abigail taught me a technique that seems to bring the pain to a more manageable level. How about you?"

"I haven't had one for some time now. I can only hope that continues."

Abigail had introduced Emma to the owner and was now giving her a tour of the store. The two ladies seemed to be getting along well, but that came as no surprise to Michael. They both loved books which gave them a common element to share.

"It doesn't feel right to use Emma as bait," Michael said.

Ashbury sighed. "True. But these are unusual circumstances. What choice do we have?"

"I keep wondering if we should tell her what's happening."

"The thought crossed my mind as well, but would it serve any purpose other than to appease your feelings of guilt?"

Michael thought it over yet again, just as he had most of the night. "I'm reluctant to try to explain to her that her uncle lives, let alone what he might be involved in."

"I have to agree. Telling her now would only hurt her. Until we know more or have solid proof, I don't see how it would help."

Emma browsed through the shelves of books while Abigail spoke with the owner. Emma stopped abruptly and, with care, drew a book from the shelf before her. A look of utter delight crossed her face as she ran her fingers over the leather bound cover. Her pleasure continued as she opened the book and carefully turned the page.

"Looks as if she found something."

"Hmm...the problem is that she won't buy it for herself, nor will she accept a gift." He remembered all too well how she'd refused a ride in his carriage not so long ago. And how she'd seemed less than pleased at the basket of food he'd sent to her family. The woman had a problem accepting assistance. Heaven help him when she discovered what else he'd done.

"I'm certain you can find a way around that. You're a smart man."

Michael used to think so as well, at least until he'd renewed his acquaintance with Emma Grisby. Since then, he seemed to have lost his wits. Why else would he share kisses with a woman who drew forth the very passion he'd been so careful to avoid, especially when he was engaged to another?

"I followed Lord Weston around a bit but he doesn't seem to be doin' anything interestin'." Vincent bit into the apple he'd copped from a street vendor. It tasted all the sweeter knowing he'd stolen it himself. He didn't want his skills to become rusty. Who knew what the future held?

According to his uncle, the paper he'd stolen had provided lots of money. Soon they'd be moving to better quarters. Though moving was a pain in the arse, he looked forward to a few finer comforts than the hovel in which they currently resided.

"We need to find out whether Ashbury or Weston has the meteorite," his uncle said but didn't lift his head from his reading.

Vincent stepped closer, realizing it was the

same book his uncle always seemed to be looking at, *Treatise on Electricity and Magnetism* by Patrick Clerk Maxwell. Vincent thought by now, he'd have the thing memorized.

"How am I supposed to determine which one has the bloody stone? They went together to some bookstore, but I didn't learn anything of interest there. I can't follow either of them closely. They might recognize me. Nor can I follow both of them at the same time."

"We must use the opportunities presented to us wisely."

Vincent rolled his eyes at his uncle's back. Advice like that was useless as far as he was concerned.

"Once we determine who has the meteorite, we can obtain it by whatever means necessary."

Vincent perked up at that. Though he'd used *necessary means* on both the museum guard and the bloke with the papers only to have his uncle become displeased with him. "Seems like a lot of effort for one rock. Ye sure the ones we have aren't enough?"

"The more we have, the stronger we can make the devices."

His uncle continued to study the book as Vincent ate his apple and tried to think of ways to find out who had the bloody rock. He'd followed each of the lords at different times over the past few days but that hadn't gotten him anywhere.

He still couldn't believe the Bradford woman and Lord Ashbury were engaged. They should be thanking him for bringing them together. Now Lord Weston seemed to be escorting the woman staying at his grandmother's.

"Remember your niece? The oldest one from the *other* side of the family?" Vincent asked.

His uncle stilled. "Emma. Of course. Why do you ask?"

"The woman Weston is sniffin' after reminds me of her."

"You must find out for me, Vincent. I need to know for certain."

Vincent's brow rose at the intensity of his uncle's words. "I'll see what I can do."

Emma rose early the next morning, eager to spend the day with her family. The viscountess had suggested she take a day to visit them. A break from the social events and people after a week of non-stop activity would be most welcome.

For awhile, she could be herself again.

She looked at the beautiful gowns that had been provided to her and realized those would never do. She couldn't return home looking as if she were pretending to be someone else. Besides, they weren't really hers.

In short order, she was dressed in her serviceable grey gown. Odd how uncomfortable the rough wool fabric felt against her skin. She avoided looking at herself in the mirror, not certain what she'd find there.

Ignoring her mixed emotions, she tried to think of something she could take her family. Since she had no wages to share, there had to be something else she might give them. Yet in reality, none of the things in this room were truly hers.

Despite her feelings of guilt, she selected one of her blue hair ribbons for Tessa, a small cameo pin for her mother as she had two, and a tin of candies for Patrick. With her meager gifts tucked in her pocket, she made her way down the stairs.

"Shall I call a carriage for you, miss?" the footman asked.

"Oh, no. That's not necessary."

"But the viscountess said you should take it so you'd have more time to spend with your family."

The idea was tempting. Her home was a long walk from here.

"It will only take a few moments."

"Very well. Thank you."

Soon the carriage had delivered her to the neighborhood on Trenary Lane. The street looked even more dismal than it had a week ago. Shaking off the thought, she ignored the stares of passersby as the footman assisted her to the ground.

"When should we return, miss?"

"Perhaps just before dusk?" These streets could be dangerous at night. She didn't want to take unnecessary risks. Nor did she want to be away from her duties for the viscountess too long.

With a bow, the footman took his leave.

Hurrying now, she entered the lodging house and climbed the stairs, her mind on her family. She hoped Tessa was doing well. Had the landlord returned to collect the rent payment? Did her family have anything to eat other than cabbage soup?

She knocked on the door so as not to startle her mother before using her key to let herself in. "Good morning."

The sitting room area and kitchen was empty, but at the sound of her call, her mother came out of Tessa's room.

"Emma. How lovely to see you." There was a tightness in her mother's face that scared Emma. She gave her a hug, Emma clinging a moment longer than normal. "Let me see you."

Emma pulled back to look closer at her mother as well. "I've come to spend the day with you." Well aware that Tessa would be listening to every word, she whispered, "How is she?"

Her mother's smile faltered. That was all the

answer Emma needed. She squeezed her mother's hands, trying to lend her support.

"Emma?" Tessa's voice from the small bedroom sounded weak and tired.

Emma hurried toward her sister, anxious to see her for herself. "Tessa, darling. How are you?"

"Much better now that you're here. How lovely to see you." The shadows under her eyes told of a bad night. She struggled to sit up in bed.

"No need to sit up on my account. Rest. I'm here all day. We'll have plenty of time to visit."

Tessa nodded as Emma gave her a kiss on her forehead and stroked her hair.

"Close your eyes and rest while I put on the tea kettle."

"But I want to hear everything."

"And I will tell you all of it but after you rest."

She didn't argue any further, and that alone nearly broke Emma's heart.

Her mother stood staring out the narrow window in the front room, her hands idle, her shoulders sagging.

Emma crossed the small room to hug her from behind, wanting to give her some of her strength. "I love you, Mother."

She patted Emma's arm. "I love you as well." When she turned to face Emma, she had a smile on her face. "How is everything going with the viscountess?"

"Very well." She swallowed her guilt at not having told her mother the full truth of her position. Even as her mouth opened, she stopped. She couldn't think of any way to say it that made it sound less mercenary. "Unfortunately, I don't yet have my wages to give to you."

"But money was in the basket you sent us."

"What basket?"

Her mother pointed to a basket that sat in the corner on the floor. "It was so kind of you to send the food and blankets as well. I gave one of the blankets to Mrs. Dobbs. She's been so worked up of late. Her predictions are more crazed each time I speak with her." She shook her head. "Oh, I wanted to ask if you already paid the landlord."

At Emma's questioning look, she went on, "When I attempted to pay him, he said he'd already received payment."

Michael. As though she didn't owe him enough already. But how very kind of him to think to perform such a generous gesture. Her heart swelled at his thoughtfulness. How was she to hold back her feelings when he continually did such things?

She wasn't certain her mother would think it wise to accept such a gift from a gentleman though, so she simply smiled. "I must've forgotten to mention it. Where is Patrick?"

"Mr. Smith paid him to run a few errands this morning."

"Tessa had a bad night?" she whispered, hoping Tessa couldn't hear them discussing her.

"Poor dear. Her coughing has grown worse."

"Should I fetch the doctor?"

"I suggested it last night, but of course she wouldn't hear of it. She insists we spend some of the money to make Patrick new clothes and that we save the rest."

Emma sighed. Money had been so tight for so long, it would be difficult to convince Tessa that they had enough to pay the doctor. "I'll go speak with Dr. Barnes now while she's resting."

"Take some of the money you sent and put it toward our account."

Emma tucked the money in her pocket and let herself out of their flat, trying to be as quiet as possible. If Tessa heard her leaving, she'd be upset. No need to cause her any worry.

Now she was glad she'd worn her old grey

dress. Walking these streets in one of her newer ones would've drawn far too much attention.

As she began her brisk walk to the doctor's home, the sensation of being watched came over her. She paused on a street corner, waiting for traffic to clear and took the opportunity to glance around. People of all sorts lined the sidewalk but no one seemed to pay any attention to her.

A man with a bowler hat caught her gaze but quickly looked away. He probably wondered why she was staring at him. She shook off the feeling and focused on what she would say to Dr. Barnes. Surely the money she carried would pay enough of their bill that he would come to see Tessa.

At last she reached the doctor's red brick home on Villiers Street and rang the bell. The servant who answered showed her to his office. Apparently she was early enough that he hadn't yet started to see patients.

"Miss Grisby, what can I do for you today?" Dr. Barnes asked with a smile.

"First, I'd like to put some money on our account."

The doctor's brows rose with surprise at the notes she held out. "Thank you."

"I realize this isn't enough, but I hope it will allow you to pay a visit to Tessa. She had a difficult night."

"Tell me about it."

Soon they agreed on a time and Emma showed herself out.

She hurried back home, trying to figure a way to repay Michael for his kindness. The man seemed to lack for nothing, but somehow there had to be a way for her to return the favor.

Patrick had returned home by the time she arrived and Tessa had awakened. They spent an enjoyable time together catching up. Emma shared as much as she could of the balls and even the contents of the museum.

"You went to the museum with the viscount?" her mother asked.

"Yes. He was kind enough to offer."

"But what of the viscountess? Didn't she go with you?"

"She said she had no interest in rocks and minerals."

"But I thought you were *her* companion?" Patrick asked with a frown.

Heat filled Emma's cheeks. That was the problem with lying. It created all sorts of tangles that could be avoided with the truth. Yet how could she tell them the truth now? The only thing she could do was downplay the outing.

"The viscountess had heard me speak of Uncle Grisby and how he liked to show us interesting rocks and things. So she thought I might enjoy the outing. We weren't gone very long, and I was properly chaperoned of course."

"Of course," her mother agreed, though she frowned as she watched Emma.

"Remember when Uncle Grisby took us to the park and had us dig for rocks and a constable interrupted us and insisted we put them all back?" Tessa chuckled at the memory.

Emma laughed as well, partly from relief at the change in subject and partly at the memory.

Patrick still looked none too pleased. "I don't remember that. Was I there?"

"Yes, but you were quite young at the time." Emma tousled his dark hair, sad that he had so few memories of better times. He seemed to have grown even more in the short time she'd been gone.

"I don't remember him."

"No, you were quite young when we lost him. You would've loved him just as much as we did." Emma shared a look with Tessa.

She hated that he had to work at such a young age. He should be in school. Though their mother had told him she'd rather he attend school, Patrick had flatly refused, insisting he was the man of the house and needed to help put food on the table.

Everything would've been so much different if that terrible accident hadn't taken Uncle Grisby. They would've had a decent home, food on the table, money to pay for Tessa's doctor, and Patrick would've been in school.

Emma's heart ached with the loss.

But no. She couldn't allow herself to wish for things that weren't—that couldn't be. All she could do was continue with her plan. If she married, they could have all that. At least she hoped they could.

Michael was right in one respect. Finding another job as a governess would do no good. It would solve nothing. She couldn't turn back from her plan now.

Michael waited in the library of the red-brick house on Villiers Street. He'd told the servant he had a business matter to discuss with the doctor.

In reality, he wanted to discover what the doctor would tell him about Emma. She'd come to see him twice now. He assumed it had to do with her ill sister, but part of him couldn't help but wonder if the doctor had a connection to the professor. Somehow, Michael doubted it, but he had to know for certain.

"Lord Weston. To what do I owe the honor of your visit?" Dr. Barnes had a thick grey mustache and long sideburns, both a shade darker than the hair on his head.

"I wonder if I might inquire as to your acquaintance with Emma Grisby."

The man frowned and took a seat behind his desk. "Why do you ask?"

"She's been serving as companion to my grandmother, and I've grown to care for her." He refused to consider how true that statement was. "I want to be certain all is well."

"Emma Grisby is fine. I'm afraid it's her younger sister who is ill."

"I'm sorry to hear that. Nothing serious, I hope."

"Very serious. Consumption. Terrible thing."

Michael nearly groaned with dismay. The disease was serious and chances of surviving it were slim. Poor Emma. He knew all too well how important her family was to her.

"I fear her prognosis isn't good, but Emma is quite determined to see her better."

Michael nearly smiled. That sounded just like Emma. "I hope you're able to help."

"With the family's limited resources, there is little I can do." Doctor Barnes shook his head. "Unless their situation changes and the young lady can receive improved nutrition and even more critical, clean air, her survival is doubtful."

Here was something he could do, a way he could help Emma. With luck, she'd never know. He made arrangements to pay the balance on their account and advanced the doctor enough to see them through the coming months.

"I'll be paying a visit to the younger Miss Grisby today and will do all I can to aid her." He shook his head. "I can't say it will make a difference, but I'll try. What has helped many is spending a few months in a sanatorium, but that is not an option for Miss Grisby."

Michael couldn't help but wonder if Emma would allow him to make arrangements for such a trip. He'd have to wait until he further gained her trust before he broached that subject with her. He moved toward the door. "I'd rather you didn't say that I assisted in any way."

"As you wish," Doctor Barnes agreed and Michael took his leave.

No wonder Emma had so desperately needed that governess position with his cousin. Consumption was a nasty disease which slowly drained the life out of its victim. He would do everything in his power to make certain that didn't happen to Emma's sister.

CHAPTER ELEVEN

"Lord Tagart to see Miss Grisby," the footman announced, surprising Emma as she and Viscountess Weston chatted in the drawing room the next afternoon.

Emma looked at the older woman, uncertain what to do.

The viscountess smiled in delight. "Isn't that lovely? Show him in."

Though flowers had arrived over the past few days, including a lovely bouquet from Lord Tagart, he was her first official caller.

"Good day to you, my lady, Miss Grisby." The man had his usual smile in place and a sparkle in his brown eyes. He seemed to have a permanent sunny disposition.

"Please join us." The viscountess gestured toward a chair. "How are you this fine day?"

Though flattered, Emma wasn't certain what to say or do. She'd never had a gentleman call on her.

Viscountess Weston glanced at her with a raised brow, making her realize she needed to join the conversation. Unfortunately, no topic came to mind.

She could hardly share the events of the previous day, nor did she care to discuss her family. Not yet anyway. What did that leave her with? The exchange of niceties had ended, leaving an awkward silence in its wake.

"Did you happen to read the article in this morning's paper regarding the continuing unrest in Egypt?" she asked.

Both Lord Tagart and the viscountess looked rather surprised at her question. "Indeed," Lord Tagart replied. "The Suez Canal is of great importance to England. British troops may have to intervene. I didn't realize you were interested in world events."

Though worried she should've chosen to speak of the weather instead, she soon relaxed as Lord Tagart shared his views on the problems in Egypt, and an entertaining conversation followed.

Emma genuinely liked Lord Tagart. He didn't pretend to be something he wasn't. He didn't stare at her as if he intended to devour her. Instead, he spoke with her as though he enjoyed hearing her opinion.

He was in the middle of an amusing story when Michael arrived. His brow rose as he caught sight of Lord Tagart occupying what she'd discovered was his favorite chair.

Emma didn't appreciate the scowl on his face. The last thing she wanted was for Michael to discourage Lord Tagart.

Michael caught her glare and gave her a questioning look. Surely he understood her meaning. He was just being deliberately obtuse.

Lord Tagart cleared his throat and paused, obviously uncomfortable now that Michael had joined them.

"Please do finish your story," Emma urged him with another pointed look at Michael.

"Yes, don't allow me to interrupt," Michael added.

The lord haltingly finished what he was

saying, then stood and quickly said his goodbyes. Emma placed the reason for his quick departure directly on Michael.

"Wonderful that Lord Tagart called on you, Emma. That is a very good sign indeed." The viscountess seemed to notice her grandson's scowl at her words. "Lovely of you to call on us as well, my dear." She rose from her seat. "Excuse me while I speak with the cook about this evening's meal."

As soon as she departed, Emma moved to stand before him. "Why did you do that?"

"Do what?"

"Chase away Lord Tagart."

"I did no such thing."

"I beg to differ." Emma knew she was acting like a shrew but couldn't help herself. "Didn't you notice how quickly the conversation ended once you arrived?"

"That is hardly my fault." Michael stepped closer, his gaze narrowing.

"I'm attempting to find a husband. Having you chase off a potential one defeats the whole purpose of my efforts."

"I am not chasing away anyone. Perhaps you should consider that the fault might lay with you."

Emma's jaw dropped. "What?"

"You have erected a barrier to keep the rest of the world at bay."

"I have done no such thing!"

"Oh, please. You might as well have a notice posted that you think yourself far superior to everyone else."

Emma couldn't believe he'd said such a thing. "That is not true."

He drew even closer, causing her to tip her head back in order to continue meeting his eyes. "You've had that particular attitude since I found you sitting in my library, asking for a reference."

"I have not." Heat speared through her at his proximity. How was she to think when he was so close? When she could see the dark flecks in his blue eyes? When the scent of the woods and bay rum that was uniquely his curled through her?

"In fact, there has been only one time since we renewed our acquaintance when you did not portray that attitude."

"When?"

"When I kissed you."

"Which time?" she asked, unable to keep the sarcasm from her tone.

He looked taken aback for a moment. That was all the invitation she needed to prove she did not put up a barrier. Two could play at this game.

She lifted up on her toes and kissed him. His body went rigid with surprise. *Good*, she thought briefly. Now he knew what it was like to have astonishment steal his breath.

Her thoughts fled as she felt the firmness of his lips beneath hers. His hands cupped her elbows, whether to hold her back or bring her closer, she couldn't tell. Determined for it to be the latter, she tilted her head ever so slightly to better fit his mouth to hers.

Yes.

Desire speared through her, casting a glow deep inside her that spread.

He released her elbows and her heart stopped, afraid he intended to push her away. But no. Instead, he drew her into his arms, deepening their kiss. He held her as though she were precious, as though nothing else in the world mattered. His tongue swirled with hers and increased her desire with each pass. He pulled back only to murmur her name and wrap her in his arms. "Emma."

Realizing he felt the same desire for her that she had for him was a wondrous thing and gave her a feminine sense of power. Yet she dare not risk too much. His engagement stood between them. With luck, she soon would be engaged as well.

Immediately she regretted her impulsive behavior and, with much regret, pulled back.

But Michael didn't let go. His eyes held hers, their darkness evidence of his passion for her. That made this all the more difficult. "Emma," he said again, this time in protest.

She shifted, suddenly anxious to remove his hands, unable to bear his touch when he couldn't be hers. "No. You are engaged, and I soon will be."

He ran a hand through his hair. "That is an obligation, something I cannot change." He turned away briefly only to turn back. "You do things to me. Make me feel things that I thought— That are better left buried. For me, marriage is merely a business agreement. I cannot follow the path of my parents."

"I don't understand."

He was quiet for so long she didn't think he'd answer. "Their passion for each other was their undoing. They couldn't live together, nor could they live apart."

Emma frowned, uncertain what he meant. She'd never known anyone like that. The only thing she could compare it to was how she felt about Michael. And that was no comparison at all. Surely she didn't love this man. In truth, she barely knew him.

Besides, love wasn't something she could afford. It had no place in her world. The only thing she could hope for was to marry someone whom she could like and respect.

With a heavy sigh, Michael continued. "My father loved my mother deeply. He grew wildly jealous if she even looked at another man, and she used that to manipulate Father. If he displeased her, she flirted simply to enrage him. Their fights became legendary as they didn't wait to have them in the privacy of their home." He shook his head. "They fought in ballrooms, at the theater, it didn't matter where they were. Those arguments grew more and more physical. They would strike each other violently then kiss in the same manner."

Emma gasped at the image of a young Michael witnessing such a heated exchange.

"Weeks might pass when they refused to speak to one another. Instead, they used me to pass each other messages, all while attempting to persuade me they were in the right. I was never sure whether it was better when they weren't speaking to each other but spoke to me, or when they ignored me completely."

He met her gaze for a long moment, allowing her to see the depth of his pain. "One evening, not long after your uncle's death, my father shot my mother before taking his own life." He rubbed his hands over his eyes. "I discovered their bodies in the library, holding each other. Ironic."

The bitterness in his voice squeezed her heart. "I am so sorry, Michael."

"As am I. That is why my marriage will be a business agreement and nothing more. The arrangement is done and I cannot change it."

"I'm not asking you to. I only hope you'll be happy with your plans." Perhaps she needed to follow Michael's example and consider marriage as a business agreement. The thought only made her heart hurt more.

"Women are complicated creatures." Michael couldn't remove Emma or their kiss...or rather, kisses...out of his mind.

Ashbury snorted. "You're just now realizing this?"

They walked along one of the busy streets near the docks the next morning. Another lead had surfaced as to a location rented to Leon Smith, the name that had been used to lease several locations they believed the professor had used. Unfortunately, they'd missed him each time.

This morning, Michael's man of business had discovered another lease agreement in a variation of the name, and they'd wasted no time in going to investigate the location.

"Are things not going well with Miss Vandimer?" Ashbury asked.

Michael wasn't certain how his relationship was progressing with Catherine. In truth, it didn't really matter. And that was the problem. *She* didn't matter. At least not to him.

"My engagement is merely a business arrangement."

"Are you telling me that, or yourself?"

Michael didn't answer, uncertain what was wrong with him.

At his long silence, Ashbury tried again. "So if it isn't your fiancé, of whom are you speaking?" He glanced at Michael. "Ah, you're referring to Miss Grisby. How interesting."

"What is that supposed to mean?"

"Nothing. I simply find it interesting that she is the one who occupies your thoughts rather than Catherine."

"She kissed me."

"Catherine?"

"No. Emma."

Ashbury chuckled. "She has more fortitude than I had thought. The question is, did you like it?"

"Well, I—" Michael stopped as he realized he

was about to lie to his best friend. Why bother? Ashbury knew him well enough to ferret out the truth, most likely before they arrived at their destination. "Far too much, I'm afraid."

"And?" The interested expression on Ashbury's face surprised him. No judgment. Just interest.

"Emma Grisby turns me inside out quicker than..." He paused, unable to think of an appropriate comparison. He shook his head. "None of that matters. I am engaged. Soon to be married. I should not be kissing any other woman, let alone the one staying in my grandmother's home."

"It's complicated."

"As I said." Michael was grateful his friend understood. "Much too complicated to allow any involvement."

"With who?"

"Emma. Keep up with the conversation."

"I merely wanted to clarify who was the problem."

"She's not a problem. It's me, or rather, our relationship that's the problem."

"Do you have a relationship?"

Michael came to a halt. "Whose side are you on?"

"Squarely on yours. Merely clarifying the details of the—er—issue."

"Right." Michael continued, his pace slow as his mind churned. "In truth, it's a business arrangement. Nothing more."

"With Emma?"

"No. With Catherine. Please do try to stay with me."

Ashbury gave him a bland look. "Yes, of course."

"So it doesn't matter what my feelings are on that score. Feelings have nothing to do with business."

"None at all."

"Excellent. Thank you for helping me resolve the issue."

This time, it was Ashbury who stopped. "What exactly did you resolve?"

Michael stared at him as what had seemed so clear a moment before shattered. What had he resolved? Nothing. His feelings—he nearly shuddered at the thought of admitting he had them—had not changed. Something about Emma lit a spark within him that he could not deny.

And he had no idea what to do about it.

"Listen, Weston, I am well aware all this is none of my business, but I'd remind you that you're the one who raised it." He held up his hand when Michael started to protest. "Hear me out. I appreciate how you've put back together everything your father tore down. But is shackling yourself to a woman like Miss Vandimer worth it? Can you imagine having children with her? Growing old with her?"

Michael hadn't thought of his engagement in that way. He'd been so focused on gaining back the holding, he hadn't pictured anything beyond that.

"I mean no disrespect," Ashbury continued after a moment, "but as your friend, I must say, Miss Vandimer is not an especially nice person."

Michael scoffed. "There's more truth to that than you know. But I fear I'm too far down this path. There's my grandmother to consider as well."

Ashbury nodded. "Family is another complication, isn't it?"

"I must press on with my plans." Michael could see no other choice. Allowing Catherine's father to keep that holding was not an option. It had been in Michael's family for centuries. Losing it had been the blow that had set his parents' toward their final destruction. Their arguments had been brutal after his father had lost it in a game of cards.

His great grandfather would come back from the grave for Michael's head if he failed to gain it back when he had the opportunity. His grandmother had been born there. After all she'd done for him, he would do anything for her. Anything.

Somehow, he needed to set aside the desire he carried for Emma. Never mind that *desire* seemed too tame a word. The feelings he had for her served no purpose. He'd learned that all too well from his parents. But the idea of keeping Emma at arm's length put him in a dismal mood.

Emma stood with Viscountess Weston at a ball that evening. She'd already danced several times and now longed for some fresh air. The day had been quite warm and the ballroom seemed to have absorbed the heat.

Her gown this evening was amber and one of her favorites thus far. The ruffles were narrow and made of the same fabric as her gown. They ran along the neckline and sleeves, and in a swirling circular pattern on the skirt. She'd never seen anything like it before. She hoped that meant it was unique rather than out of fashion. With a sigh, she pushed aside her worry. The only thing that mattered was how she felt in the dress and she felt lovely. Based on the amount of attention she'd received from the men here, she wasn't the only one who thought so.

An uneasy awareness filled her, and she glanced over her shoulder to find Mr. Vandimer standing behind her.

"Good evening, Miss Grisby." He smiled slyly,

as if he knew something she didn't.

The sensation made her uncomfortable. She took a step back, unable not to, as she returned his greeting. The man made her nervous and not in a pleasant way.

"Would you honor me with this dance?"

She paused, trying to think of any possible reason to refuse. Her face heated as she realized several people nearby turned to stare as she delayed her answer. Left with no choice as she didn't want to offend him, she smiled politely. "That would be lovely."

The viscountess frowned as Mr. Vandimer took her hand. "Don't be long, my dear. I have need of you."

Grateful that the older woman seemed to have sensed her disquiet, she nodded. "Of course."

With a deep breath, she allowed Mr. Vandimer to escort her to the dance floor. The strains of a waltz began and she nearly groaned. He smiled knowingly, and it crossed her mind that he had somehow arranged it.

Determined to try to enjoy the dance, she returned his smile and tried to relax, flowing with the music.

"You look lovely this evening, Miss Grisby."

"Thank you."

"You're a beautiful woman."

"My, you are full of compliments." But they didn't make her feel good, not to mention how much his superior smile was beginning to annoy her. "One might worry why."

He raised his brow. The way he watched her made her feel as though he'd already taken liberties. "Do you wonder if I have an ulterior motive?"

"Surely not." She held her smile in place, hoping he didn't. Somehow, she was certain that whatever it might be, it wouldn't be good.

"I hope spending more time in your company is not considered an ulterior motive."

"I suppose it depends on why you wish to do so."

There was that smile again. Rather than continue to look at him, she looked out across the crowd, her gaze automatically searching for Michael. He would not be pleased if he knew the identity of her dance partner.

"I find your intellect quite stimulating. So different from the other silly women here." Her gaze met his, and the heat she saw there was unmistakable.

"And are you on the hunt for a wife?" What better defense than to make her own intentions clear?

He chuckled. "Heaven forbid. I am most anxious to see my daughter married, but not me. I found a wife quite inconvenient."

She didn't want to hazard a guess as to what he meant.

"However," he squeezed her waist, "I do enjoy more pleasurable pursuits."

Her mind went blank. She had no idea how to respond to his comments. Would this dance never end? "I confess I love to read and spend time with my family."

Another chuckle. "I would hope that you have other interests, perhaps those of a more physical nature?" He raised his brows suggestively.

"Oh. Indeed. Nothing like a brisk walk in the park." At last, the notes of the waltz faded. Emma wasted no time stepping away. "Thank you."

He didn't release her. Instead, he kept his arm about her waist, forcing her to remain at his side unless she wanted to cause a scene.

"I believe the viscountess is in need of me." She met his gaze, refusing to be intimidated by his outrageous behavior.

"An intelligent woman such as yourself shouldn't be at the beck and call of an old woman." He pulled her closer, and she had no choice but to allow it. "You should be covered in jewels, hosting parties more interesting than this one."

She attempted to remove his hand from her waist without success. Fear curled in her stomach. "What are you suggesting?"

"Good evening." Michael's greeting had never been so welcome, but the look he sent her was less so.

"Weston." Mr. Vandimer nodded. "I was just going to escort Miss Grisby back to your grandmother."

"No need," Michael said with a smile as he offered his elbow to her. "I believe you promised me this dance?"

The glitter of anger in his eyes belied his friendly words. She'd prefer his anger over the continued presence of Mr. Vandimer any day. "I'd nearly forgotten."

With a nod at Mr. Vandimer, Michael led her to the dance floor. "I thought we agreed you'd keep your distance from him."

"Manners leave me little choice but to accept when he asks me to dance."

"Invent an excuse."

"Next time, I'll try harder."

Michael's eyes narrowed as he looked closely at her as though sensing her unease. "What did he say to you?"

"Nothing of import." The movements of the dance prevented them from speaking further. As they floated along, the magic of being in Michael's arms took over. How could dancing be such a totally different experience with this man than with any other?

With Michael, the rhythm of the music took

precedence over the intricacies of the steps. Her focus narrowed to him, to the blue of his eyes, the arch of his brow. Why did he have to be the one who stirred her so? Who made her long for things that could never be? She closed her eyes briefly as she spun, holding back her emotions as best she could.

But wait. She had this moment with him, and maybe, if she was lucky, a few more. Why should she waste them? She wanted to enjoy each one and store them away. No matter what happened in the coming weeks, she'd have these times to remember. No one could take them away from her.

"What is it?" he asked, eyeing her smile warily.

She considered giving him a lighthearted answer, but what came out surprised her. "I'm pleased you're here."

He blinked, obviously uncertain how to respond.

That only made her smile more. She set aside her worries and gave herself over to the music, to the feel of being in Michael's arms, even if it was temporary. The joy of it filled her, and she couldn't help but laugh when they executed a turn.

"I remember the night your mother taught you to waltz," Michael said with a smile.

"That was an enjoyable evening." It had been one of the last light-hearted times she could remember. Soon after that, her uncle had been killed, and their lives had never been the same.

All too soon, the dance ended. Michael tucked her hand in the crook of his elbow and moved toward his grandmother.

Emma caught her breath as the Marchioness of Warkshire paused before them.

"Weston." Her greeting held a distinct chill.

"Dear, Cousin. Lovely to see you, as always."

Michael bowed but didn't release Emma's hand.

The marchioness's gaze shifted to Emma then narrowed. "Have we met?"

Emma could think of nothing to say. If the marchioness remembered interviewing her for the governess position and decided to declare her a fraud—

"Allow me to introduce you to Miss Emma Grisby."

Emma curtsied, her stomach in knots. With effort she found her voice. "It's a pleasure to meet you, my lady."

The beautiful woman acknowledged the greeting with a simple nod. "Indeed." With one last glance at Emma, she turned and walked away.

As Emma breathed a sigh of relief, she heard Michael whisper in her ear. "I told you she doesn't like me."

Before she could respond, Catherine moved into their path. She spared a glance at Emma though she offered her no greeting. "When did you arrive?" she asked Michael.

Emma did her best to hide her surprise. He'd come to her rescue before finding his fiancé? But no, she couldn't read anything into that small act.

"A short time ago," Michael answered.

Catherine's eyes narrowed but she said nothing more. She turned toward Emma, and Emma knew she searched for a derogatory comment to make.

Before she could come up with one, Emma excused herself. "I think the viscountess is in need of me." With a parting glance at Michael, she left the pair. Between Mr. Vandimer and his daughter, Michael was going to have his hands full in the coming years. She didn't envy him.

Emma was pleased to find Abigail visiting with the viscountess. She liked the other woman.

Abigail seemed so comfortable with who she was and what she wanted. Her interest in financial matters fascinated Emma. She'd never known another woman who did something like that.

The three women chatted about everything from the weather to some of the gowns to the flowers that decorated the room.

Lord Tagart appeared at her elbow. "Good evening, Miss Grisby. May I say how lovely you look this evening?"

She couldn't help but return his smile. Warmth spread through her as they exchanged pleasantries. But it was far different from the heat she felt in Michael's presence. Nor was it anything like the rather unpleasant awareness Mr. Vandimer caused. With a sigh, she realized that while she genuinely liked Lord Tagart, the idea of kissing him was unappealing.

Where did that leave her in her quest for marriage? As they continued to visit, she glanced about the room for the other men she'd met of late. Some had seemed nice enough, others she hadn't cared for at all. Should she try to meet others to see where that led? Or should she spend more time with Lord Tagart and see if her feelings for him grew into something more?

"Is all well?" Lord Tagart asked, his brown eyes filled with concern. "I hope nothing is troubling you."

She had to restrain herself from sighing again. He was so nice. Surely he would make a good husband. Surely he would care for her family as much as she did.

"I enjoyed our discussion earlier," she said, hoping he'd resume the conversation. Perhaps if she tried harder, she'd grow to care more. That would have to be enough.

CHAPTER TWELVE

Michael stood visiting with Catherine, her father, and one of Catherine's friends after Emma took her leave. Why was he filled with regret that he couldn't go after her? Catherine and Adolphus Vandimer would soon be part of his family. He should enjoy spending time with them.

In truth, he didn't.

Catherine was involved in a discussion about a new dressmaker with her companion. From the look on the other lady's face, he assumed she didn't appreciate Catherine's remarks. That happened far too often. Michael sighed. Catherine seemed to have no idea how much her comments annoyed others.

He glanced at her father, wondering why he did not curtail his daughter's behavior. But as he looked at the older man, he realized he wasn't paying any attention to Catherine. Instead, Vandimer stared across the room.

At Emma.

Anger flickered through Michael before he tamped it down. While he needed to be prepared for Emma to marry, the idea of Adolphus being interested in her infuriated Michael. From what he'd garnered from his conversations with the man, he had no intention of marrying again. So why was he interested in Emma?

Michael nearly shook his head at his own stupidity.

One look at her was enough to answer that. She was intelligent, beautiful, and radiated something special. Something unique.

Lord Tagart stood next to her, but he wasn't the only lord nearby. Yet she seemed unaware of the stir she caused. That only added to her charm. Rather than batting her eyes and acting coy, she took the time to genuinely engage with each person who spoke to her.

Who was Michael kidding? He at least needed to be honest with himself. It didn't matter in whom she was interested. Michael wouldn't like it.

But at the top of that list was Adolphus Vandimer. Michael would be damned before he'd allow the older man to charm Emma into becoming his mistress.

His thoughts on how he might manage that were interrupted when Ashbury appeared at his elbow.

"I have terrible news," Ashbury said, his face grim.

"What is it?"

"Lord Berkmond was killed last night."

Michael stilled. While he hadn't known Lucas's older brother well, his death came as a shock. "That's terrible. What happened?"

"He was shot on his way home from a ball."

"Here in town?"

Ashbury nodded.

"I just spoke with him a few days past. He said he hadn't heard from Lucas in months." His younger brother's choice to move to Brazil had never set well with Berkmond. Michael imagined that Lucas had never shared the full extent of his injuries from the electromagnetic accident. Hell, he hadn't even told Michael and Ashbury how it had truly affected him.

"Did they catch the culprit?" Michael asked.

"Not as of earlier today."

"Christ. I suppose this means Lucas will return to England." Michael remained quiet as he thought over his last conversation with Berkmond. He'd seemed so hale and hearty. "Life as we know it can change at any given moment."

"Do you think this has anything to do with...recent events?"

Michael ran his hand through his hair. Though the idea was terrible to consider, it would be naive of them not to. "You know I don't believe in coincidences."

"That means we have a lead the police do not."

"Unfortunately, I don't think they'd consider it much of a lead."

"Perhaps we need to make some inquiries of our own."

"Can you request your associates to see if any rumors are circulating?" The effectiveness of Ashbury's network never ceased to amaze Michael. Though some were only children, they often learned more than a detective from Scotland Yard could.

"Yes. Someone has to know something."

"If I remember correctly, Berkmond's wife died in childbirth several years ago. The twin girls will be alone now."

"Terrible to lose both your parents at such a young age. Lucas will return to a ready-made family."

"Perhaps he already has a family of his own."

"Somehow, I doubt that."

"His life is about to become much more complicated."

"Surely he will return from Brazil when he receives the news. Those two little girls will need him." The doubt in Ashbury's voice echoed Michael's thoughts. "Though he held little regard for his father or his brother, Lucas was never one to shirk his duties."

"True, but he may have changed. Living abroad can do that." Michael shook his head. "The least we can do is attempt to find his brother's murderer."

"I believe we agreed you would make it look like an accident."

The disapproval in his uncle's voice grated on Vincent. "I told ye 'twas a bad idea in the first place."

"And I told you it had to be done. There was no other way to force Lucas to return from Brazil unless we did away with his brother."

"I still don't understand why ye need all three of them here. The two lords are enough trouble as it is. A man can hardly walk the streets without one of their spies followin'."

"The number three holds magic. That's been proven since ancient times. The three of them together might produce a vortex of sorts."

Simmons turned away to roll his eyes. "Here I thought you were a man of science."

"What was that?"

"Nothing." He shook his head. "What's done is done. I can't very well undo it."

"It would've been much simpler if you'd at least made it appear as if the man took his own life."

"I tried. The bloody man wouldn't cooperate. You'd think that being the one with the weapon would give me the upper hand. Funny how some men don't think that way." He couldn't help but think back to the other time he'd killed a lord.

That one hadn't cooperated either. Some men refused to back down. That cost them their lives.

"Are you certain no one saw you?"

Vincent hesitated as he ran the events through his mind again. Out of the corner of his eye, he'd thought he'd seen someone...a boy perhaps? But when he'd turned to look, the figure was gone. If he'd been there at all.

What harm could one boy cause?

"No. No one saw me."

"Very well then. Soon everything we need will be in place. We'll proceed with the next step of our plan while we wait for Lucas to return." Uncle Grisby chuckled.

The eerie sound caused a chill to creep down Vincent's back.

"The devices need to be tested again. See if you can find some subjects willing to spend some time with us. Though we need more meteorites to provide consistent power, we'll continue testing with what we have. A few more experiments and we will know if it's successful. Then the world will bow at our feet. We'll have more riches than we ever dreamed possible."

Vincent sighed as he looked around the new hovel they currently called home. Despite the money they'd recently gained and his uncle's positive words, he wasn't so sure they were any closer to accomplishing what Uncle Grisby thought they were. Now he was supposed to find more 'volunteers'. Involving others is what had gotten them in trouble last time.

Good thing he didn't have a conscience. Else he'd be tortured by all the harm they'd caused thus far.

Emma felt the weight of Michael's gaze all the way home. While she wasn't quite clear on why he'd decided to escort them home from the ball, she could hazard a guess. Somehow he thought she'd encouraged Mr. Vandimer's interest in her and decided he must speak to her about it.

She sighed. While she had no intention of encouraging the man, she wasn't comfortable being rude either. Where was the line between those two options?

The viscountess chatted about several people Emma didn't know, remarking on this person and their ridiculous attire and that person and their clever grandson. She seemed to require little if any response, so Emma allowed the conversation to continue without commenting. Determined not to look at Michael again, she kept her gaze on the passing buildings as they made their way through the dark, quiet streets.

Soon they arrived home and entered the drawing room. The viscountess dismissed the yawning footman and requested that Michael pour them each a libation. Emma breathed a sigh of relief as the viscountess sat in her favorite chair. At least she wouldn't be left to defend her actions to Michael. He could hardly raise the topic when his grandmother was here.

"I don't care for Miss Vandimer's father. His behavior is odd, don't you think?" The viscountess looked up at Michael.

Emma nearly groaned.

"Perhaps we could ask Miss Grisby her opinion of him. She spent quite a bit of time with him this evening." Michael raised a brow at her.

"I danced with him, we spoke for a few moments afterward, and then you arrived. That's hardly enough time for me to form an opinion." She took a long sip of sherry, hoping the topic was now closed.

"What did he speak to you about?" the viscountess asked.

All too aware of the heat filling her face, she took another sip before answering. She had no desire to tell them that he'd told her she deserved more than to be the viscountess's companion. Never would she hurt her feelings. "Nothing of importance. Odd comments, really."

Michael's gaze narrowed as he studied her. "I'd prefer you stay away from him."

She could only guess how angry he'd be if he knew exactly what Mr. Vandimer had said. "Would you have me refuse next time he asks me to dance?"

"She can hardly do that, Michael. What would you have her do?"

Emma looked at him expectantly. "Yes, what would you have me do?" She knew she had the sherry to thank for her false bravado along with the presence of his grandmother, but why not take advantage of both while she had the chance?

"I don't think he is on your list of potential suitors, so do not seek him out."

"I have no intention of doing so."

"Excellent. Now that we're in agreement, I'm going to retire for the evening," the viscountess announced and rose to her feet.

Emma stood as well, relieved the conversation was over. "Perhaps you'd like to read some more of our novel?"

"Not this evening, my dear. You keep Michael company while he finishes his drink. I'm so tired I believe I'll sleep the moment my eyes close." She moved to Michael and offered her cheek.

The tenderness Michael always showed her squeezed Emma's heart. He really was a good man, despite what he seemed to think of her.

"Good night," Emma said as she kissed the viscountess's cheek as well.

The older woman patted her arm and winked. Emma stared at her, wondering what that was all about.

She left the room, closing the door firmly behind her.

An awkward silence descended as Michael stared at the amber liquid in his glass, and Emma continued sipping her sherry.

"May I ask what he said to you?" Michael came over to sit beside her on the settee, glass dangling from his fingers.

"What am I supposed to do when he speaks to me? Turn away? I thought it unwise to be rude to your fiancé's father."

He set down his glass. "I realize that. I'm sorry I suggested otherwise. Will you tell me what he said?"

She told him, feeling as though somehow it was her fault. After all, Mr. Vandimer wasn't the first man to make inappropriate comments to her. Life had been easier when she'd worn her governess disguise, though that hadn't always been completely effective either.

Michael shook his head as he leaned back and rested his arm along the edge of the settee behind her. "Do be careful. He is not someone to be crossed. The less you engage with him the better. As I said, he's not searching for a wife."

"Do you think he's showing interest in me because of my association with you?"

Michael smiled. "No, I don't."

"Then what?"

Michael rose and offered his hand.

Uncertain what he intended, she set down her empty glass and put her hand in his, her stomach leaping as he pulled her up to stand before him. "What?" she asked as he continued to look down at her.

"I wish you could see yourself as I see you. As

others see you. You are a very attractive woman."

Embarrassed, she shook her head as she tried to tug her hand from his.

"Come here." He kept a tight hold on her hand and led her to the large mirror that hung on one wall of the drawing room. He positioned her in front of him and stood directly behind her, looking at her reflection with her. "See?"

"See what?" She could only see the handsome man behind her, the dim light glittering in the blue of his eyes.

"How stunning you are." He trailed his finger along the line of her jaw.

She caught her breath, fascinated by the sight of him touching her in the mirror.

"Skin like alabaster. Hair as soft as satin." He traced the arch of her brow, the hollow of her cheek.

Her mouth parted in response. She was no longer sure if it was the sherry she'd had or the feel of his fingers on her skin that heated her. No. That wasn't true. It was him. Of that she had no doubt.

"Do you see it?" His voice was low and, combined with his gentle touch and heated gaze, held her in place. He swallowed hard. She watched as he bent his head to nuzzle her neck.

She tipped her head to allow him better access, the feelings his mouth evoked setting loose a flurry of butterflies in her stomach. The image in the mirror held her transfixed, and she couldn't look away.

As he pressed kisses just below her ear, his fingers trailed along her collarbone on the other side. They dipped progressively lower, toward the neckline of her gown. Her breasts tingled in anticipation. She watched as those clever fingers disappeared in the top of her gown. The sight and the sensation caught her breath as he lifted her breast above the fabric.

The shock of seeing her breast displayed in the open, with Michael's hands on it, on her, weakened her knees. The sensations he evoked hardened her nipple, and desire shot through her core. She felt so wanton but couldn't have stopped him if her life depended on it.

"So beautiful," he murmured in her ear, his lips continuing their exploration.

Heat pooled low in her belly. She wanted more. With a moan, she tried to turn to face him, but he held her in place.

"Watch. See what I see." His gaze met hers in the mirror then dropped to her breast. His fingers kneaded the flesh there before touching the very tip.

Her center throbbed with need. She felt helpless, pinned beneath his hands, held captive by their images in the mirror. He shifted to stand beside her and to her surprise, took her nipple into his mouth, sucking gently, then harder. "Oh. Michael. I—"

"Shh. Let me show you." Again, he licked her breast as he freed the other one from the constraint of her gown and repeated his sweet torture.

Watching him in the mirror, his dark head against the paleness of her skin, caused all thoughts to stop. She could only feel.

"You are an amazing woman." His words heated her further. "It makes me wonder what other passions of which you are capable."

He eased behind her once more, continuing his assault on her senses. She watched where his gaze fell, watched where his hands lingered, watched his mouth move across her heated flesh.

When he raised his head, the desire etched in his face only made her hotter. "I would see you bloom in full, Emma. Will you let me?" He kissed her neck again and the cool air of the room brushed her thigh.

She glanced lower in the mirror to see his hand easing up the hem of her gown. Her breath caught in anticipation until at last, his warm fingers touched her thigh. Again, she moaned.

"Oh, yes. Such passion," he whispered. "Just as I thought." He eased the skirts higher. "Let me touch you, Emma. Let me give you this adventure."

Passion of which she hadn't known she was capable held her in its grip. Refusing was not an option. This was Michael. The man she loved. No longer did she doubt that. If she had this one and only time with him, she'd take it. She'd grab it with both hands and hold it tight. "Yes. Touch me."

He closed his eyes as though relieved at her acquiescence as his mouth returned to nibble on her ear. A mixture of heat and shivers coursed down her flesh. She eased her head back to rest on his shoulder, giving him better access, her eyes closing as sensations poured over her, through her.

His fingers found their way to her hip, his touch hot through the thin fabric of her chemise. Then his fingers found the bare flesh above her stocking, and she jerked upright only to encounter their reflection in the mirror.

The wanton woman there was no one she recognized. Strands of hair had come loose from her chignon. Her eyes were glazed with desire, her cheeks rosy red, her bare breasts pressed up and heaving with each breath. Despite the shock of the sight, her gaze fixed on Michael.

His dark hair beckoned her touch, and she threaded her fingers through it. He raised his head long enough to kiss her fingers, then drew one of them into his mouth, sucking gently.

"Oh!" she cried, aching everywhere.

He brushed her inner thigh, moving up to her center lightly then again more firmly. "So soft. So beautiful."

She throbbed with need. He slid his fingers into her soft folds and her knees gave way. He held her waist as he continued to touch and rub in places she'd never realized could make her feel like this. She moaned once more, her breath coming in gasps. "Michael?"

"Yes, yes, just let go. I have you."

Again, his fingers danced along her moist center, taking her higher, and suddenly stars exploded. Her whole body throbbed as she flew.

Michael turned her at last and held her tight, wrapping her in his strong arms, holding her like he'd never let her go.

A sob caught in her throat at the bittersweet moment. To be this close to him but know he was not hers made her heart hurt. For right now, she did the only thing she could—held on tight to Michael, wanting to keep this moment etched in her heart forever.

CHAPTER THIRTEEN

Emma stared at the message that had arrived that morning, her heart racing. Her mother's carefully penned words caused fear to tighten her throat.

Your sister is very ill. Please come home.

The situation must be dire for her mother to send for her. Guilt flooded her. While she'd been enjoying herself, her sister was worsening.

Within moments, she'd gathered her cloak and gloves. She hurried to the viscountess's bedroom and knocked on the door.

"Come in." The older woman was sitting at her desk, pen in hand. She took one look at Emma and seemed to realize something was amiss. "What is it, my dear?"

"My mother has sent for me as my sister has taken ill." Emma's heart squeezed. Saying it aloud made it more real.

"Oh, dear. I do hope it's nothing too terrible."

"I'm afraid it is...quite serious." Her eyes filled with tears at the thought.

She hadn't told the viscountess about her sister's illness. She was so used to keeping her personal life to herself that she hadn't shared much about her family. That had been a mistake. Viscountess Weston had brought her into her home and showed her nothing but kindness. Emma had kept her at arm's length, and now she regretted that. Her habit of trusting no one might protect her, but it kept everyone else out.

"Take the carriage. Stay as long as you need."

"Thank you." Emma turned to leave.

The viscountess grabbed her hand. "Emma, send word if you need anything. Anything at all."

"Thank you so much," she managed through her tears before hurrying out.

In short order, the carriage rumbled along the busy streets. Each time they were delayed by some conveyance or other, Emma wanted to scream. She could not arrive quickly enough.

When they finally drew to a halt before the lodging house, she opened the door and alighted without waiting for the footman. She ran up the stairs as fast as her gown permitted and used her key to unlock the door.

Her mother greeted her, her brow creased with worry. Her normally neat appearance was disheveled. Weary eyes dark with fear filled with tears at the sight of Emma. "I'm so glad you're here."

"What is it? What's happened?" She reached out and squeezed her mother's hands.

"Tessa has worsened considerably the past two days. I'm not certain how to help her."

"Did you send for Dr. Barnes?" Emma took off her cloak and set it on a chair.

"No. Tessa wouldn't hear of it."

The distress in her mother's voice tugged at Emma. She held her tight for a long moment then leaned back to look in her eyes, wanting to reassure her. "Let us see what can be done."

Emma moved toward the bedroom, part of her anxious to see her sister and the other part dreading how much worse she'd find her.

Tessa lay sleeping, her face so very pale in the

morning light. She looked positively haggard. Her eyes had large dark circles and her cheeks were sunken. Even her hair appeared limp and dull.

"Oh, dear," Emma muttered. She glanced at her mother, devastated to see how poorly her sister appeared.

"I know," her mother whispered. "She was doing fairly well until two days ago."

Emma sank down beside her sister on the edge of the bed to rest her hand on Tessa's forehead for a moment. "She feels warm, don't you think?"

Her mother nodded and stepped forward to touch her forehead then the back of her neck. "Yes. Her fever was even worse last night."

"Does she have any additional symptoms?"

"Her nose is congested and her cough is worse."

"I'll fetch Dr. Barnes."

"But there's very little money left. I purchased some fabric for pants for Patrick as well as some more food."

"'Tis fine, Mother. I'll work something out with the doctor."

Much to Emma's surprise, the carriage still waited on the street. The footman told her the viscountess had advised him to wait for Emma if possible. Relieved, Emma gave him the doctor's address.

Unfortunately, the doctor was not at home but was expected to return soon. Emma left an urgent request for him to visit Tessa as soon as possible.

She swallowed hard as she returned in the carriage. What could she do if he refused to come? Should she offer to trade her services again? She covered her face with her hands, so angry with herself. Why had she wasted so much time in trying to find a husband? No, that wasn't the worst of it.

She'd spent her time longing for a man she couldn't possibly have.

Michael.

Memories of the previous evening flowed through her mind and body. The way he'd looked at her, the way he'd made her look at herself, had changed something deep inside her. She knew the passion they shared was a gift to be treasured. But what he'd endured with his parents had scarred him, and there was no changing that, not when he wasn't willing to do so. Besides, as he'd said, his engagement was in already in place.

She needed to set aside her feelings for him and be practical. He had no intention of marrying her despite the attraction they shared. Many people said their vows for practical purposes. She could do the same. All she needed to do was select a man for whom she could grow to care.

For a long moment, she considered Adolphus Vandimer. His wealth would solve all their problems. And even if serving as his mistress was only temporary, wouldn't that be better than marrying and spending the rest of her life with a man she didn't love?

With a sob, she put her hands over her face. No. She couldn't do it. Not with him.

Marriage to a man with whom she could find companionship might work, but she wouldn't be someone's mistress. She would try harder with Lord Tagart or Lord Calverton and see what came of that.

As the carriage arrived at her home, she told herself she was relieved she'd made a decision. Now she could focus on helping Tessa.

The day passed slowly with her sister sleeping most of it. Emma felt so helpless. There seemed to be very little they could do to help her. Emma was certain that was what wore on their mother more than anything—simply waiting and hoping.

Half the day had passed before Emma realized she had yet to see Patrick.

"He's running errands again," her mother advised her. "He thought the money he'd earn might help pay for the doctor."

Emma nodded. At least Patrick would feel like he was contributing. That had to be better than sitting here, listening to Tessa's rattled breathing.

Dr. Barnes arrived mid-afternoon. Emma had never been so pleased to see him. To her surprise, he didn't mention needing payment. Instead, he focused on Tessa.

"You say she's been running a fever?" He examined her eyes, then looked in her mouth.

"It started two nights past. She's been so tired and had little appetite." Emma's mother shook her head, her worried gaze watching the doctor.

"It appears as though she's caught the chills in addition to her other ailment. With some rest and food once her appetite returns, she should recover within the next day or two. Be certain she has plenty to drink as well."

Her mother sank into a chair with relief. Emma reached out and squeezed her mother's shoulder, grateful for the good news.

The doctor left a potion in a bottle for Tessa's cough then bid Tessa and her mother goodbye. Emma walked him to the door.

"Could I come by again and help with your notes?" she offered, hoping he'd permit a trade.

"That's not necessary," he said with a smile, "though I do appreciate your help. Your account has been paid in advance."

"I'm sorry?" Emma was certain she hadn't heard correctly.

"Viscount Weston asked me not to tell you unless you inquired, but since it's your account, you have a right to know."

Stunned, Emma thanked him, pleased when he said he'd be back on the morrow to see how Tessa fared. Just when she'd been certain she could set aside her feelings for Michael, he did something to breach her defenses.

"While the fever she has is certainly complicating matters," Dr. Barnes continued, "what she really needs for the consumption is a long rest in a sanatorium. Many patients benefit from doing so. That might not be within your means, but I would be remiss in my duties if I didn't mention it."

After he took his leave, Emma shut the door behind him and leaned against it. He was right in that an extended stay in a sanatorium was impossible at this point.

With a sigh, she stood upright. She couldn't afford to allow Michael's kindness and generosity to change her goal. Her family needed her. She needed to continue her pursuit of a marriage proposal and could only pray it was one she could live with.

"Two men were fished out of the Thames yesterday." Michael stared out the window of Ashbury's library, frustration mounting at their lack of success in tracking down the professor. Their former mentor had to be stopped, especially if he'd had anything to do with Berkmond's murder. Lord only knew what he'd do next.

"And?" Ashbury rose from his desk, his brow creased.

"The detective I spoke with mentioned they had strange burn marks on their bodies."

"You think it could be Grisby?"

"Perhaps he's experimenting on people again as he did before to test the electromagnetic devices. This time, he's not limiting himself to using children."

"Unbelievable."

Michael turned to face his friend. "They came from the workhouse. From what the police have been able to discover from their families, they believed they'd found a few days' work for a scientist."

"Christ." Ashbury spun away to pace the room. "He must be stopped. But how? We can't even find him."

"Perhaps we should ask Farley to speak with the victims' families, see if he can discover anything the police couldn't." Ashbury's partner in the gaming hell easily blended in with those who lived near the docks or in the East End.

"He'd be pleased to help. If he could find out where they were contacted or where they were to report to work, that might lead us somewhere. We must find Grisby before he causes any further harm."

"I don't understand what his purpose is. How did he go from wanting to use those blasted devices to heal people to this?" Michael ran his hand through his hair.

"I've wondered the same thing. Did the accident damage him so much that he is not the same person?"

"If we knew why and what he is attempting to accomplish, we could gain the advantage."

"To what end does he experiment on...people?"

"If it's not to heal, then it must be to harm. There is no in between."

Ashbury looked at him in alarm. "I suppose I never thought of it in quite that way. But for what purpose?"

"I have no idea." Michael scowled. "Given the size of the devices, I'd hazard a guess it isn't to use on just one person."

"Blast it! If Simmons hadn't died, surely we could've convinced him to tell us more."

A footman opened the door. "Markus to see you, my lord."

"Send him in."

Michael watched as Markus, one of Ashbury's 'associates' entered the room. The young lad swaggered in and bowed, his usual grin tempered. Another lad followed him, this one no more than thirteen or fourteen if Michael had to guess. Something about his eyes looked familiar.

"Afternoon, my lords."

"What brings you here, Markus?" Ashbury asked.

"My companion, Patrick, is one of our newer associates. He saw something the other night I thought you might want to hear."

Patrick swallowed hard then glanced at Markus who nodded in encouragement.

"You're in safe company, Patrick," Michael added, hoping to encourage the lad.

"Two nights past, I—" He hesitated. "I saw a man murdered."

The hair on the back of Michael's neck rose. "Who?"

"Don't know his name. A lord by the look of his clothes."

Michael turned to look at Ashbury to see if his friend had the same suspicion he did. Then Michael turned back to the boy. "Where was this?"

The boy described the street, matching the location of where Lord Berkmond had been killed.

"Did you see who did it?"

"I didn't recognize him, if that's what ye mean. He was pretty tall, thin, wore a bowler hat." The boy shook his head. "It was dark, so I didn't see much more." He shrugged. "I heard voices arguing and went closer to see what was happening. Then I saw the gun and realized what he was about."

"Did he see you?"

"I don't think so. I think he saw me move, but I

don't think he had a good look at me. He didn't chase me or anything."

"Good." Ashbury stepped forward to grasp the boy's shoulder. "You did the right thing. No point would be served by you confronting the man. Your personal safety comes first. Always."

The boy seemed relieved to hear that he wasn't expected to play the part of hero.

"Patrick, would you be willing to speak with the police? To tell them what you saw?"

"But I didn't really see him."

"Yes, but what you tell them might tie into what they've already learned or provide enough of a clue that they can continue their investigation."

He shrugged again. "If ye think it's important, I will."

Ashbury offered to have the police come to his home on Park Lane so Patrick didn't have to attempt to navigate to the police station on his own. He told the boy he'd send word once he'd made arrangements with the police and the boys took their leave.

"It appears as though we've just found a witness to Berkmond's murder," Ashbury said.

"I haven't heard of any other lords being murdered in the past two days. It had to be Berkmond."

"Interesting description of the murderer."

Michael glanced at his friend. "Because it matches Simmons' description."

Ashbury nodded. "Perhaps the professor isn't the only one who didn't stay dead."

Emma returned to Viscountess Weston's home after spending the night with her family. Though feeling a bit guilty for abandoning the older woman so abruptly, she'd wanted to allow her mother to have a good night's rest. Emma had stayed with Tessa in her room, assisting her through the night and helping to calm her restlessness. Her mother looked better for having slept and had promised to send word if she needed anything.

Tessa's condition appeared to have improved during the night, for which Emma was very grateful. The doctor planned to come by again. While accepting more of Michael's financial assistance made her uncomfortable, Tessa's wellbeing was more important. Now she needed to thank him.

Emma found the viscountess in the drawing room with her needlework; a basket of thread sat within reach on the nearby table.

"Good morning, my dear," the viscountess said with a warmth in her smile that warmed Emma's heart. "How is your sister?"

Emma sat and closed her eyes for a moment. "She gave us quite a scare."

"I'm terribly sorry to hear that. Is she better now?"

How like the viscountess not to inquire as to what had happened. Good manners won out over curiosity.

Slowly, haltingly, Emma shared her sister's condition, surprised at how difficult it was to speak about such a personal matter. It was so much easier to keep people at a distance to protect herself and her family.

But the viscountess was different. Emma believed that with all her heart and would be sad to lose contact with her once her time here was over.

As Emma expected, the viscountess showed great concern over Tessa, going so far as to ask, "Is there anything I can do?"

"Viscount Weston was kind enough to assist with the doctor's bill. I don't know how I'll ever pay him back."

"Sometimes, we need to simply accept the help of those who reach out."

"I just wish there was some way I could return the favor. For everything." She rose and looked out the window at the garden for a long moment. "I feel undeserving of his generosity. And of yours." Emma turned to face the viscountess.

She waved off Emma's comment with one graceful hand. "I've enjoyed every moment of your company. While I hope your mission is a success, I'll be quite lonely when our time together is over." There was that warm smile again.

"I couldn't agree more." Emma walked forward and took her hand. "You have been so kind and gracious."

"As have you, my dear. Now, we'll have some refreshments and discuss our schedule for the coming days. With luck, we'll find a wonderful husband for you, allowing us to continue our friendship."

Emma smiled and hoped it might be true.

Michael heaved a sigh as he entered the Larkby's home later that evening. Musicals were not among his favorite things. In fact, they didn't even make the list of events he normally attended. Listening to young ladies attempt to play instruments and sing had proven quite painful in the past. So painful that he made it a point to avoid them.

But the message from his grandmother had made it quite clear that his presence was required. Though he longed to spend more time in

Emma's company, he also knew it would be a mistake. Especially after the other night. Watching her come alive in his arms had been something he'd never forget. She deserved happiness with a man who would treasure her, who could—

He caught himself before his thoughts carried him any further down the path. His priority should be Catherine, not Emma.

A tug of guilt had him shifting. He should've inquired as to whether Catherine would be present. He'd been remiss in his obligations to his fiancé of late. It bothered him that he hadn't missed her in the least. Escorting Emma and chasing after the professor had taken up most of his time.

The footman directed him to the music room where the performers prepared. He remained at the back of the room, searching for his grandmother.

The lovely back of a dark-haired woman standing across the room caught his eye. Emma looked amazing this evening. The graceful line of her shoulders along with the creamy smoothness of her skin held his gaze. Her hair was upswept, revealing an elegant neck which begged to be nibbled. The deep plum of her gown made her glow with health and vitality. All his senses stirred as he watched her.

His breath caught as a strange burning sensation spread through his chest. *Christ.* Even from the back, she stirred him. When she turned, providing him with a better view, he nearly moaned. The dress fit her to perfection, hinting at her generous breasts and the curve of her hips.

She was so beautiful and now held herself with confidence. As she stepped to the side, he saw his grandmother in front of her. Emma said something, causing her to laugh. Emma had been wonderful to his grandmother, and for that he was truly grateful.

Movement in his line of sight caught his attention and he realized Catherine had indeed attended. He took the opportunity to watch her for a few moments. Odd, but he felt nothing as he looked at her. She was attractive as well, but in his mind, she held no appeal compared to Emma. At least not to him.

As usual, Catherine was dressed in the height of fashion, though the gown carried far too many striped frills for Michael's taste. And he feared she might fall out of it if she bent forward. The young lady Catherine spoke with smiled shyly then nodded at something she said. Catherine's gaze moved up and down the lady's attire as she spoke again. Suddenly, the smile the young lady wore fell away and her eyes widened with hurt.

Michael grimaced. He could only imagine what rude comment Catherine had made. He was convinced that she said such things to make herself feel better, to feel as though she belonged amongst the nobility since she hadn't grown up in the *ton*. The comments she'd said to Abigail, Ashbury's fiancé, on more than one occasion had made him say something to Catherine. But she didn't seem to understand—or care—if she hurt someone's feelings. He was coming to realize how very self-centered she was.

Like father like daughter, he thought.

The young lady turned and fled toward the other side of the room, moving past Emma and his grandmother. Emma had apparently witnessed the exchange for she glared at Catherine and caught the young lady's attention as she neared.

With a smile, Emma greeted her and gestured toward the lady's gown, offering a compliment if Michael were to hazard a guess. The young lady glanced down, still uncertain. Emma kept her smile firmly in place as she sent one last glare at Catherine who turned away, obviously miffed at Emma's action. Emma hooked her arm through the young lady's and turned her toward his grandmother. The three chatted companionably for a few moments before their hostess requested that everyone take their seats.

Doubt filled Michael as he considered what he'd seen. He needed to put aside his personal feelings toward Catherine in order to ensure the future of his family seat, a responsibility he took seriously. However, the idea of aligning himself with her for the rest of his life caused a knot of unease to form in the pit of his stomach. He'd never concerned himself with being overly nice, but Catherine's behavior was unacceptable. The question was, what was he willing to do about it?

CHAPTER FOURTEEN

Lord Tagart invited Emma for a ride in Hyde Park the next day. As they left Viscountess Weston's, Emma eyed the grey clouds which threatened rain.

"I am told by the highest authority that it will not rain," Lord Tagart said with a smile as he assisted her into her seat.

"That relieves my worries considerably." She couldn't help but smile in return.

"Are you comfortable?" he asked as they settled into his landau with the folding hoods left open so they could take in the sights.

"Quite. Thank you." Emma held his gaze, waiting and hoping for something—a flutter—anything to prove he would make a wonderful husband.

But she felt nothing other than the start of a friendship. Was that enough? In truth, it was more than many married couples experienced. The problem was that she couldn't help but compare her feelings for Lord Tagart with her feelings for Michael. And the two were as similar as night and day.

He gave a flick of the reins and the pair of matching blacks with white stockings sped into a trot. A groom was seated behind them. The

elegant conveyance was well sprung and the
interior lush, making the short journey to Hyde
Park enjoyable.

"Might I say you look lovely today?" He glanced
at her with his customary smile, his warm brown
eyes steady on hers.

"How kind of you." She returned his smile,
determined to enjoy herself.

She relaxed back in the seat, drawing a deep
breath of fresh air, or rather, as fresh as London
air could be. The park was busy, filled with many
on horseback, in carriages, and some even on foot.
Emma looked about with curiosity and realized
others were staring at her. It was an odd feeling,
and she straightened her posture in response.

As they made their way along the path, she
struggled to think of an appropriate topic to
discuss.

"Did you know that Hyde Park was created by
Henry VIII in 1536?" She immediately berated
herself. Now he'd definitely think her too bookish.

"Truly? Your knowledge amazes me, Miss
Grisby." He appeared interested in the topic, and
she couldn't help but add one more fact.

"It remained a private hunting ground until
1637." More than anything, she wanted to inquire
as to his family. Was that too personal?

"Have you always lived in London?" she asked,
hoping that might bring him to speak of more
personal matters.

"Only during the season. I have an estate in
the country where I spend much of the year."

Silence ensued, and she could think of no other
way to gain the knowledge she wanted other than
to inquire. At least if she asked her questions here
with some privacy, no one would be the wiser. "Do
you have brothers and sisters?"

"I'm the eldest with two brothers and two
sisters. My mother remains in the country. She

doesn't care for the air in London and most of her friends live near our estate."

Now they were getting somewhere. "What do you enjoy doing?"

"When in the country I fish and ride, though most of my time is taken with managing the estate. Tenants to see to and all that. What of you, Miss Grisby?"

Her cheeks heated. How honest should she be at this point? "I haven't had much free time in the past, but I enjoy learning new things."

"That's something we have in common," he said as he negotiated around a halted carriage.

Their conversation moved on to the weather. He pointed out a few of the people they'd spoken with at balls. Her nerves settled as they visited. She realized that not only was he nice, he was amusing. She appreciated that very much.

Yet as the hour continued, she became more convinced that while she truly liked him, her feelings were more brotherly than husbandly. *Was that so wrong?* Some married couples couldn't even claim that much. Some remained virtual strangers the balance of their lives.

The real question was, would those feelings be enough for her? Would it sustain both her and him in the years ahead, assuming he cared enough to offer her marriage?

Uncertainty filled her, leaving a knot in her stomach she couldn't ignore. It seemed impossible to separate the pressure she felt to marry quickly and her true feelings. How could she follow her instincts as to whether the marriage would be a success?

What better test would there be for the relationship than to see how he reacted when she spoke of her family? If he didn't care for what she told him, she'd have her answer. She drew a breath and began. "I have siblings as well. A younger sister and brother. Unfortunately, my sister is quite ill."

She watched him carefully for his reaction as she continued, relieved when he showed only concern. Perhaps she could find a way to make this work after all.

Michael entered his grandmother's drawing room, his gaze automatically sweeping the room for Emma.

But she wasn't there.

"And here I thought you'd come to visit me." His grandmother's dry tone made him smile.

"Never doubt that I did." Yet he couldn't help but glance at the mirror, the memory of Emma in his arms making him ache.

"I beg to differ," his grandmother argued even as he bent to kiss her cheek. "I believe it is my companion whom you seek."

"Emma? Where is she?" He should've known his grandmother would pick up on his interest.

"Lord Tagart invited her for a ride in the park."

"How nice." He forced his smile to remain in place, though he'd rather have scowled with displeasure. He didn't care to examine the reason for it too closely.

"Surely you're happy for her. Your plan is proceeding as you'd hoped." Those blue eyes, so much like his, saw far too much; she knew him too well. "I would expect at least two offers by the end of the month."

Her prediction struck him to the core. He turned away before his grandmother saw more than she should.

"Michael." Her inflection said it was too late.

Masking his emotions, he turned to face her.

"Yes?"

"What are you doing?"

"Visiting with you." He came to sit beside her and squeezed her hand. "One of the finest pleasures in my life."

"If visiting with an old woman is one of your finest pleasures, we need to talk."

He scoffed.

"I speak the truth. While I know you love me, and I truly do appreciate that, there should be so much more to your life than that."

"There is more to my life. I'm engaged, remember?"

"Why?"

"Why what?"

"Why are you marrying Miss Vandimer?"

"She's the perfect wife for me."

"How so?"

Michael rose to pace the room, uncertain where his grandmother was going with this conversation. "She's a good match. Surely you see that."

"No, actually, I don't."

Surprised, he turned to face her. "You don't approve?"

She leveled him a glare that took him aback. "No." She rose to stand before him. "Michael, I do not care for her at all. How can you imagine yourself growing old with her?"

He closed his eyes, the image her question presented far from pleasant. But that didn't change things. "I must marry her."

"Why?"

"It's the only way to gain back Langford Hall." He turned away to pace again. "I've made every attempt to buy it from Vandimer, even under a false name. But he won't accept any offers, no matter how outrageous."

"That drafty old place? Whatever will you do

with it?"

He turned to stare at her, wondering for the first time if her advanced age had affected her mind. "It's been in our family for centuries. When Father lost it—"

"Your father was a fool."

Michael raised a brow. Never had she spoken of her only son so poorly.

She shook her head, her eyes sad. "I loved him very much. Perhaps too much. When your grandfather and I first married, I feared for years I would never have a child. And when your father finally came, I wanted to give him everything, anything to make him happy, to make him smile. I have often wondered if I am the one who created the seeds of destruction in him."

The tears in her eyes nearly broke his heart. "No. That is simply not true. It was him. He and my mother together were...not good for each other. But none of that matters. In a few months, Langford will be ours again. In our family just as it has always been."

"Why are you so insistent on picking up the mess he made? Have you ever thought that perhaps what he tore down should remain so?"

"But it's my responsibility to put the family estate back together. I have the opportunity to make it better than it was before."

"You already have. I know how hard you've worked. You can't imagine how much I appreciate the excellent care you've given me. But I would be happy anywhere. I don't need a home with more rooms than I have need. As long as I have you and friends and a roof over my head, I would be happy."

Michael had been so driven to pay off the debts, to attempt to restore honor to the Weston name, had he so misunderstood what his grandmother wanted? "I don't know what to say.

Langford Hall was the home in which you were born. How could you not want to see it returned to Weston hands?"

"Michael, it's a lovely house. But it's old. It's drafty. The roof leaks."

He raised his brow.

"I have some wonderful recollections of my childhood there. And both you and your father were born there. No one can take those memories from me. I will keep those always. I don't need to wander the halls of that house to remember."

Not gain back Langford Hall? He couldn't imagine such an idea. Not when that had been his goal for so many years. "I thought it meant more to you. Everyone knows Father lost it in a bet. To restore our family honor, I must—"

She raised her finger in the air to stop him. "No. You've already restored our family's honor threefold. Now you should concentrate on being happy."

"But it's within my grasp to gain it back. How can I walk away from the history of our family?"

Anger flared in her eyes. "My son died there. He killed his wife then killed himself there. Why would I want to remember that?"

The images from that terrible night crept over him despite the years that had passed.

His grandmother sighed. "I do not care if you regain Langford Hall. I have no desire to go there again. If that is all that holds you to marrying Miss Vandimer then set it aside. These are modern times. Marriage should be more than a business arrangement."

Michael glanced away, not certain he could explain why he had to be careful, how treating his life like a business arrangement was so much safer. His ability to read success and failures in auras had made it very easy to keep all of his relationships professional.

"What is it?"

He should've known she could tell there was more to his decision to marry Catherine than what he'd revealed thus far. "I think I would be better off if I honored my promise to Catherine."

"How do you mean?"

"I am my father's son." He turned away, unable to meet her eyes for fear he'd see confirmation of his fear there. "How can I possibly allow myself to love? The moment my father did, look what happened. He destroyed himself and my mother. He lost everything, all in the pursuit of *love*."

"Surely you see what they felt for each other was not love but something much darker. Besides you are not your father."

He met her gaze, wishing he could believe that was true. Yet those few moments here in this room with Emma had confirmed his worst fears. His passion for her could so easily burn too brightly and turn down a dark path.

"As we're speaking candidly, I will ask you this point blank." She stepped forward to grasp both his hands in hers, forcing him to hold her gaze. "Do you have feelings for Emma?"

Nonplussed, he could only stare at her, wondering if his regard for her was so obvious. Yet after all he'd told his grandmother today, why lie now? "Yes. I'm afraid I do."

"She's a lovely person." She paused as though waiting for him to agree.

"Yes, she is."

"Lovely inside and out."

He reluctantly nodded, wondering what her point might be.

"I find it impossible to see how loving someone like her could cause you to become as violently jealous as your father. You are not him. Emma is nothing like your mother." She seemed to realize she had not yet convinced him. "You must decide how you feel about Emma."

"I don't know what I feel. I'm not sure I'm prepared to put a label on it." He released her hands to fiddle with a figurine on the table. "I can say that what I feel for Emma is not comparable to what I feel for Catherine."

Emma froze at the doorway of the drawing room unable to breathe. The tiny flicker of hope she'd held that Michael felt something for her extinguished, leaving a dark void. She blinked back the tears in her eyes.

Of course, he loved Catherine. She was beautiful and of his world. She would fit in perfectly.

Emma backed up as quietly as she could and made her way up the stairs to her room, the heaviness in her heart making each step an effort. Lord Tagart had proposed. She'd requested time to consider it. Though she'd thought to refuse him when she gave him an answer in a few days' time, now she was no longer sure.

Michael obviously didn't feel the same way for her as she felt for him. But her family still needed help.

She closed the bedroom door behind her and let her tears fall. Rarely did she indulge in crying. Tears only made her feel worse. But sometimes no other release would suffice. The dream she hadn't realized was forming now lay in ashes at her feet, right beside her heart.

The next morning, Michael awaited Catherine in the drawing room at her home. He dreaded the encounter before him yet was eager to see the deed done. A weight had been lifted from his shoulders after his visit with his grandmother.

He'd spent a long night weighing his decision but realized there was no other recourse. He couldn't marry Catherine. The idea of a lifetime of being subjected to her petty comments and belittling of others was now unbearable.

During the long night, he'd realized the depth of his mistake in offering marriage to her. In truth, he'd felt trapped into doing so. He'd tried every possible way to gain back his family's holding to no avail. Perhaps that had been Vandimer's intent all along—to force him into offering marriage to his daughter.

In many ways, not regaining their estate was a relief. As his grandmother had said, why would they want to stay in the very place where so much heartache had occurred?

His decision had nothing to do with Emma, he told himself. What he felt for her was a separate issue—one he wasn't certain how to deal with at the moment. If he could control the passion he felt for her and focus on helping her and her family, then all would be well. At least he hoped so. Losing control of his desire for her would only harm them both. He could not, would not, allow that to happen. He need only hold back, to maintain some distance between them. That would keep him objective enough to properly handle their relationship, assuming she had feelings for him as well.

He reined in his impatience as he wondered how long Catherine would make him wait. Based on past experience, he knew it could be an hour or more. He'd considered sending her a message first, but had decided against it. He didn't want to give her time to prepare. Better to keep her off balance.

Too restless to sit, he rose to look around. While he'd been in this room before, he hadn't really noticed it. The wallpaper was the very best in quality, the color and pattern the latest fashion. The room was decorated very well, but felt so different than his grandmother's. Nothing here revealed anything about the people who lived in this house. The items in here, from the fabric of the settee to the knickknack that sat on the low table, seemed to have been chosen for appearance's sake only.

Time passed with excruciating slowness until he wanted to seek out Catherine in her bedroom and speak with her there. At last she appeared in the doorway, pausing as though to give him a chance to admire her. How long had he ignored how calculated her every move was?

"Michael, darling. This is an unexpected surprise." Her pink and white gown showed off her narrow waist. While her figure was merely average, her dresses always made the most of it.

"I'm sorry to arrive unannounced, but I had something rather important to discuss with you."

She smiled as she neared him to wrap her hand around his arm. "I know exactly what you have in mind." She looked up at him from under her lashes.

"I don't believe you do," he said, fighting the urge to remove her hand.

"Of course I do. I can practically read your mind. After all, I'll soon be your wife."

"Catherine—" He had to stop her before she made what he had to say even worse.

"No. Allow me to finish. It's time to set the date for our wedding, isn't it?" She smiled triumphantly.

"Actually, that isn't it." He gave in to the urge to remove her hand. Her gaze narrowed with anger. Or was it suspicion?

"Oh?"

"I'm afraid I am not able to marry you after all."

"What!" The shriek took him aback. "How dare you! Do you think to make a fool out of me? Make me the laughing stock of the *ton*?"

"No, of course not." How like her to be more upset at the idea of being made a fool than not marrying him. "I'll give you three days to call off our engagement. You can say you've changed your mind, or whatever you'd like."

"No. This is not happening." She spun away to pace the room, hands on hips. "My father will not allow you to break your word."

"Your father has no say in this."

She stalked up to him and slapped him across the face, catching him by surprise. "You bastard. Who do you think you are?"

"I—"

She drew back her hand to slap him again, but he grabbed her wrist and held tight. "Enough," he demanded in a voice that brooked no argument.

"Let me go!" Her voice shrieked loud enough to bring a footman to the open doorway.

"Is all well, miss?" the burly man asked, looking suspiciously at Michael who quickly released her.

"Leave us," she yelled at the footman.

The servant's mouth tightened as he shot a warning glare at Michael, but he backed out of the room.

"Who is she?"

"What?" he asked, puzzled at the sudden change in topic.

"The doxie who's caught your interest." She gasped, eyes wide. "It's that woman who's staying with your grandmother, isn't it? I saw how you look at her."

"This has nothing to do with another woman. This is about my realization that we will not suit." He touched the corner of his sore mouth. Her behavior confirmed how right he was to end the engagement.

She tipped her head back and laughed, the sound grating on his nerves. "Not suit? You must be joking. What does that have to do with marriage?"

"Catherine—"

"Didn't you learn from what happened to your parents that passion and marriage should never be mixed?"

He stilled as the pain of her barb struck.

"Darling," her voice softened as she drew near, running her hand down his chest, "I only say that because I care for you. I want the best for you, and that is me."

His stomach churned as he looked at her. How had he ever thought he could marry her? "I appreciate that. However, this is for both of our benefits. Trust me."

"I did trust you and look where that got me." She spun away again, all attempts at sweetness dissolved like sugar in hot water. "I've wasted all this time on you. I knew I should've set my sights higher."

"No doubt. I'm certain there's a duke in your future. Three days, Catherine."

"What if I don't?" she asked, brow raised.

"Then I'll call it off. I'm doing everything in my power to protect you—"

"If that were true, you'd have kept your word."

"I'm sorry. I never meant to hurt you."

"I intend to hurt you. You will pay for this, Michael. You will pay dearly."

Though he'd expected her to threaten retaliation, he hadn't expected her aura to glow with the promise of success. He would have to watch her closely.

Next, Michael sought out Adolphus Vandimer at his club. The sooner all of this was over, the better. He found him visiting with another man, a drink sitting on the table at his elbow.

"Weston," he said as Michael approached.

Michael greeted both men. "Might I have a word with you?" he asked Vandimer after pleasantries were exchanged.

"Of course." He bid the other man goodbye and gestured to the vacated seat. "I'm glad you sought me out."

"Oh?"

"Indeed. I have news of the shipping venture of mine in which you invested."

The aura around the man's head dimmed, telling Michael it was not good news. "What is it?"

"Things have not gone according to plan. The shipment will be delayed by at least a fortnight. Maybe more."

Why did he feel he wasn't being told the truth? He waited a long moment, but Vandimer said nothing more. "A delay is inconvenient, but not disastrous, wouldn't you say?"

"Difficult to say at this point." The man stared across the room, making Michael wonder what more there was to the story. But the investment was the least of his worries today.

"I'm afraid I have some unfortunate news of my own. My circumstances have changed." Michael cleared his throat, uncertain how to word his news. "I've asked Catherine to call off our engagement."

"What?" The anger in Vandimer's expression didn't surprise Michael. Anything that could potentially harm his daughter was not allowed.

"I'm no longer able to marry her."

Vandimer rose to his feet, leaving Michael no choice but to stand as well. "You bastard."

"I'm sorry." Michael waited, knowing there would be more.

"I will sue you for breach of promise. I'll drag your name through the dirt."

"I hope you won't. That would not help you or your daughter." Michael had recently read in the newssheet of a case won for breach of promise. Suing for broken engagements appeared to be quite the rage these days.

"What in hell is wrong with you?" Vandimer demanded, fists clenched at his sides.

"I've realized we wouldn't suit. I would spare her from spending her life with me as I do not have the power to make her happy." That was as kindly as he could put it and still speak the truth. God knew she certainly couldn't make him happy. He had no doubt he would've made her miserable by marrying her when he didn't even respect her. Without respect, what was there?

"Do you realize what this means? You will never again own Langford Hall."

That fact still bothered Michael despite what his grandmother had said. He didn't care to be the one to break centuries of family tradition. But he'd finally realized it wasn't worth tying himself to Catherine or her father. "If you ever decide to sell it—"

"You'd be the last person to whom I'd sell. I'd rather burn the place to the ground than see it in your hands." Vandimer took two steps forward to grab Michael's shirtfront and shove him into the wall. "I'm going to bury you."

"Release me." Already Michael could feel the stares of several men who entered the room to watch.

The glittering look in Vandimer's eyes spoke of rage. Michael braced himself, unwilling to allow the older man to strike him. A public disagreement would only provide tinder for the gossip mill, something Michael preferred to avoid. The dimming light of Vandimer's aura gave Michael the confidence to push away his hands.

"Weston? Is all well here?"

Michael glanced out of the corner of his eye to see Ashbury approaching. "Fine, thank you." He looked back at Vandimer. "As I told Catherine, she has three days to publicly call it off. I will take full blame for the broken engagement." Michael straightened his clothing, doing his best to ignore their audience.

"You'd better." Vandimer glanced at Ashbury then back at Michael. "If my daughter's reputation suffers because of your actions, have no doubt. You will pay."

Ashbury drew closer as Vandimer grabbed his drink from the table and left the room. "What was that all about?"

"I requested that Catherine break our engagement."

Ashbury's gaze caught on the corner of Michael's mouth. "Did he strike you?"

"No, but his daughter did." He touched the tender spot with a grimace.

"It will be unfortunate to have her angry with you. But not as unfortunate as it would be to have married her." He grinned. "I for one applaud you for coming to your senses."

Michael raised his brow, surprised at Ashbury's comment. "Truly?"

"Indeed. She's not the most pleasant person."

"We'll see how truly unpleasant she is over the coming weeks. What brings you here?"

"Looking for you. I have news."

CHAPTER FIFTEEN

"Hold him still."

"Can't ye see I'm tryin'?" Vincent glared at his uncle. "These straps won't tighten any further."

The thin man wrenched against the leather bands, his brown eyes rolling with fear. The buckles loosened a bit with each movement. His muffled moans caused by the rag tied over his mouth grated on Vincent's nerves but were preferable to his screams. Blood trickled down the man's wrist where the leather cut into his skin as he jerked to and fro.

Vincent sighed. While using the street urchins for these experiments had been much easier, it had stirred up too much trouble. Luring adults from the workhouse with the promise of good pay had been fairly easy. It was strapping them into place that was a bit more difficult. The chloroform drugged them but lifting them into place made Vincent's back complain.

"Vincent, he cannot move so much." His uncle limped from behind the electromagnetic device that stood on one side of the large room. "I have enough trouble aiming this without him squirming."

"What would ye have me do? If we use more chloroform, ye won't be able to see the affects."

The man strapped to the table whimpered and fought harder against the restraints.

Vincent turned to see how the woman fared. She was also strapped to a table but appeared dazed. He must've used too much chloroform on her. "Mayhap ye should try the woman first."

"Very well." His uncle seemed quite put out by the change in plans. "Though she hardly appears coherent."

Vincent grumbled under his breath, trying not to look at the struggling man. He missed the early days when they'd used objects to test rather than people. It'd been so much easier.

His uncle's pursuit of the ability to animate bodies using electromagnetism seemed impossible. Yet last time, he'd managed to make a man's arm move, so there appeared to be something to it. Of course, that had been before the man had caught on fire. No one had said this wasn't without risks. Vincent shuddered at the memory of the smell, not to mention the sight.

"Step back, Vincent."

With one last glance at the woman, Vincent joined his uncle by the power source. The three devices stood taller than Vincent and equal distances apart with the tables in the center.

"Watch her carefully to see if her limbs move."

"How can I tell when she's strapped down like that?"

"Watch her fingers. If they shift, we'll remove her bindings and measure the full extent of movement."

Uncle Grisby powered on the device, and the machine whirred to life with a high-pitched hum. He allowed the currents to build then aimed the gun at the woman. Electrical current filled the air, making the hair on the back of Vincent's neck stand on end. He squinted at the blue-white light that shot between the devices, then out of the gun.

The woman's body jerked, her back arched, her hands twitched.

"Yes!" His uncle shouted. What must've been a smile twisted his scarred lips. "That's it!"

A sudden pounding on the door of the building halted their progress.

"Who could that be?" Vincent asked.

"I have no idea." Uncle Grisby glared at him as though it was his fault. "Rid us of whoever it is. We cannot be interrupted now."

The knocking started again. Vincent hurried toward the door, his stomach lurching at the image of the police banging on their door. Heaven forbid if they found the two strapped to the table.

Vincent rubbed his sweaty palms against his trousers, heart racing. He cleared his throat. "Who is it?"

"Open up," a gravelly voice demanded. Vincent paused, trying to determine if the voice was familiar. "Open up, Simmons. I know yer in there."

Vincent swallowed hard, still unable to place that voice. He didn't have much choice but to open the door, not with whoever was on the other side yelling like that. Lord knew who might be walking past and come to investigate the noise.

He unlocked the door, eased it open a crack and peeked out. The sight was not a welcome one. "Mikey?"

The man's appearance had changed little since Vincent had last seen him a few weeks past. The same battered hat was pulled low on his brow. His dark, greasy hair was longer and shaggier than before. It was his flat, black eyes and short, stocky form that worried Vincent. Mikey had assisted Vincent in gathering some of the boys from the workhouse when Uncle Grisby had first started his experiments but had soon proved too difficult to manage.

"Yeah, 'tis me. Surprised?" Mikey asked.

"Ye might say that. What brings ye here?" Whatever it was, Vincent knew it couldn't be good.

"I heard a rumor and came to see if it be true."

"Oh?"

"Seems someone offed a lord a few nights past." Mikey leaned against the doorframe, a smirk on his full lips.

Bile rose in the back of Vincent's throat. He glanced over his shoulder to make sure his uncle wasn't listening to any of this conversation. He turned back to Mikey, trying to play dumb. "Haven't heard anything about it."

"Yeah, right." Mikey stepped closer, and it was all Vincent could do not to slam the door in his face so he could run and hide. The man made him nervous on a normal day let alone when guilt weighed on him. "Funny, but the description of the killer reminded me of ye."

"Yeah, that's funny all right."

Mikey leaned forward and looked him up and down. "'Tis the spittin' image of ye, in fact."

"Who's startin' these rumors?" If Mikey would give him the name, Vincent could be rid of him quickly.

"I bet it wouldn't surprise ye to learn it was a lad who swears he saw ye."

Vincent's stomach sunk. Bloody hell. Just as he'd feared. How could the lad have seen anything on that dark street?

"Says he had a pretty good look at the man's face when the street light hit it for a moment."

"I don't know what yer talkin' about."

"Vincent!" His uncle's impatient voice called from the other room.

"Comin'." He looked back at Mikey. "Sorry. I don't know anything about it." He made to close the door, but Mikey's boot stopped him.

"I'm sayin' ye do. And I think 'tis worth a few

shillings for me to keep my mouth shut."

Vincent pondered his options. Mikey was like a dog with a bone. Giving up on his attempt to play dumb, Vincent tried another tactic. "It would be worth even more if ye shared the name of that lad."

Mikey nodded in satisfaction. "How much ye offerin'?"

"Six bob."

"That's not nearly enough. 'Twould cost ye at least twenty."

"I don't have that kind of money."

"Ye better look for it. The price fer my silence goes up each day."

Vincent sputtered in protest.

"If ye can't find it, I'll have to take advantage of the reward the police offered fer information." Mikey grabbed the brim of his hat as he stepped back, those flat black eyes on Vincent. "I'll be back in two days' time. By then, I should have the information yer lookin' fer. And you'd better have the money."

"Vincent!"

Not bothering to watch Mikey walk away, Vincent closed the door and leaned against it. Now he had an even bigger problem on his hands. The good news was that the police thought him dead. The bad news was they'd soon learn otherwise if Mikey had his way. Even if he managed to find the money to pay Mikey, how much more would it take to buy the man's silence forever?

Emma settled into a chair in the drawing room to do some mending while Viscountess Weston rested upstairs. Michael had just left, but Emma chose to remain in her room during his call. She told herself it was because she wanted to give them a chance to speak in private without her being there. In truth, she was avoiding him. She no longer knew how to act around him.

Her attraction for Michael grew each day. Even now, she admitted she'd selected this chair as it was the one in which he always sat during his visits. With a sigh, she smoothed the arms where Michael might have done the same.

Heaven forbid he realized how much she cared for him. Her face heated at the very idea of it. She could imagine the look of pity he'd give her as he reminded her that he was engaged. Just because he'd kissed her—touched her even—didn't mean he felt anything for her. He'd been trying to make a point, not express his feelings.

With a shake of her head, she admonished herself. She could never allow him to know the depth of her feelings. Somehow she had to find the strength to control her reaction to his presence.

She reached for the basket of thread on the floor to find the proper shade to mend the viscountess's gloves when a folded piece of paper near the basket caught her eye. She opened the stiff paper to see if she could determine to whom it belonged.

Words penned in strong, powerful strokes lined the page. Michael's perhaps? She hadn't seen enough of his writing to be certain. She started to fold it up to give to the viscountess, only to have her surname catch her eye. Only it wasn't in reference to her.

Professor Grisby alive? How?

Her breath caught. Why would Michael think her uncle might be alive? He'd been gone for over ten years. Unable to help herself, she read the rest of the words, her stomach tightening with each one as bile rose in her throat.

Electromagnetic devices.
Leon Smith—alternate name for Grisby.
Charles Nulty—chief warder at prison.
Experiments on people—what is purpose?
Emma involved?
Meteorite stolen at museum—murder there.
Vincent Simmons dead—did Grisby kill him?
Burnt bodies found in Thames—killed in experiment?
Berkmond murdered—to force Lucas to return?

Her heart squeezed as her gaze returned to the line with her name. Was that what he thought? Had he only offered to help her because he thought her somehow involved with her uncle? She couldn't wrap her mind around the idea that Uncle Grisby had somehow survived that terrible accident. Why wouldn't he have contacted them?

Her heart ached on every level as her mind reeled. Lies! Everything she'd believed, everything she'd been told, had been a lie. She felt betrayed. Devastated. Hot tears filled her eyes.

What a fool she'd been. How could she have thought for even a moment that she belonged in this world? That anyone would want her in their lives? How many times did she need to be taught that she was not worthy of love? From her father to Uncle Grisby and now Michael. He'd only pretended friendship to provide him with the opportunity to see if she was involved with whatever her uncle was doing.

Could it be true? Could he have survived? None of it made any sense. A thousand questions ran through her mind, but there was no one she could ask. Certainly not Michael. Nothing he said could be trusted. Where did that leave her?

Alone again.

With a sob, she rose, leaving the paper on the chair with the gloves as she fled to her room. She couldn't possibly stay here. Not after all she'd learned.

Tears clouding her vision, she wrote a brief message of gratitude to the viscountess, a part of her wondering if the older woman had known Michael's true intent. She would miss the viscountess terribly, but she couldn't face her now. She donned her old grey gown, packed the few things she could call her own, and left the rest behind.

She glanced around the room that had begun to feel like her own despite its splendor. The future seemed bleaker than ever, yet she had no choice except to leave. She'd been here under false circumstances. The helpless, angry feeling that filled her was far from pleasant and all too familiar.

She shut the bedroom door behind her, her tattered bag in hand as she hurried down the stairs to let herself quietly out the front door. The walk ahead of her was a long one, but she welcomed it. She needed to calm herself, to determine what, if anything, she would tell her mother about her uncle's possible survival.

The rain started to fall as she turned the corner, following the same path down her face as her tears.

"Good morning, Grandmother. I came as soon as I received your message."

The look of concern on her face had Michael's stomach dropping. It took a serious matter to upset her. "What is it?" He glanced about the room. "Where's Emma?"

"Gone."

"Where?"

"I can only assume she's returned home." She

held up a piece of paper that looked quite familiar. "I believe she found this. Perhaps you'd care to explain."

The sight of the paper had his heart sinking. It must've fallen out of his pocket when he'd visited the previous day. He reached for it, glancing at the words he'd noted. The words Emma must've read. "Oh, no."

"Quite. What is going on?"

He spun away to stalk across the room, raking his fingers through his hair as his stomach clenched. "Why wouldn't she have given me a chance to explain?"

His grandmother raised her brow. "You suspect her uncle somehow survived that terrible accident ten years past, your notes imply he's up to no good, and that you suspect Emma might be involved. Why would she want to speak with you at all?"

"No, it's not like that. Well, perhaps I suspected her at first, but who could spend time with Emma and suspect her of anything?"

"I certainly don't believe it."

"The coincidence of her appearing on my doorstep within weeks of Ashbury and me suspecting Professor Grisby not only survived but was performing experiments on people with his electromagnetic devices was too much to believe."

"What experiments?"

Michael shook his head. "We don't know, but we suspect it's not for good."

"You didn't tell Emma any of this?"

"I'm not certain what is true and what is speculation at this point. I knew how much it would hurt her to hear that her uncle may have survived and hidden himself away, so I hesitated to tell her. How could I advise her before I knew the truth? I didn't want to put her through any more pain than she's already experienced."

"But there are so many items on this paper. Surely you have enough that it warrants speaking to her about it all now."

"I should've. Ashbury and I thought her uncle would attempt to contact Emma and, with her in our midst, we would be able to monitor the situation." His explanation sounded weak even to his own ears.

"And possibly catch the professor? Were you using her as bait?"

"Yes. No." Michael put a hand to his suddenly pounding head. "At first, perhaps, but..." He paused, trying to find the words to explain, to quell the panic that he'd lost her. Again. "All of this has been complicated by my...feelings for Emma. You should know that I've asked Catherine to call off our engagement."

"I'm happy to hear that, at least." The look of approval on his grandmother's face eased his worry. Though she'd said she didn't mind losing their country estate, a part of him feared that wasn't true.

"My feelings for Emma have grown into...something more." Silence greeted his statement, and he realized she waited for an explanation. But how could he explain what he didn't yet understand himself?

"Are you going after her?" she asked.

How like her not to ask more than he could answer. "Yes. Yes, I am."

She rose and took his hands. "Then I'll wish you luck, for I think you'll need it. You have much to explain and an apology to offer."

Equal parts of urgency and worry filled him. "Indeed, I do." He bent and kissed her soft cheek. "Thank you."

"For what?"

"For always giving me sound advice. I can't imagine what I'd do without you."

"Lucky for you, you won't have to find out for quite some time."

He smiled and turned for the door.

"Michael?"

"Yes?" He looked back to find a frown on her face.

"Do be careful. The word 'murder' appears more than once on that list of yours."

"All the more reason we need to keep Emma close. With luck, I will convince her to allow me to explain." But in his heart, he feared she wouldn't be willing to listen.

During the long day and night since Emma had returned home, she'd cried until she had no more tears. The most she'd been able to tell her family was that circumstances had changed and she'd decided to search for a new position.

"Are you certain?" her mother had asked. "You seemed so happy at your last visit."

"I'm quite sure." How could she even begin to explain the depth of Michael's deception or that she'd fallen in love with him when he was soon to be married? The only thing she could do was try to put it behind her.

It hadn't taken her long to realize that it would be even more difficult to forget Michael than she'd expected. He'd sent her family several baskets each week filled with everything from fresh fruit to hair ribbons to a newssheet he thought Tessa might enjoy to some jacks for Patrick. Also included were books and fabric along with tea and biscuits. Fresh meat arrived often as well. Not to mention him taking care of the rent and their account with the doctor.

The improved food had obviously aided her

whole family. Gone were the sharp edges to their cheekbones and shoulders. Patrick seemed to have grown even more with proper nutrition. The worry had eased somewhat from her mother's eyes, though she still watched Tessa carefully. Tessa's condition had improved as well. The shadows around her eyes had faded, and she seemed to slowly be rebuilding her strength.

Despite everything Michael had kept from her and the fact that he'd used her, she was grateful for his generosity with her and her family.

The knock on the door that afternoon didn't surprise Emma but still caused a jolt of nerves in her stomach. No one normally called on them, so she knew it had to be Michael. She'd advised her mother that she expected him to call upon her and had asked for some privacy. Now her mother squeezed her hand and joined Tessa in the bedroom, closing the door behind her.

Emma drew a deep breath and opened the door.

"Emma," Michael said, his blue eyes seeming to see right through to her very soul.

She blinked, hoping her anger would return to help protect her heart. Upon seeing his tall, handsome form, she realized what a fragile hold she had on her emotions. "Michael."

"I'd like to explain what you found and apologize, if you'll allow me." For the first time since they'd renewed their acquaintance, he appeared uncertain, a far cry from the confident man she knew.

"I have a few questions for you." She opened the door wider to allow him entrance. As he removed his hat and stepped in, their flat felt impossibly small. She shoved the thought aside as the words from his note marched through her mind.

"I'm sure you do." He stepped to the window to

look out at the grey day for a long moment before turning to face her, his gaze meeting hers. "I am truly sorry. It was never my intent to hurt you."

She swallowed hard, fighting back tears. She didn't want his apology. Not until she understood what was happening. "Do you honestly believe my uncle is alive?" She kept her voice low, hoping her mother and sister couldn't hear them.

Michael glanced at the closed door, seeming to understand, for his reply was but a whisper. "Yes, I do."

"You've believed this ever since the accident?" Her throat tightened at the thought of him keeping such a secret all that time.

"No." He shook his head. "Only for a few weeks now." His eyes closed for a moment before seeking hers again. "Several weeks ago, Lord Ashbury and Miss Bradford were attempting to locate a man who was supposed to have hung for killing her father, yet she'd caught sight of him outside her home. Then Ashbury heard rumors of boys missing from a workhouse. The two problems ended up being connected. Simmons, who we soon discovered was working for your uncle, was gathering the boys to use in an experiment."

"Experiment?"

"We didn't understand at first. I started helping Ashbury with the missing boys then Miss Bradford almost became one of the missing."

"How terrible." The idea of the lady she knew involved in something so dangerous was frightening.

"I'll save that story for another time. At any rate, Simmons managed to take Miss Bradford's two younger sisters along with the boys. In the end, we found their location and were able to free them."

He shook his head. "Sounds crazed, does it not? I thought so when Ashbury first came to me with all this. As we investigated further, we had some suspicions which came from several different sources that hinted at your uncle. But after we freed the boys, we received a message signed by him. No one saw him, other than describing him as a cloaked man who walked with a cane."

"What did the message say?"

"Something to the effect that the time has almost come for Stephen, Lucas and I to be rejoined with him."

"I don't understand any of this. How could he have survived?"

"I thought the same. Back at university, when we were testing electromagnetism, your uncle thought it might be capable of healing people. But now, from what little we've learned, it appears as though he has something else in mind, something much more dangerous."

"You think he's become a criminal?" The idea of the man she'd known and loved involved on the wrong side of the law was impossible to believe.

"We have wondered if perhaps the accident changed him." Michael looked away for a long moment.

"Did it change you?" His expression made her ask even though she told herself she didn't want to know.

He looked back at her, his gaze narrowing.

"You were injured during the experiment," she said. "Did you have lasting affects?"

"A scar." He tapped his stomach. "Headaches, but not as severe as Ashbury's." He shrugged. "Too minor to complain about."

"What else?" In the last fortnight, she'd gotten to know him even better than she'd realized. The look on his face told her there was something he wasn't telling her. She was certain of it.

"Nothing of import."

She raised her brow, holding her silence, a

tactic she'd often used on her charges with much success.

He heaved a sigh as he glanced at her hair. "I see auras."

Surprised, she pondered the meaning. "As in the field of energy said to surround some people?"

"I should've known you'd be familiar with them," he said wryly. "The breadth and depth of your knowledge amazes me."

She refused to acknowledge the warmth that stirred within her at his words. "What do the auras look like?"

He shifted, obviously uncomfortable with the topic. "Basically light or dark as I only see success or failure." At her questioning look, he added, "If someone intends to do something, I can usually tell if they will be successful or not."

She thought over his words, something niggling at the back of her mind. "That is how you knew I wouldn't win the position with your cousin."

"Yes."

"Interesting." She studied Michael, additional questions floating through her mind. But now was not the time for that topic. "Has my uncle contacted you?"

"No, but evidence suggests he continues to conduct these experiments."

"The bodies found in the Thames with burn marks." The words on that piece of paper had made little sense until now.

"Yes."

"What do you think happened at the museum? My uncle murdered the guard in order to obtain a meteorite?" That seemed impossible to believe.

"While he has become more ruthless than the man we used to know, I think he remains the same at his core—a man of intellect. The man who serves as his assistant, who murdered Abigail's father, Vincent Simmons—"

Emma gasped as a memory stirred. "He is a cousin of mine. Always in trouble of one sort or another."

"We wondered if that was the case. It appears your uncle created a rather elaborate scheme to free Simmons from prison after he was convicted of killing Abigail's father."

"I'm surprised Uncle would do so as he rarely had anything good to say about Vincent. He told us that Vincent was always searching for an easy path through life. He didn't share our uncle's love of learning like the rest of us."

"He did your uncle's bidding for a time, at least the unsavory side of it. But we were told Simmons died in prison shortly after you came to stay at my grandmother's. I'd hazard a guess that your uncle found someone else to do his dirty work, but we don't know who."

"What of the lord who was killed, Lord Berkmond? How does he fit into all this?"

"You may remember our friend, Lucas. He was with us one of the times we stopped by your home."

Emma nodded, vaguely remembering the quiet man who'd accompanied Michael and Lord Ashbury.

"Lord Berkmond was his elder brother. Lucas left for Brazil soon after the accident and never returned. Now that he's inherited, he'll be forced to return to England."

"I don't understand why my uncle would want that. Having a lord murdered with the hope that Lucas would come home seems a bit farfetched."

"Indeed it does. But that's not the only piece of this puzzle that's difficult to believe."

All of this information made Emma's head spin. The one question that had no answer was why? Why had her uncle done this? If he was truly alive. Yet how could she believe otherwise with all Michael had told her?

CHAPTER SIXTEEN

"Emma," Michael pulled his chair directly in front of hers, knowing he hadn't yet convinced her of anything. With gentle hands, he clasped hers. Her brown eyes watched him warily, making him wish he knew the secret to gaining her trust. "You have to know I don't believe for a moment that you have anything to do with all this."

"But you did."

"When you appeared so soon after all those events, I couldn't help but assume you were somehow aiding your uncle."

"I wasn't."

"I know. I determined that in short order."

Those intelligent eyes narrowed in speculation. "Then why did you do all this for me? For my family?"

He wanted to pour out his heart to her, to tell her how he truly felt. Would she believe him? Would it make a difference? "Because I care for you. I—"

The doorknob shook, rattling the door on its hinges.

"What on earth?" Emma rose with Michael directly beside her.

They took a step toward the door as a young lad burst into the apartment and slammed the door behind him, locking it.

His eyes were wild with fear, his breath coming in great heaves as though he'd been running the breadth of London.

"Patrick, whatever is the matter?" Emma asked.

"Do you know this boy?" Michael asked, unable to believe the very lad who had witnessed Lord Berkmund's murder was standing in Emma's home.

"Of course. This is my brother," Emma put a protective arm around the boy's shoulders, her back ramrod straight. "Why?"

"Yer one of the lords Markus took me to see." The boy's gaze narrowed. "Thanks to ye, I've got someone tryin' to do me in."

"What?" Michael shared a glance with Emma as they both asked the question.

"Patrick, please explain." She glared at Michael, who in turn looked at Patrick. It seemed only fair that Patrick be the first one to face his sister's wrath, at least until Michael understood the facts of the situation.

The boy shifted his feet and glanced at the closed bedroom door. "I didn't want to upset Ma—"

"Mother," Emma corrected.

Patrick sent her an impatient glance but repeated the proper term none-the-less. "Mother. So I didn't tell anyone what happened." His lips tightened as he stared at Michael. "I didn't realize the whole bleedin' country was going to know it was me who saw the murder. How did that come to pass?"

"I have no idea. The police—"

"Can't be trusted." Patrick paused as though waiting for Michael to contradict him, but Michael wasn't sure he could. What other explanation could exist for Patrick being pursued?

Footsteps sounded in the hall, slowing as they

passed.

"I don't think they know which flat I live in," Patrick whispered.

Michael neared the door, ready to confront whoever it was, but the footsteps didn't return. "Do you know who they are?"

"I've seen the one man around before, but I don't know his name." Patrick rubbed his brow as he looked at his sister with worry in his eyes.

"Emma? Is all well?" The soft voice came from behind the closed bedroom door.

Emma walked over to open the door. "Perhaps you should come and hear what Patrick has to tell us."

"I am coming too," Tessa pushed back the covers as though to rise.

"No. You stay there. You'll be able to hear everything," Emma reassured her.

The sight of Emma's sister tugged at Michael. Her pale, thin face spoke of a long illness, but there was a spark in the depth of her eyes that said she was far from giving up.

Emma's mother gave him a questioning look, but as he wasn't certain what Emma had told her, he didn't know how to respond. "Good day, Mrs. Grisby."

She curtsied. "Lord Weston." She turned to her two children. "Which of you is going to tell me what's happened?"

"If you'd allow me?" Michael asked Emma. At her nod, he turned back to her mother. "Patrick may be in danger. He witnessed a murder. If that's been discovered, your entire family might be in danger as well."

"Murder? Patrick, what exactly have you been up to?" Mrs. Grisby asked her son then glanced back at Michael and Emma, her eyes wide with fear.

"Might I suggest we discuss the details once we

know you are safe? I'd like all of you to stay with my grandmother until this is resolved."

"But Tessa can't be moved."

"Yes I can," Tessa called from the bedroom.

Michael held Mrs. Grisby's gaze. "I fear she may need to in order for all of you to remain safe. I'd be pleased if you'd allow me to see to her transport."

Mrs. Grisby raised a brow at Emma, as though to verify her opinion. When Emma nodded, she looked back to Michael. "If you feel it is truly necessary. We will gather a few things and be on our way."

Then Mrs. Grisby turned to Patrick. "I expect a full explanation as soon as we are settled, including why you haven't told us all of this before."

"Yes, Mother." Patrick hung his head.

Emma closed her eyes for a brief moment. Michael could only imagine the turmoil going on inside her after all the worries the past twenty-four hours had brought. He wanted to go to her, draw her into his arms and hold her until her worry eased. But he did nothing, hoping that he would soon be able to tell her the depth of his feelings for her. That would have to wait until they had some privacy.

"I'll send my footman to fetch the coach," Michael advised. "We'll have more room for all of you and your things. Patrick, stay out of sight. It's unfortunate that we don't have some sort of disguise for you."

"I have an idea," Tessa called from the next room, humor evident in her tone.

Patrick groaned. "I don't think I'll like whatever suggestion she has."

Michael patted him on the back. "I'm sure it will be easier than outrunning your pursuers."

The boy did not look convinced but headed

toward the bedroom to hear what his sister had in mind.

"I'll see if anyone is watching. Somehow, I doubt whoever it is will be looking for me," Michael said, though he had no intention of drawing attention to himself in this neighborhood. "Do not open the door to anyone else."

"Of course," Emma agreed.

He turned to go, but Emma took his arm. "Michael, please be careful."

He lifted her hand to his lips, noting with both hope and pleasure the way her eyes widened. "I will if you promise to as well."

Emma and her family waited for Michael's coach to arrive, tensing each time they heard footsteps in the hall. Tessa had cleverly suggested they disguise Patrick as a girl in one of her old dresses, complete with a hat.

Though he'd argued heatedly, their mother had given him a stern look. She'd mentioned something about "that was what he got for being in the wrong place at the wrong time when he should've been home," and he'd complied readily enough.

When the coach arrived, Michael carried Tessa with Emma directly behind. Tessa had breathed deeply in the fresh air and looked about in wonder as they'd left the lodging house, making Emma realize with a pang of guilt how long it had been since she'd left their small apartment. Somehow, she needed to determine a way to help Tessa venture outside more often.

Michael had told them all not to look about or act nervous, but instead act as though they were going on an outing. Emma had breathed a sigh of relief when they were all tucked inside the luxurious coach. Michael had the driver take a circuitous route to make certain no one followed them. In a short time, they'd been delivered to the viscountess's.

As the others alighted, Emma's mother pulled her aside. "Perhaps we should enter using the servants' entrance. My attire is more suited to that than pretending to be a guest here."

"You are a guest here," Michael added, not looking the least bit embarrassed for having eavesdropped. "My grandmother invited you to stay with her."

Her mother didn't look convinced, but when Michael offered his arm to her, she took it with a shy smile, and they led the way up the steps to the front door before Michael returned to carry Tessa inside.

Viscountess Weston awaited them in the foyer and greeted them with a warm welcome. "Do come in. I'm so pleased you're all here." She smiled at Tessa whom Michael held. "Would you prefer to settle in your room or do you feel well enough to have tea with us in the drawing room?"

Tears filled Tessa's eyes as she shared a look with Emma. "I would love to visit with you and have tea, my lady. Thank you."

For once, Tessa would partake instead of merely listening to Emma's description of an event. While it seemed a simple thing, Emma knew how much it meant to Tessa.

"Tea sounds lovely," Michael said as he carried her sister into the drawing room ahead of them.

The viscountess peered over Emma's shoulder and caught sight of Patrick's odd looking attire. "Lovely dress, my dear."

"We thought—that is—I had to disguise—" His face turned red as he tried to explain, tugging at the ribbon that kept the hat in place.

"No need to explain, Patrick," she said with a smile. "Do you want to change before you help yourself to the sandwiches and biscuits cook has for us?"

Emma chuckled. Her brother looked torn. "You can change first," she told him as she shared a smile with the viscountess. "We'll hold tea until you return."

They gathered in the drawing room, the viscountess asking many questions. Apparently, Michael had sent her a note with only the briefest of information. Michael soon took his leave, saying he had several things he needed to see to. Emma could only hope he'd be careful with whatever he was doing.

Patrick had quickly returned in his normal clothes, declared himself to be starving, and eyed the food hungrily. When wasn't he hungry?

"Please help yourself, Patrick," the viscountess directed him with a wave of her hand.

Emma was relieved to see him take modest portions and eat with some manners. As Emma had hoped, her mother and the viscountess already seemed to enjoy each other's company. While Emma could tell her mother felt self-conscious as she continued to glance at both the viscountess's elegant attire then her own well-mended gown, then around the room, she seemed to relax as the conversation continued.

When Tessa began to wilt, Emma excused them and accompanied her to her room with one of the footman carrying her. He set her on the bed, leaving them with a smile and a bow.

"Oh, my," Tessa said as she looked around the room. The entire room was done in shades of yellow, from the pale shade on the walls, to the deeper shade on overstuffed settee and stool, to the medium shade on the bedding. Pillows, a lamp shade, and the bottles on the dresser carried touches of robin's egg blue that accented the room.

Emma smiled as she sat on the bed beside her. "Amazing, isn't it?"

"How can I possibly sleep here?"

Emma leaned forward and whispered, "I had the same exact thought when I first stepped into my room. I didn't want to disturb it."

"The viscountess is very kind."

"Yes, she is." Guilt struck Emma as she remembered the brief note she'd left. Yet despite that, the viscountess had taken them all in with open arms.

Tessa touched the satin coverlet on the bed. "It's so smooth."

"Let's settle you beneath it so you can rest." Emma moved to the wardrobe and found Tessa's few things had already been unpacked.

"How can I possibly stay in my room with all that is happening? What if I miss something?" Emotion thickened Tessa's voice.

"I'll keep you up-to-date on all events," Emma promised as she helped Tessa unfasten her gown.

"The way you have been of late?"

"I don't know what you mean," Emma protested even as guilt seeped through her. The news of their uncle's survival jumped to mind. But Emma had already decided not to tell her family quite yet. Didn't Tessa realize the reason Emma didn't share everything was to protect her? In her fragile state, Emma wasn't certain what news she could handle.

"For one thing, what is going on between you and the viscount?"

Shock paused Emma's hands. "Why do you think anything is happening?"

"'Tis obvious." Tessa's voice was muffled through the gown Emma drew over her head.

"You're mistaken. He has been very kind to me. That is all. He's engaged, you know."

Tessa pulled her gown off her head to stare at Emma. "No."

"Yes," Emma said, as much to confirm it to Tessa as to remind herself. "To Miss Catherine Vandimer."

"I don't understand."

"What's not to understand?" Emma asked, suddenly impatient with her sister. This was not a subject she cared to dwell on, not when it made her heart ache so.

"I was so sure he cared for you."

Oh, the pain! It came in waves and tightened her throat. But she couldn't allow anyone to see how deep her feelings for Michael were. "I'm sure he does, but as an acquaintance, or perhaps a distant cousin."

Tessa scowled but said nothing more.

"We have many other things with which to be concerned." Emma drew back the covers on the bed and Tessa climbed in. "Beginning with how Patrick managed to witness a murder. That greatly concerns me."

Tessa sighed. "I feel as if that's my fault."

"How could it possibly be *your* fault?"

"If I weren't so ill, then Mother would pay more attention to what Patrick is doing and where he goes." She lay back against the pillows, her face pale with exhaustion.

"Tessa, you can't believe that for a moment. Even if you were feeling better, Patrick would not be able to stay in our flat all day long. He'd make us all crazed, enclosed in such a small space with all his energy."

The image coaxed a small smile from Tessa. "That is true, but I still think—"

"No. What's done is done. No regrets." How many times had she told herself that over the past few days? It applied to this situation as well. "We need only focus on what happens next."

"Thank goodness Viscount Weston and his grandmother are willing to help us."

If only Tessa knew how tied Michael was to the situation, then she'd better understand why he was assisting them. A part of Emma couldn't help but wonder if he was continuing to use her to try to find her uncle. Obviously, it was doing no good as her uncle hadn't bothered to tell them he lived.

The pain from his abandonment of them had formed a crevice she didn't think could be repaired. To think he'd leave them to survive on their own hurt deeply. Had he not realized there were nights they went hungry? That there were times when Emma had not been certain they'd be able to keep a roof over their heads? When the cold had seeped into their flat, leaving them so chilled they couldn't sleep at night?

She swallowed hard, trying to push back all those memories. Somehow, she needed to do as she'd told Tessa. What had passed was passed. They had survived. And they would continue to do so. Emma had found a way to keep them housed and fed before, and she would do so again. Never mind the thought made her so tired that she was tempted to lay down beside Tessa and close her eyes.

Tessa's breathing evened out as Emma continued to stroke her sister's hair until at last, Emma was certain she slept deeply. As quietly as she could, she rose and returned to the drawing room.

"Your mother and brother have gone upstairs to settle into their rooms and rest before supper," the viscountess said as Emma came in. "How is Tessa? I hope we didn't tire her overmuch."

"She'll be fine. She's truly enjoyed stepping out of her bedroom and seeing something different for a change."

"Poor dear. How are you holding up with all

this?"

Emma shook her head, amazed at the viscountess. "How can you possibly be so kind and welcome us all into your home when I left so abruptly?"

She smiled and clasped Emma's hand. "I saw the list you found. I would've done the same thing in your shoes. How could you stay here if you believed Michael suspected you of being involved?"

Emma's eyes filled with tears. "It means so much to me to hear you say that. But I still must apologize. You've done many things for me for which I can never repay. I'm sorry I left without speaking to you first."

"You forget how much you've done for me, Emma. I've enjoyed your company very much. The house felt quite empty without you. It is truly a pleasure to have your family here. And I'm pleased to be able to help keep all of you safe."

"Thank you." Emma's throat tightened, making it difficult to speak. She released the viscountess's hand so she could give her a hug.

"You are a treasure, Emma," the viscountess said as she returned the hug. "Always remember that."

"As are you, my lady," Emma replied, so grateful she'd had the chance to meet this amazing woman.

"Now, tell me, what would you like to do? Do we proceed with our plan or keep all of you hidden away here?"

"I suppose I hadn't thought that far ahead."

"I believe we should continue our normal activities unless something arises." She clapped her hands together like a young girl. "This will be more fun than I've had in years."

Emma could only smile, her heart feeling lighter than it had for some time.

Matters were getting more and more curious, Emma thought, as she entered the drawing room the next morning. Miss Catherine Vandimer awaited her on the settee, having asked specifically to see her.

Emma couldn't imagine what the woman could possibly want, unless it had something to do with Mr. Vandimer. Even so, Emma had no desire to speak to her. But good manners dictated that she do so, whether she wanted to or not.

"Good day, Miss Vandimer."

Catherine didn't bother to rise, and the expression on her face was far from pleasant. Her mouth twisted in distaste as she scrutinized Emma's gown.

Emma inwardly sighed, restraining herself from turning around and leaving the room. If the woman criticized her attire that was exactly what she'd do. "To what do I owe the...honor of this visit?" Emma asked.

Catherine took her time answering. "I had to speak to you to ask you if you realize you're ruining Viscount Weston's life."

Emma stared at her in shock. "What could you possibly mean?"

"Surely it's obvious. You're spending far too much time with him. People are beginning to gossip."

Anger brought a reply to Emma's lips, but she held her tongue. There had to be something more to this conversation. What the woman said made no sense. "I'm afraid you'll have to clarify that."

"I know Michael far better than you." Catherine tipped up her chin as though to convince herself it was true. "You may not realize that his one desire is to regain his family's holding. Upon our marriage, it will once again be in Weston hands as it had been for centuries before."

Ah. That explained so much, and in a way, relieved her. So that was why he planned to marry Catherine. "I don't see how that has anything to do with me."

"We both know you don't belong here. You don't fit in. You should return to from wherever it is you came." She raised a brow, as if daring Emma to disagree.

Emma's breath caught in her throat. Wasn't that exactly what she'd convinced herself? That she didn't belong in this world? Should she do as Catherine said and leave? Perhaps that would be the best solution for everyone. She stared at Catherine as she tried to decide what she should do.

A gleam came in the woman's eye which Emma could only interpret as superiority. That smug look suggested she knew she'd won.

Anger rose unexpectedly in Emma, straightening her spine. "No."

A flash of surprise crossed Catherine's face. "What?"

"No. How dare you suggest that I leave to suit your purpose. I belong here just as much as you."

"You have acted inappropriately and—"

"No, I haven't." At least not in public, Emma told herself. "Besides, my behavior is no concern of yours."

"I should've expected this sort of response from you." Catherine rose, her thin lips tightening. "You leave me no choice but to call off my engagement with Michael. It will be your fault that he'll lose his family holding."

Emma's heart sunk as guilt struck. She had no desire to be the reason their engagement ended. What could she do? Should she leave after all?

No. Resolve filled her. None of this was her fault. As much as she worried she didn't belong here, she knew even better that her family didn't belong in their tiny flat which filled with coal dust each day. Nor did they deserve to go hungry at night.

"This is between you and Viscount Weston. I suggest you speak with him if you're having second thoughts about the marriage."

Catherine stormed out without so much as a goodbye. *Good riddance*, Emma thought. While she hated the idea of Michael not regaining his family estate, he would surely be better off without Catherine. He deserved a wife who would make him happy. A deep pang of longing filled her. How she wished things were different.

But she'd learned long ago that wishing brought nothing. It only made you sadder. In her younger days, she hadn't realized life would be quite so difficult. Hope had kept her moving forward through many challenges they'd faced. Maybe it was time to let go of hope. It filled her with longing for things that could never be. Her focus needed to stay on what was, on the next step before her. And that meant this evening.

She needed to prepare for the ball tonight and decide if she could accept Lord Tagart's offer.

This ache in her heart would fade eventually. At least she hoped it would. *Damn.* There was that word again.

CHAPTER SEVENTEEN

Michael studied the crowded ballroom, wondering what the night would bring. Had Catherine done as he requested and called off their betrothal? Surely by now she'd told a few of her friends that she'd changed her mind. Such news would spread quickly. A man could hope anyway.

He knew exactly for whom he searched. He'd deliberately stayed away from his grandmother's since delivering Emma and her family there two days past. While the distance had not been easy, he thought it best, at least until certain events had settled. His top priority was to keep them safe from whatever crazed plan Professor Grisby was attempting.

He looked forward to becoming better acquainted with her family. Patrick was an intelligent lad who was doing well despite the lack of a male role model in his life. Michael could certainly relate to that. His own father had been less than helpful in guiding his life. Tessa was a lovely young lady. He hoped she regained her health and intended to do everything in his power to make certain she did so. Emma's mother had always been kind to him and was a pleasure to spend time with. It was easy to see where Emma had gained many of her attributes.

Which brought him to Emma.

Though he needed to wait a reasonable amount of time after his broken engagement before declaring his feelings for her, he wasn't sure how long he could wait. Each moment with her made his feelings grow. Hence, his reason for keeping his distance. This was his opportunity to learn to control his feelings, to contain them so they didn't turn into something disastrous.

But this crowded ballroom might provide him with the opportunity he desired. At the very least, he'd be able to dance with her. Having her in his arms even for a short time might serve to appease him temporarily.

Or make matters worse.

He was willing to take the risk.

At last he spotted her as she left the dance floor, her partner returning her to his grandmother's side. Irritation filled him at the number of men surrounding her. Her entry into society had been far more successful than he'd imagined. While the knowledge should please him, it didn't.

He eased through the crowd, greeting a few acquaintances, disappointed when no one mentioned his broken engagement. Apparently he'd need to make a few comments of his own if Catherine had truly failed to spread the news.

As he neared Emma, he couldn't help but notice how animated those around her appeared, as though they truly enjoyed her company. They listened with interest to what she said and responded in kind. He wasn't the only one who was attracted to her. Tagart was at the front of the group. Rather than elbow his way through her suitors, he moved nearby to where his grandmother visited with friends.

"How are you faring this evening?" he asked

after delivering his customary kiss.

"Quite well, thank you."

"And how is everything at home?" They'd been careful to keep the whereabouts of Emma's family a secret. Extra footmen had been added to the household to keep watch and serve as protectors if needed.

"All is fine thus far. I hated to leave them to their own devices for the evening, but we thought it best to make things appear normal."

"With luck, it will only be for a short time. Then you'll have your home back to yourself."

"I'm quite enjoying all the company. It will be far too quiet once they leave."

"Your protégée continues to gain in popularity." Michael watched as Emma smiled at something Tagart said, annoyed with the pang of jealousy that struck him.

"Indeed. I believe she can expect several offers in addition to Lord Tagart's soon."

"Tagart proposed?" Michael could hardly believe his ears.

"I thought she'd told you."

"No, she didn't." A weight settled on his chest and wouldn't release. "What did she answer?"

"She asked for a few days to consider."

His gaze sought Emma, noting the graceful curve of her neck, the sparkle in her eyes, the hint of rose in her cheeks. Then he studied her companions, wondering which other man might offer for her.

In many ways, she was just finding her way, only now becoming comfortable in her new persona which fit her so well. He wondered if she realized that. It was almost as if the events she'd been through in her life had prepared her for this. Her confidence had grown in the past fortnight, making her even more attractive, more appealing. Obviously, he wasn't the only one who thought so.

Uncertainty filled him, adding to the weight in his chest. Here she was finally coming into herself, and he selfishly wanted to keep her as his own. How could he possibly ask her to step away from all this and become his? She couldn't make a decision until she'd fully tasted success, until she'd sampled what life had to offer.

He scowled, displeased at the thought. He didn't want to wait. He'd done some sampling of his own and found her more than appealing. Why should he delay? Surely he could make her happy.

"Whatever is the matter?" his grandmother asked. "You look as though you've eaten something that didn't agree with you."

"It's nothing. Excuse me, please." He parted the group that stood between him and Emma, using an elbow or two when necessary until he reached her. "Would you do me the honor of dancing with me?"

She looked up at him, those brown eyes showing her hesitation, reluctance even. He couldn't help but wonder why. "Thank you, my lord. Of course."

She excused herself from her companions and took his elbow. An extra layer of reserve seemed to sit between them. He didn't care for it but wasn't certain how to remove it, at least not here.

The deep blue of her dress set off her smooth skin. The neckline hinted at the curves she'd so successfully hidden in the past, tantalizing him with memories of those lovely breasts. He forced his gaze to her face before his body betrayed him, only to realize she'd stopped smiling since he'd taken her in his arms.

"Is your family settling in?" he asked when the dance permitted an opportunity to speak.

"Yes. Patrick is a bit restless, but otherwise, all is well."

"We've posted a few people to watch your

lodging house, hoping to discover who was threatening Patrick."

She nodded but said nothing more. The silence drew long, making him wonder at her thoughts.

"I prefer your laughter when we dance." He smiled but she remained somber.

"You don't have to do this anymore," she said quietly.

"Do what?"

"Dance with me."

"You think I only do it out of duty?" He missed a step at the thought.

"Don't you?" She dropped her gaze for a moment before meeting his again. "Perhaps it would be best if we spent less time together."

He studied her closely, desperate to understand why she'd said that. Surely he hadn't misread her feelings toward him. The mask of cool indifference she wore made him long to kiss her until she kissed him back, until she held him tight, until desire gripped her as hard as it gripped him. "Why?"

She blinked as though surprised he'd asked the reason. "Because you're engaged." She paused for a moment as though that should be enough of a reason. It would be if that were still true. But it wasn't. "In fact, your fiancé called upon me this morning."

Hell and damnation. Damn Catherine. How long would it take him to be rid of her? "What did she say?"

Emma looked away and in that moment, Michael knew he wouldn't gain the full truth of the matter. "She reminded me that you're engaged. In truth, I was grateful to her. I would never want to do anything to jeopardize your happiness."

Her eyes met his again. His breath caught in his throat at the depth of emotion he saw there.

He drew to a halt in the middle of the dance floor. "Emma, there's something you should know."

"Michael, darling." A hand on his arm jolted him out of the moment. "I'm so pleased I found you," Catherine said. "I'm sorry I'm late. I hope you didn't miss me overmuch."

Emma stepped away as Catherine took her place. Before Michael could say anything, Emma turned and walked away.

Michael had to draw a breath to control his anger as he watched Emma disappear into the throng. He shifted his gaze to Catherine, wanting nothing more than to put his hands around her neck and squeeze that smug smile off her face. "I don't believe you've taken the opportunity I offered."

She lifted her hands as though to begin to dance, but Michael didn't move. He stood there with his hands folded before him. He refused to play her games. He would not be manipulated by her. Catherine glanced around as people began to stare.

She dropped her hands, eyes narrowing as she glared at him. "Surely *you* of all people aren't going to make a scene."

"I believe you're the one doing that." Never would he have believed he'd allow himself to make a public display like this. But he refused to allow her to manipulate him.

"Do you think you have the upper hand? Our engagement will only end when *I* decide it. Not you." Her voice rose, causing even more people to stare. Her gaze took in the onlookers and a small smile came over her lips.

"I gave you the opportunity to save face, but that's coming to an end. When the clock strikes midnight, your opportunity to end it will be over. At that time, I will take matters into my own hands."

"Do you think to be so easily rid of me? I don't think so." The venom in her gaze only made him shake his head despite the brightness of her aura which clearly showed her success at whatever she plotted.

"Do not trifle with me, Catherine. You will regret it."

"We shall see who regrets this, Michael. But I can promise you, it won't be me. Meet me on the terrace at quarter past the hour. Then we will resolve this." Head held high, she spun on her heel and left him standing on the dance floor.

Michael didn't bother to watch her go. Instead, he moved in the opposite direction to where he'd spotted Ashbury earlier.

"Evening, Weston."

"Ashbury."

"That was a lovely bit of drama on the dance floor. So unlike you." Ashbury grinned, clearly amused at Michael's situation. "Making your life difficult, is she?"

"Annoying, not difficult." He glanced at some of the other people he knew in the room. "I need some information to spread. The quicker the better."

Ashbury feigned disbelief. "She refuses to cooperate? How surprising. Are you planning to make this unpleasant for her?"

"No. I only want it to end."

"In all honesty, you may need to play a stronger hand than you had intended if you wish to make your point."

Michael pondered Ashbury's words, considering his options. Then his gaze caught on a man with a bright purple vest and matching stripped cravat. "Doesn't Lord Thompson have a reputation as a gossip?"

"I believe he does. That should aid your cause. I can share the news of your broken engagement with an acquaintance or two as well." He paused as he glanced around to find a target. Then his gaze caught on someone across the room. "I wonder what our ladies are speaking about so intently."

Our ladies? Michael's gaze followed Ashbury's to where Abigail stood. Ah. She spoke with Emma. The sight of her calmed Michael. With luck, soon Emma *would* be his lady. "I, too, would be interested in that, but first I must take care of this matter."

"I'll see who I can find to mention it to as well."

"Excellent. The sooner everyone hears, the better. Remember, she's the one who called it off."

"Shall I explain how devastated you are?"

"Hell no. No need to lie anymore than I am already." Michael crossed the room to where Lord Thompson stood visiting with another man.

"Weston." Thompson turned to face him. "Heard you were searching for a meteorite."

Michael frowned. "Where did you learn that?"

"Professor Embersley attended the most recent Association for the Advancement of Science meeting to ask if anyone had any new findings on rhodite. Said you and Ashbury had come by his home inquiring about it and also had interest in meteorites."

"Did anyone have information for him?"

"One man shared that a substantial shipment coming from Brazil had disappeared. But that was all." Thompson tucked his thumbs in his coat pockets and rocked back on his heels. "Congratulations on your upcoming nuptials."

Michael nearly smiled at the perfect entry into the conversation he wanted to have. "I fear Miss Vandimer has changed her mind. We will not be marrying after all."

"Oh? Terribly sorry to hear that."

"Probably for the best."

The older man, still unmarried, much to his mother's dismay, raised his brows in interest. "How so?"

Michael couldn't resist. He leaned closer to whisper in his ear. "She's more demanding than most men could handle, if you know what I mean." He eased back and gave him a knowing look.

"More, you say?" A gleam came into his eye.

"So much more." Michael slapped him on the back. "Perhaps she'd be better suited to someone with your abilities."

Thompson's eyes grew wide. "Truly?"

"Worth a try if you're in the market for a wife. You know, she mentioned you only a few days past."

The man straightened his shoulders and puffed out his chest. "Did she? Wouldn't surprise me in the least."

"Women are attracted to mature men like yourself."

"I've found that to be true. Perhaps I'll go ask her to dance." He frowned as he caught sight of her near the garden door. "Is she leaving?"

"I believe she's in need of some fresh air and is going out onto the terrace. You could join her there. Always nice to have an opportunity for a private conversation."

Lord Thompson smiled. "Indeed. You sure you don't mind?"

"Not at all. In fact, I wish you luck." *You're going to need it*, he whispered under his breath. "Be sure to tell her you're sorry to hear about the broken engagement, but that you understand why she decided to call it off."

"Yes, yes, that's exactly what I'll tell her." Without even bidding Michael goodbye, he headed directly toward where Catherine had exited the room with a lift in his step that made Michael smile.

Emma could only sigh as she watched Abigail study Lord Ashbury across the room. "You truly love him, don't you?"

Abigail turned back to Emma with a smile. "In truth, it still amazes me. What I feel for him is so...big. It's a bit difficult to describe." As though she couldn't resist, she glanced again at her fiancé.

The look on Abigail's face sent a sharp pang of longing through Emma. "What you have together is very special."

Abigail turned back to face Emma with a smile. "Indeed. I'm very lucky. Of that I have no doubt. It's all a bit of a shock considering how much we irritated each other when we first met."

"Well, you did shoot him, didn't you?" Emma still found the story difficult to believe.

"That was not my fault. At least it wasn't *all* my fault." She waved a hand in the air. "That's behind us now. We're attempting to focus on the future. Though that's rather difficult with recent events." She sent a worried glance at Emma. "I'm sorry. I didn't mean to concern you."

"Yes, recent events." She shook her head. "I still can't believe my uncle lives, nor that he has been the cause of so many problems. That's not the man I knew and loved. It's very difficult to understand how he could be capable of the things Lord Weston has shared with me."

Abigail took her hand and squeezed. "Let us not speak of such dismal things this evening. I have something else I wanted to discuss with you."

"Oh?" Emma asked, quite curious as Abigail focused her blue eyes on her.

"Have you ever considered writing a book?"

Emma frowned. "I'm not certain I'm qualified. I have no talent for poetry or the like."

"Well, I'm in need of something especially suited to your talents. I want a handbook to aid beginning governesses. Something with a logical order that would provide the more helpful things you've learned over the years."

"I don't think I'm the right person," Emma denied. "I don't have any exceptional knowledge or techniques."

Abigail faced her, her blue eyes holding an intensity that Emma couldn't deny. "In the bookstore the other day, when you were telling me of some of your experiences and how you handled your charges, I thought it quite brilliant. I'm certain others would find it very helpful, especially those women who are only beginning their careers."

Emma looked across the ballroom as she considered the idea. "I suppose I might actually know enough to write an entire book on the topic."

"Tell me you'll think about it. Maybe even take the time to jot down some thoughts on the various topics it might cover and how it could be organized to be the most helpful. Think of what you wished you'd known when you first began as a governess."

"I'll give it serious thought," Emma said, flattered Abigail thought enough of her knowledge to suggest such a project.

"I'd be willing to pay an advance and an additional payment when you provide us with the completed manuscript."

Emma hadn't really considered that she would receive any significant payment for it. When Abigail named the sum she had in mind, Emma could only stare. "Are you quite serious?"

"Of course. I never jest about financial

matters."

"That seems far too generous of an offer."

"Not at all. It's purely a business matter. One from which I think we could both benefit."

"I'm very honored that you'd think of me. I know I would enjoy working with you," Emma said with a smile, excitement filling her at the thought.

"I couldn't agree more. We'll speak further after you've had a chance to consider it and begin your notes."

"I'll work on them on the morrow."

A stir rose in the ballroom, catching their attention. Loud shouts could be heard above the murmurs of the crowd. Emma turned to where everyone stared and caught sight of an angry Mr. Vandimer emerging from the terrace door with his daughter and Lord Thompson directly behind. She looked furious but Lord Thompson appeared quite pleased with himself.

"I wonder what all that was about?" Emma asked.

"I have no idea but I'd be interested to find out." Abigail's attention shifted as she saw Lord Ashbury approaching. "I believe my fiancé is here to claim the next dance."

"Enjoy. Thank you again." Emma smiled as she watched the couple greet each other, their expressions showing how much they cared for each other. She closed her eyes for a moment at the longing that filled her, willing away the ache. That sort of relationship was for a lucky few. Not her.

What an interesting evening this had been. She had much to consider. Now she wanted only to return to her family to see how they fared.

Michael escorted Emma and his grandmother home. He'd told the footmen to keep a close watch for anyone following them. With Patrick being pursued and the continued search for the professor, he didn't want to take any chances.

But seeing the ladies home safely wasn't his only reason for accompanying them. He hoped for the opportunity to speak with Emma. While he couldn't declare himself publicly, he wanted to tell Emma he was no longer engaged. Now that he knew Tagart had proposed, Michael felt an urgency to speak to her.

The silence drew long in the carriage. His grandmother yawned behind her hand while Emma seemed preoccupied. He didn't bother to make conversation.

They soon arrived at his grandmother's, and he alighted to assist his grandmother, and then Emma. "Allow me." He offered his arm to each of them and they mounted the stairs.

"Thank you," Emma said as they entered the hall. "I'll bid you both good night as I want to check on my family."

"Of course." His grandmother turned to the drawing room. "Shall we have a nightcap, Michael?"

Michael watched Emma hurry up the stairs, seeing his opportunity to speak with her disappear. He scowled as he followed his grandmother in the opposite direction.

"May I pour you a sherry?" he asked.

"I would prefer something stronger." She nodded as he lifted the decanter of brandy in question.

"Someone mentioned your broken engagement to me. Thank you for that. Soon afterward the oddest event occurred."

"Oh?" He waited, wondering to what she

referred.

"Rumor has it that Mr. Vandimer discovered Catherine on the terrace with Lord Thompson in a rather compromising position."

He nearly spit out the drink he'd taken. "So that was what she had planned." When his grandmother raised a brow at him, he explained. "She demanded that I meet her on the terrace at a particular time. Obviously, she still thought to proceed with our engagement and intended to have her father discover us."

His grandmother chuckled. "But Lord Thompson joined her instead. Hoisted with her own petard, eh?"

"So it seems. We shall see if she finds herself engaged to Lord Thompson." He ignored the small twinge of guilt he felt for his part in the drama. After all, if she hadn't tried to trap him, she wouldn't be in this predicament.

"Did you see Lady Callum's gown? The color made her look like a turnip."

They visited for a few more minutes about the ball and then she rose. "I'll leave you to finish your drink in peace. Good night."

He settled back in his chair after she'd left and pondered his options. In truth, there was only one. As soon as the movements upstairs quieted, he left his drink unfinished on the table and headed up the stairs as quietly as possible. Hoping Emma remained in the same room, he knocked quietly on her door.

A long moment of silence passed, making him wonder if she was with her mother or sister. Unwilling to leave without speaking to her, he raised his hand to knock again when the door opened. The look of surprise on her face was priceless.

"Michael?" His given name on her lips after the formality of the evening sent a spear of longing through him.

"May I speak with you for a moment?" he whispered. "Please," he added when she hesitated.

"All right." She opened the door wider to allow him in even as she tightened the belt of the thin white wrapper she wore.

She must've only recently retired for a candle still burned on her bedside table and her hair remained in the chignon she'd had it in at the ball. "What is it?"

"How is your family?"

"Fine. As well as can be expected, I suppose. Have you discovered anything new about who was following Patrick?"

"No, not yet, but we are still keeping watch."

She shifted, her body silhouetted in the candlelight. Those large brown eyes full of secrets watched him, and all coherent thoughts flew from his mind. In its place was an ache so deep, he could hardly breathe. He looked away for a moment, closing his eyes as he tried to contain his desire and gather his thoughts.

"Is something wrong?" she asked, drawing closer until her sweet scent enveloped him.

Gritting his teeth, he attempted to hold back the need that filled him. He focused on saying what he wanted to say so he could escape the sweet torture of her presence. Being so close to her only made him want her more. "I wanted to advise you that my engagement has come to an end."

Those eyes held his, deep pools of an emotion he couldn't name. Perhaps this news meant nothing to her. Disappointment filled him at the thought.

"Because of what happened this evening on the terrace?"

He frowned, trying to grasp what she was speaking about.

"With Lord Thompson?" she added.

"No. I asked Catherine to call it off several days ago. Lord Thompson fell into a trap that I believe she had set for me."

She frowned, hardly the reaction he was hoping for. "If anything I did caused you to—"

"Emma." He took her hands in his to stop her apology, for he knew that was what she was going to say. "I couldn't marry Catherine when... When I have feelings for you."

Her hands trembled in his. "You do?"

Unable to resist, he released her hand to trail a finger along the soft line of her jaw. "I thought for so long that passion wasn't safe. That I carry the same seeds of destruction my parents had. That if I free what I feel for you, it would lead to harm. But over the past weeks, I've realized there must be more to life than business agreements. I simply can't deny how I feel when I'm with you."

She kissed his hand that still held hers. The sweet gesture nearly buckled his knees. When she raised her eyes to meet his, they were filled with tears. "I love you."

"Emma." His heart soared with joy even as he realized he couldn't say the words back to her. Those three words had been tossed about throughout his childhood, used as both a lure and a weapon. He didn't trust himself to know what love was.

But he knew how he felt right now, in this very moment. The tender passion filling him could not be denied.

He cupped her face with his hands and kissed her, molding those soft lips to his. Desire jolted through him as she responded. Never had a kiss been so brimming with promise. As sharp as his desire was for her, he cared deeply for her as well. He eased back to rest his forehead against hers, tamping down his passion as best he could. "Will you wait for me? Wait until I am free to be with you? As much as I'm coming to dislike Catherine, I don't want to hurt her by immediately courting you."

She eased out of his embrace to look up at him, a frown marring her brow. "Michael, I must ask if you're certain? I have nothing to offer you. No dowry, no chance to gain back your family's holding. Nothing." She shook her head. "Why would you choose me?"

CHAPTER EIGHTEEN

Emma waited, trying to gauge Michael's reaction, wondering if he truly cared for her. She realized he hadn't told her he loved her, nor had he asked her to marry him. Her heart pounded with worry as his silence drew long until at last he spoke.

"I couldn't be more certain. None of that matters. Believe me. Only you matter."

Relief flooded her. In this moment, it was enough to know he had feelings for her.

She rose up on her toes to press a kiss on his lips. Despite his words, she couldn't erase the trace of doubt that lingered. She didn't deserve him and certainly had nothing to offer him. Why did he want her?

As she tried to form the words to question him further, he drew her closer, molding her thinly clad body to his. His hardness pressed against her, leaving no doubt he wanted her. Wasn't that enough?

He tilted his head and deepened the kiss, his firm lips capturing her heart along with her lips. How could she doubt anything when he kissed her like this?

He moved to press kisses along her cheek, her ear, then down her neck. She sighed in response, desire swirling inside her. She wrapped her arms around his shoulders, her fingers tangling in the hair that brushed his collar.

"I'll never forget the sight of you in my library," he whispered. "I decided you were my little grey mouse. How wrong I was. You are nothing of the sort."

She smiled up at him. "My disguise was quite effective."

"What made you decide to don it?"

She glanced away as unwanted memories assailed her. "At my last post, the lord decided a governess should provide more than just lessons."

The concerned expression on his face changed to anger in an instant. "Who was he? What did he do?"

"Very little before his wife discovered us." She shook her head. "It doesn't matter. Besides, in some ways, he brought me to you."

Michael's expression eased. "For that, I am grateful. But if you'd care to share his name, I'll make certain he is no longer capable of bothering any governesses."

"I believe his wife is now aware of his antics and watches him like a hawk."

He reluctantly smiled. "I'm sure she's more effective than anything I might do. Once again, your strength amazes me."

"Me? You're the one who is strong." She ran her hands along his shoulders and down his arms, enjoying every inch of his muscled form.

"You've been the anchor for your family, the main support financially and emotionally, you've been a role model for your siblings, a sounding board for your mother, all while holding an important position."

She blinked at the sudden moisture in her eyes, touched that he saw her that way. "You have a unique way of seeing things."

"No. I have an objective view, thank you very much. I don't know how you've done it all these years, especially with the pressure placed on you."

"All of my family has contributed. We worked together." She'd be nothing without them.

"I spoke with the doctor."

She closed her eyes for a brief moment. "Michael, you've been far too generous."

He waved that away. "Dr. Barnes told me of the trade you offered him. In fact, he asked if there was any chance of you returning to aid him with a new project he had in mind. He said your organizational skills were outstanding."

"Truly?" She wasn't certain she believed him.

"I told him you were no longer available, but I would ask if you had anyone else you'd recommend." He gathered her close again to hold her tight. "I'm sorry."

"For what?" she asked, reveling in the feel of being held like he'd never let her go.

"For not finding you after your uncle—after we thought your uncle had passed. I came to your home, but the neighbors said you'd moved. They didn't know where you'd gone. Then I went to the university. They didn't know where you'd gone either, but they told me that the professor's pension had been paid out, so I was certain you would be all right."

"Pension? What pension?"

"Didn't you receive payment from the university for his pension?"

"No. Nothing."

He tipped his head back. "The professor must've collected that himself. I wondered where he'd obtained the money on which to live. I should've investigated more closely, but my parents died soon after."

"I'm sorry. I didn't know." A knot loosened deep inside her. That explained so much.

"It was a difficult time for both of us, it seems."

"All that is behind us now."

A shadow crossed his eyes, making her wonder, but he nodded. "Yes. And we're together now."

He wrapped her in his arms and drew her against the hardness of his body. "I am grateful for every moment we have together, for the feel of you in my arms, for the sweet scent of you, for the softness of your skin." He pressed his lips to hers, allowing his tongue to slide in and move with hers. "For the taste of you. I am eager to make you mine. Have no doubt. But we must wait."

"No." She shook her head, unable to bear the thought of delaying even one more moment, let alone weeks. Life was far too short. The future was uncertain. But this moment was so clear. She knew exactly what she wanted, what she needed. "I want to be yours now."

"But—"

"Shh," she murmured, pressing her finger to his lips. "If you want me, I am yours."

"You tempt me beyond measure and leave me no choice."

Again, he gathered her in his arms. The heat of his body felt so right. She intended to enjoy every moment of this.

She bent her head as he nibbled near her ear. The sensation was glorious. Heat spread through her from the very center of her body. She'd dreamed of this for so long. It felt as though she'd waited an eternity for it. For Michael. Oh, but the wait had been worth it. His lips sent shivers down her body.

As good as she felt, she wanted Michael to feel the same. To feel desire pulsing through his body. She wanted him to experience at least a part of what she did.

She ran her hands along his broad shoulders, amazed at his strength. Fingers trembling, she moved to his shirt, displeased with all the layers of clothing that separated them.

As though he read her mind, he unfastened his jacket and shrugged out of it, then unbuttoned his vest. The smooth linen of his shirt allowed her to feel the sculpted form of his chest and the flat plane of his stomach.

"You are so beautiful." He glided his fingers along a strand of her hair that had come loose from her chignon. He bent his head and captured her lips once again, his tongue dancing with hers before he eased back. "Do you have any idea what you do to me?"

His words stirred her as much as his kisses. She unfastened his shirt, eager to see what she'd only guessed at. Dark hair covered his muscled chest. She couldn't help but run her fingers over the wiry hair, surprised at its texture. A long puckered mark crossed diagonally along his stomach.

She drew back to study it. "What happened?"

"Some debris caught me the night of the accident with your uncle."

"How terrible. That night changed so many things."

Her exploration continued down to the rippled contours of his stomach, then the narrowness of his hips. As she brushed the back of her hand across his belly, he jerked in reaction. Pleased, she did it again.

"Emma." He grabbed her hand and swallowed hard. "You undo me. I can only take so much before I—"

She waited but he didn't finish the sentence. He placed her hand on his shoulder instead.

"My turn," he whispered. With slow, gentle movements, he untied the belt of her wrapper then eased it from her shoulders. He trailed his fingers along her shoulders and down to the neckline of her nightgown, dipping lower with each pass until her nipples tightened in response. "You're so soft."

Luckily, he didn't seem to expect an answer, for she wasn't sure she could give one. The sparks alighting inside her erased her thoughts, making speech impossible. Those sparks turned to fire as he molded his hands to her torso, the fine linen of her nightgown enhancing the feel of his touch.

Her breath caught as he tugged at the ribbon holding her gown. Uncertainty filled her despite her desire. Her body was nothing like the beautiful women she'd seen at the ball, those women who were his equal. "Michael?" She placed a hand on his. "I'm not...that is to say..." She shook her head, unsure how to explain the self-doubt that filled her.

"You are beautiful. That I know." He kissed her again. A long slow kiss that erased all her qualms. "But we will wait—"

"No." She refused to allow her insecurities to ruin this moment when she so desperately wanted to grab it with both hands. With a deep breath, she took a tiny step back and eased the nightgown from her shoulders.

He froze, his gaze locked on the skin she'd revealed, whether from surprise or pleasure, she didn't know. Then the thin linen fell to the floor, leaving her naked before him.

"Damn me." His softly muttered oath made her smile as he obviously liked what he saw. "So perfect in every way."

"We should rid you of this." She stepped forward to lift his shirt from those broad shoulders, allowing her hands to linger along the way. All those bulging muscles made her feel weak.

"Yes." He smiled as he removed his shirt and drew her into his arms.

As his chest rubbed against her, she caught her breath. Then she moved along him once again, amazed at the sensation, at how very different they were. Her nipples tingled in response, tightening each time she brushed him.

His low growl brought her gaze up to meet his. "As I said before, you have no idea what you do to me, Emma."

He released her to remove his shoes, then took her hand and moved toward the bed. "Though I want you so much that I'd make love with you anywhere, it would best serve us in the comfort of a bed."

She realized what he was doing—giving her time to make sure she hadn't changed her mind. That made her love him all the more. They neared the bed where the covers were already pulled down.

Oh, Lord. She was nervous. Though she had a basic idea of what would happen, experiencing it was another matter. She must've frowned for he touched the spot between her brows.

"If you've change your mind, you've only to say so. I'd be pleased to simply hold you." He cupped her cheek then trailed his finger down her face and neck to linger on her collarbone.

She rose up on her toes and pressed her lips along his neck, then the smoothness of his shoulder as she ran her fingers through the crisp hair of his chest. Her fingers brushed his nipple and he jerked in reaction. Delighted, she did it again before lowering her hands to his waist.

Braver now, she kissed his chest and was rewarded by his soft moan. He gathered her tight and kissed her until her head spun. His hands released their hold to wander along the curves of her body, and she arched into his touch. His fingers grazed the sides of her breasts, his thumbs caressing her nipples. Liquid heat poured through her and she gasped in response. He leaned down to kiss the top of her breast, easing down toward her nipple. With a lick, then a kiss, then a gentle sucking that had her gasping in response.

"So beautiful." He said it so reverently she felt as though it were true. He lifted her to cradle her in his arms, his strength filling her with weakness. Effortlessly, he knelt on the bed and set her down then lay beside her.

Again, he kissed her then eased lower, leaving a trail of heat as he nibbled. He ran a hand along the curve of her calf, then up to her thigh, sending desire spearing through her.

"Soft, warm, so passionate." He took her nipple in his mouth as his hand touched her very center, stroking her moist heat.

"Michael." Her breath came quickly as her body quivered with need. Her hips shifted, moving to a rhythm of their own accord. His lips suckled as his hand caressed her.

"Yes," he murmured between licks. "Let it happen, Emma. I've got you."

"No." He immediately stopped to look at her, his brow creased. "Not without you. I want to feel you inside me. To be one with you."

He closed his eyes, whether in relief or desire, she wasn't sure. "Are you certain?"

"Yes." She reached for the fastening of his trousers and felt his belly tremble as her fingers brushed against him.

"Wait." He took her hands in his, closed his eyes and drew a deep breath before opening them again. "I want you so much."

The heat in his eyes sent awareness sliding over her skin. "Then I am yours."

He moved off the bed, unfastening and shedding his pants to toss them carelessly aside. She smiled to realize she had the power to make him forget to be tidy. As he turned, she saw him in full, his naked body rippling in the candlelight, his strength even more evident by the shadows cast in the dim light.

His manhood was significantly larger than she expected. Curious, she reached out to trail a finger along the shaft.

"Emma. Christ. You'll have me done before we start."

"It's so soft. But so hard." Unable to resist, she touched him once more.

He groaned in response, his breath heaving. His reaction fascinated her as much as his body. To think her touch made him tremble so.

"You are a siren," he muttered as his body jerked at her hand. "Sent to test my limits."

"I think your limits are quite high, my lord."

He smiled even as he groaned again. "No more." He moved onto the bed beside her, the heat of his body enveloping her. His lips took hers as his hands claimed her body. His caresses were everywhere, leaving no part of her untouched. At last his fingers found her moist center. "Yes, Emma, yes. So hot. So wet."

Her only response was to moan as her hips thrust toward his hand. She reached for him, her fingers traveling downward until she reached his shaft. Her hand curled around it, amazed as his hips moved back and forth, sending the hot length of him through her fingers.

He shifted, his lips capturing her breast as his fingers continued their sweet torment. But he moved out of her reach. She needed to hold him, to caress him, so found the hard pebble of his nipple to squeeze. He groaned, muttering her name.

"Michael?" She could bear no more. She needed something...anything to end this, to release the ache deep inside her.

"Yes." He shifted to rise over her and positioned himself between her legs.

The tip of his manhood touched her and all she could think was yes. This. Now. Her hips tilted to capture him. As his body eased forward, the tightness shocked her. She felt as though she was stretching, adjusting to fit him. "Oh." The unfamiliar sensation felt so odd, yet so right.

"Hold on to me," Michael urged as he eased slowly forward. "Give me a moment."

But she didn't want to wait. She wanted more. She grasped his hips and pulled him into her. The feeling of being one stole her breath. She held him there, unable to move, only able to feel. "Oh, my."

With a groan, Michael pulled back and thrust forward, the friction leaving her gasping. Already her body seemed to have adjusted to him, the tightness easing, leaving a glorious heat in its wake.

More. That was all she could think. Whatever this was, she wanted more.

"You feel so good, my sweet. So damned good." He seemed to be trying to control their speed and was shaking with his efforts. He shifted, lowering onto his elbow as he reached between them to touch her intimately.

Desire spiraled through her, arching her off the bed. Each thrust, each touch, brought her closer to the edge. Then her body took flight as her emotions collided, sending light in every direction as she convulsed. "Yes!"

Michael moved back and forth one last time before pushing into her and staying there as though he never wanted to leave. The expression on his face was part agony, part ecstasy.

Oddly enough, she knew exactly how that felt. She slowly floated back to earth, the weight of Michael on top of her a wonderful sensation. Tears filled her eyes and she couldn't help but hold him tight, never wanting this moment to end.

"Emma?" His concern brought him up onto his

elbow to look down into her face. "Did I hurt you?"

"No, no," she quickly reassured him. "Quite the opposite." She swallowed hard in an attempt to stem her emotions. "You are everything I hoped for and more."

But more tears came as she realized there *was* something missing. Something stood between them, keeping them apart despite what they'd just shared, like a thin veil that allowed them to touch, but not to do so in full. A part of her feared this interlude was only temporary, that she did not deserve Michael, that she did not belong here, so he could never truly be hers in full.

"You are so special." He kissed the tears from her cheeks, his tenderness swamping her. "Please don't cry." He shifted to move off her, but she held him tight as she battled her composure.

"Michael? If we only have this moment, I would still be the happiest woman on earth."

He kissed her again. "I intend for us to have many more times exactly like this, though perhaps not in my grandmother's house."

The mention of his grandmother worried her even more. Would his grandmother approve or be appalled by their relationship? She pushed her concern aside, determined to enjoy this moment.

"I can see the wheels turning in your mind even now. All will be well, my sweet. You shall see." He kissed her as though to seal his words.

Why oh why didn't her heart believe it to be true?

CHAPTER NINETEEN

Michael sat in the chair before Ashbury's desk and tried to suppress his smile. To distract himself, he picked up the miniature electromagnetic device Ashbury had fashioned. He couldn't remember being quite this happy since...well, ever actually.

His time with Emma had made him realize how precious life was. How truly amazing it could be. Already he looked forward to when they could be together. Images of her soft curves, her sweet lips, heated him as his thoughts returned to the previous night.

He realized Ashbury was staring at him. "What?"

"Just trying to determine what has you so bloody pleased with yourself."

Michael grinned. He couldn't help it.

"Come on, man. Out with it. What happened last evening?" Ashbury leaned forward, his elbows on his desk, his green eyes lit with interest. "I heard Vandimer found his daughter and Lord Thompson in an inappropriate embrace. Tongues are wagging. Of course, rumor has it that she had already called off her engagement to you. Is all that the reason for your happiness?"

Michael chuckled. "Aren't you a fountain of

information this morning? I had no idea you were so interested in gossip these days."

Ashbury narrowed his eyes. "Abigail was kind enough to update me on the events at the ball last evening as much of it slipped my notice. However, I can see that as interesting as those facts are, none of them are responsible for your current mood."

"True."

"Well? Out with it."

Michael sighed.

"Oh," Ashbury said with exaggeration.

"Oh what?" He stared at his friend, trying to understand his rather odd intonation.

"It has to do with a woman. I would guess her name is Emma Grisby."

Michael could only smile. "Let's just say I'm pleased with the way things are progressing on many fronts." He chose to ignore the small sliver of guilt over his inability to declare his love to Emma. Yet how could he? What if by saying the words aloud, he evoked the curse his father and mother had endured? Surely by holding back a part of himself, he could protect them both. He saw no other option.

"There is one area that is not progressing," Michael said, hoping Ashbury would permit the change of subject. He didn't care to discuss his relationship with Emma any further. Not yet. It was too new. Too delicate.

Ashbury sat back in his chair, a scowl on his face. "Our mystery has yet to be resolved."

"Have you received any word on who was after Patrick?"

"His name is Mikey. Bad fellow. Bit of a brute. If Mikey was chasing him that must mean word has spread about him witnessing the murder."

"If the professor or whoever is now helping him truly murdered Lord Berkmond and Patrick witnessed it then Patrick and his family are in grave danger." Michael ran his hand through his hair. The stakes had increased even higher than he'd realized.

"Indeed. If Mikey knows this so does the professor and his new henchman. Mikey has a bunch of thugs at his disposal, which makes inquiries rather difficult. If we ask the wrong person, the penalty is steep."

"One step forward, two steps back."

"Quite. Frustrating as hell." Ashbury shook his head.

"You do realize that Emma is truly innocent in all this." Michael didn't bother to phrase it as a question.

"I came to that conclusion some time ago as well. How did she take the news that her uncle lives?"

"About as well as could be expected." Michael sighed, remembering all too well the pain on her face. He had to find a way to bring out the professor and put all this to an end. "I have another idea that might rattle the situation. Why don't I take a turn with the meteorite?"

Ashbury raised a brow. "What do you intend to do?"

"I'm not sure, but somehow, we need to stir things up a bit, don't you think? Perhaps this Mikey is somehow connected to the whole bloody mess. A word in his ear about the meteorite could shift his attention away from Patrick."

"That could be very dangerous. Won't holding yourself out as having the meteorite potentially lead the professor to Emma and Patrick?"

"Perhaps that's what we should hope for. Then the professor will finally show himself." Michael rose and drew back the curtain to stare out into the fog. "We can't allow this to continue any longer. Not with Emma's family in danger."

"Now you know how I felt when Abigail was in danger."

"I notice you didn't mention that she was often the one placing herself in danger."

Ashbury shuddered. "Don't remind me. In truth, I could see Emma doing something along those lines as well."

"I will not allow it." Even the thought of her in danger sent his pulse racing.

"I wish you luck. Women are not so easily controlled as one might think."

"I'll keep that in mind."

Ashbury opened a drawer in his desk, lifted the lining and withdrew a key. He unlocked another drawer, removed the false back and at last pulled out the meteorite and tossed it to Michael. "It's all yours."

Michael hefted the stone in his hand. "Allow us to see if this Mikey can connect us with the professor. Rumors spread so well in the ton, I'm anxious to see if it works the same way amidst the working class."

"I'm not certain Miss Grisby will appreciate your plan."

"I don't know that I'll tell her. I wouldn't want to worry her anymore than she already is."

"Do be careful," Ashbury warned. "I hope you're not asking for more than you bargained."

"Of course. I suddenly find myself with more reasons to want to live a long life than ever before."

Emma realized she'd been staring at the same page of her notes for several minutes now. She was supposed to be jotting down ideas for her book, but she couldn't seem to focus. Granted, the research material she'd chosen was rather dry. Seeing what other instruction manuals for governesses existed had seemed like a good idea, but this one was written in such a boring manner that it couldn't possibly hold anyone's interest. Or it could be that she simply couldn't concentrate today.

Happiness was a warm glow in her heart. She wanted to hold onto it tight to be certain it didn't escape.

Two days had passed since she'd shared the night with Michael. Those days had been wonderful. Her family was settling in quite nicely at the viscountess's.

Even now, her mother sat in a tufted chair, plying her skills to an intricately patterned needlework, a basket of thread at her side. The relaxed, satisfied expression on her face had Emma smiling. She seemed to be enjoying herself whether she was visiting with the viscountess or spending time with their entire family. Emma had still not told her about Uncle Grisby. Somehow, she needed to see him with her own eyes to truly believe it was possible. A part of her still felt there had to be some sort of mistake.

Emma's gaze fell on her mother's drab gown. She wished she could find different gowns for both her and Tessa to wear, but Emma's were too long for her mother and too loose for Tessa. Her mother dismissed her suggestion, saying they would look for some fabric once they returned home. The thought of returning to the tiny, dingy rooms at the lodging house made her ill. If Michael...

She stopped herself. Michael had offered nothing. She didn't know where their relationship would lead. But she knew Michael was an honorable man. He'd asked her to wait for him, and that was enough for her. For now, that had to be enough.

With a sigh, she closed her eyes. How she wished she could share recent events with her mother. Well, not all events, but just the knowledge that she and Michael had feelings for each other. He'd held her with such tenderness, had been so giving. His body could serve as a model for a marble statue—broad shoulders, narrow hips—so powerful, yet so gentle. She grew heated just thinking about him. To know that he was no longer engaged and that he cared for her was amazing and filled her with hope.

Perhaps their future would be bright after all.

Tessa had come down for breakfast but was now resting in her room. She'd mentioned sitting in the garden this afternoon, which gave Emma a little thrill. Patrick was with the tutor Michael had sent over that morning. Though her brother had protested having to take lessons, Emma thought he was secretly pleased Michael thought enough of him to hire a tutor.

Viscountess Weston paused in the doorway of the drawing room. "Jane? The dressmaker is here to take your measurements. Let us see what she has brought for us to look at."

"Dressmaker?" Emma's mother frowned. "There must be some mistake. We didn't order any gowns."

"No, but I ordered them for you." The twinkle in the viscountess's eyes make Emma chuckle. "Come along, Jane. The fabric she has is marvelous. I can't wait for you to see it."

Her mother's brows rose. "I couldn't possibly—"

"Of course you could," the viscountess interrupted. "Or at least, I could." She moved forward and held out her hand to Emma's mother. "Please say yes. It will be great fun. Come and see. I have something in mind for Tessa as well. Emma, will you join us?"

"The two of you enjoy it. I'm going to continue

working on my notes."

"Very well then. We shall keep you apprised of our decisions." The viscountess departed, clearly expecting Emma's mother to follow.

Emma's mother looked at Emma, brow raised. "Truly, no purpose is served in arguing with her, Mother. She always manages to have her way."

Her mother shook her head but followed the viscountess with a spring in her step.

Emma grinned as she picked up her pen. Life was so very sweet.

Michael nodded at the footman who opened the door at his grandmother's home.

"Good day to you, my lord," the brawny footman said.

"I trust all is well, Wilson?" Michael asked. Wilson had transferred from Michael's home to his grandmother's temporarily with orders to be on watch for anything unusual and to keep a close eye on Patrick to make certain the boy didn't venture out on his own.

"Indeed, my lord. Nothing of which to advise you. All the ladies are resting in their rooms and Mr. Patrick is with the tutor."

Hiding his disappointment that everyone was otherwise engaged, Michael waved off the footman. "I will leave a note for my grandmother then."

He walked into the drawing room to the corner where his grandmother's writing desk stood and withdrew a sheet of paper as the footman's steps faded down the hall. Indecision filled him. What he really wanted was to see Emma. He listened as the quietness of the house settled around him. An idea took hold that he couldn't deny, especially since it had worked so well once before.

Leaving the paper on the desk, he walked back into the hall to find it deserted. As quickly and quietly as possible, he ran up the stairs and in short order, arrived at Emma's door. He tapped softly.

"Yes?"

Taking her response as an invitation, he opened the door and quickly closed it behind him, not wanting to be discovered in the hall. The sight before him caught his breath.

A tub sat in the middle of the room with the object of his desire submerged in it. Water lapped at the curve of her breasts, her expression one of stunned disbelief as she stared at him with those large brown eyes. Her hair was swept up into a casual knot on her head with a few loose tendrils framing her face. She'd never looked more beautiful. "Michael?"

"Emma." Passion speared through him, sharp and sweet. He reached behind him and locked the door, so grateful he'd given in to his impulse.

"What—what are you doing here?" She covered her breasts with her hands, steam rising around her as embarrassment pinkened her cheeks.

"I've come to see you."

"Perhaps you might wait downstairs for me to finish?"

He smiled as he strolled closer. "No need to hurry on my account. I'd be happy to wait for you. Or even better, I'd be happy to aid you."

Her eyes widened even further. "Well, I..."

He removed his jacket and tossed it on a nearby chair, then loosened his cuffs so he could roll up his sleeves. "Doing so would be my pleasure and yours as well. I promise."

"Oh." She blinked up at him as he dipped a finger in the steaming water. "Oh," she repeated, making him smile.

"I've been thinking about you."

"You have?" She sounded surprised.

He leaned closer, then closer still, only a hair's breadth from her lips. "I've been dreaming of you as well."

Her chest rose and fell, ever quickening. "Truly?" Her puzzled expression caused him to shake his head.

"Have you no idea what you do to me, sweet Emma? You turn me inside out with only a look." He pressed his lips to hers, slowly, gently, wanting to make her understand what she meant to him even if he couldn't tell her. Then he eased back, determined to simply enjoy the moment and the sight before him. "I've missed you."

Her gaze lifted from his lips to his eyes, than dropped to his lips again. She stretched up and kissed him, sending all his good intentions to restrain himself out the window. Heat built quickly, spreading like fire between them. Her tongue danced with his, her tentative movements only making him hotter. He cupped her cheek with his hand, enjoying the feel of her soft skin. The fragrance of lillies that always scented her skin drifted up from the water and made him want her more.

Eager to explore, he shifted his lips to her neck then along her jaw line to her ear. She tilted her head to allow him access and sighed when he accepted her invitation.

"I thought perhaps this was all a dream," she whispered even as her heart raced.

"What was a dream?"

"You. Caring for me."

Her soft words cut through him. He knew the fault for her uncertainty lay with him. Yet still he couldn't bring himself to say those three words. Not when he could still hear the ring of them used so carelessly throughout his childhood. Instead, he did the only thing he could.

He removed his shirt and moved to stand behind her. He ran his hands along the smoothness of her shoulders, pausing to gently massage there. She shifted under his hands as though stretching to enjoy his touch. Kneeling beside the tub, he pressed kisses along her neck, the scent and feel of her soaking into his senses. He lowered his hands into the water, finding her breasts. She arched back which lifted those white globes out of the water and into view. His body hardened at the sight of her rosy pink nipples, but he clamped down on his desire, wanting to show her just how much she meant to him.

"You are so beautiful, Emma, inside and out. From all those amazing thoughts running through your clever mind, to the softness of your skin." She sighed in response, and he paused to bury his face in her neck for a moment, hoping he could control himself.

She reached up to wrap her arms around his neck which gave him even better access to her body. Unable to resist, he allowed his hands to slide down the length of her, down to the curve of her hips, to the softness of her belly. Her knees were bent to fit into the tub and he ran his hands along her legs as well. He kissed her neck again then swirled his tongue in her ear. "I want you so much."

"Yes." Her breathless agreement sent heat straight to his groin. Her responsiveness was more than any man could've asked. And she was his. Perhaps not formally, but she was his all the same.

He slipped his hand along the curve of her hip, along her leg, before easing between her thighs. Her legs tightened for a moment then relaxed to let him in. Slowly, he moved his fingers down until he reached his destination at the apex of her thighs. He slid a finger along the velvet softness of her folds.

"Oh, Michael."

"Yes, my sweet. Tell me."

"You— I— Oh. That feels so good."

His body pulsed with need at her muttered response as her body shuddered with desire. He continued to kiss her neck as he caressed her breast and stroked her center, whispering endearments and encouragements in her ear.

"Oh!" Her hips came up as her body convulsed in ecstasy. With a sigh, she leaned her head back on his shoulder as her breathing calmed.

He held her tight, gritting his teeth at the sharp pain of need that filled him. She sat up and pulled away from him, much to his dismay.

Emma breathed deeply, hoping the air would clear her head and lend strength to quivering legs. Then she rose and turned, suppressing the urge to cover herself.

Michael stood as well, his gaze taking in the sight of her wet, naked form rosy from the warm water. The heat in his eyes was her reward for her bravery. "So perfect," he muttered.

She reached for him, winding her arms around his shoulders, her breasts pressing against his chest, her wet body sliding along his until he groaned. Pleased with the results of her efforts thus far, she kissed his chest, her hands gliding along his chest, pinching his nipples.

With little effort, he lifted her out of the tub and into his arms and moved toward the bed.

"Wait. I'm all wet."

"Exactly," he muttered then took her mouth with his, his tongue playing with hers, kissing her until she couldn't think. Then he was laying her on the bed, his body pressing hers into the mattress.

His hands roamed everywhere, making her

move and shift in response, her restless movements seeming to urge him on. She pressed kisses along his neck. He shifted his head as though enjoying her efforts. Wanting to explore, she shifted to move his weight off her. Then she moved lower, pressing kisses down to his chest, then down even farther to his nipple.

"Christ, Emma."

His breathless response thrilled her, giving her the power to do more. She eased lower still, her lips finding the edge of his ribs, his puckered scar, then the firm planes of his stomach as her hands sought the fastening of his trousers.

"Hold. I only wanted to speak with you. I—"

She smiled as he seemed incapable of completing the thought. Then she eased his trousers down his hips. "I cannot wait. I need you."

With a groan, he toed off his shoes, shoved off his pants, and moved over her once again. "You drive me mad. With one look, you undo me."

She pulled him down toward her, wanting nothing more than to feel his weight on her. The ache deep inside her built until she could bear it no longer. She moved her legs to wrap them around him.

He reached down to touch her center and groaned as her hips shifted to raise herself for him.

"Michael, please. I need you. Now." This burning ache could only be cured by him. No one else made her heart race or made her legs so weak. No one made her smile like he did or made her feel both strong and weak at the same time.

His thick shaft touched her center and she whimpered with need. At last he slowly eased into her, taking her mouth as he took her body. He groaned as he paused. "So good. You feel so good."

"Yes." And then words failed her as feeling

took over completely. She soared with his every thrust, climbing higher. She met each of his moves, doing everything in her power to make him feel as good as she did. Her nails scraped his shoulders as she nipped at his chest. A golden ball of light formed deep inside her, growing by the moment until at last it burst. She shattered into a million pieces as he joined her.

Her heart swam with joy and love and hope.

CHAPTER TWENTY

The next afternoon, Emma sat in Abigail's drawing room, her tea growing cold as her stomach jumped with nerves. Abigail's complete attention was focused on the notes and sample chapters Emma had put together for the governess handbook.

After much research, she realized Abigail was right. No truly helpful instruction books for new governesses existed, at least not that one could possibly stay awake to read. Those she'd found had mostly been written by men in a condescending tone. Not only boring, but annoying as well.

Emma had thought back to her early days as a governess as well as some of the comments her uncle had made about teaching in general. She'd decided to take a more friendly approach in her book and had begun her writing as though she was a friend sharing what she knew about the profession. To make certain Abigail understood her intent, Emma had written the first three chapters in addition to an outline so Abigail could see how it might read.

As Abigail frowned at the pages, doubt assailed Emma. Perhaps she'd taken too big of a risk and been too nontraditional. She should've made it more instructional and less conversational. She should've—

"Brilliant!" Abigail turned over the last page and looked up at Emma, blue eyes shining with excitement. "Absolutely brilliant."

"You like it?" Emma held her breath.

"I believe I could take over my two younger sisters' education with this information, but don't tell them that. They'd be quite distraught at the thought." Abigail turned back to the first page of the notes. "Your tone is so friendly and helpful but not overly familiar, like I'm visiting with a cousin whom I haven't seen for a year or two."

"That's exactly what I was trying for. So many of the books available are dry and rather boring. I wanted this to be friendlier." She studied Abigail's expression, wanting to be certain she wasn't simply being nice. "You're sure you like it?"

"Absolutely. In fact, I have a proposal for you. I would like to do a whole series in this style. That way, if a governess is having a particular challenge in her current position, she could purchase the handbook on teaching art or one on keeping a restless child's interest. Perhaps one on outdoor activities. What do you think?"

"That's a wonderful idea. I would've found something like that quite helpful when I was a governess."

"Excellent! I'll have the advance sent to you shortly. We'll put the details in writing so we both know what to expect and when."

Emma smiled, something she seemed to be doing more and more of late. This feeling of happiness was foreign, but something she knew she could grow used to. Worry had been her constant companion for so long and, in many ways, had become a habit. Suddenly overwhelmed, tears filled her eyes.

"Oh, what is it? What did I say?" Abigail was at

her side in an instant, placing a comforting arm about her shoulders.

"Nothing. It's just...I'm so happy that you like the book."

"You've had many changes of late, haven't you? I apologize if I'm overstepping the bounds of our acquaintance, but I feel as if we're already good friends." She gave Emma's shoulders a squeeze. "After all the trials and tribulations, it's hard to believe things are going well, isn't it?"

Tears blurring her vision and catching her voice, Emma could only nod.

"May I ask if you decided to accept the marriage proposal you received?"

Emma shook her head, still unable to speak.

Abigail raised a brow. "No, I shouldn't ask, or no, you aren't accepting it?"

"The latter," Emma managed. She drew a deep breath to calm herself. "One of the reasons I had the choice whether or not to accept it was because of your offer to write this book. Thank you so much for that."

"I'm delighted to be of assistance, but please know that you're helping me just as much. We are going to be a great success together." Abigail gave her one last squeeze, then reached for the teapot. "Let us warm up our cups. Nothing like a bracing cup of tea to strengthen your fortitude." She handed the cup and saucer to Emma and placed a biscuit on her plate. "Now then, I'm quite anxious to hear what you think of Catherine's new engagement."

Surprised, Emma paused before lifting her cup. "I hadn't heard of it. Is it because of the other night?"

"Apparently so. Now Lord Weston is truly free." Abigail watched her closely as though waiting to see if she agreed.

Emma sipped her tea to avoid responding as

she pondered what this meant. Would Michael suggest they allow their courting to become public? A tangled mix of hope and worry filled her at the thought.

Vincent wiped his sweaty hands on his pants and glanced around the deserted dock, anxious to have this meeting with Mikey over and done with. The scent of brine in the air mingled with the odor of rotting fish. Somehow the smells seemed stronger at night when a person couldn't see from whence they came. He didn't care for the dock or for being so close to the Thames. Perhaps it was because he couldn't swim. The thought of drowning in the dark swirling water made him break out in a cold sweat. Each time he dumped a body in it, his worry increased. He could clearly picture trying to fight his way to the surface with the dead bodies dragging him back under. The image caused him to shudder.

He'd had a terrible time sneaking away from his uncle this evening, but he hadn't wanted to say where he was going or why. Somehow, he needed to resolve the problem Mikey had brought to his attention. That damned boy who'd witnessed the lord's murder had to be taken care of. Vincent did not like loose ends. He knew too well they came back to haunt you.

The experiments were not exactly proceeding according to plan, from what he could tell. He'd had to dump two more bodies with those distinctive burn marks on their skin. Each time he did so, he knew the chances increased that he'd be caught. The problems with the devices were making his uncle more agitated. His volatile mood swings were bloody hard to live with.

The whole thing made Vincent wonder if it was time to leave. But where would he go? He certainly couldn't depart without taking care of both Mikey and the lad who'd witnessed the murder. He didn't need people searching for him once he'd left. Not to mention that he needed some of the riches his uncle kept promising but had yet to share.

"Come on, Mikey. Where are ye?" he muttered. At the sound of boots scuffing the wooden dock, he spun on his heel.

Mikey strolled out of the shadows, other forms shifting behind him. Apparently he'd brought friends. "Simmons. Ye got the money?"

"I don't know. Ye got the lad?"

Mikey scowled. "Not yet. He hasn't returned to his lodging house, but it's only a matter of time. He has to go home sometime. Witnessing a murder must've scared the lad."

"Then I don't have the money." Vincent hoped his voice sounded confident despite his fear.

"Come now. My silence on yer dirty deed should be worth something."

"Indeed it is, but not nearly worth as much as that boy."

"I got his name fer ye." Mikey's flat black eyes watched him in the dim light cast by the distant street light.

Vincent shrugged. "A name is helpful, but it doesn't solve my problem."

"It gets ye one step closer to findin' him."

"Maybe. Maybe not." Vincent paused, hoping his lack of enthusiasm would lower Mikey's price. The name of the lad might make it easier to find him, but if Mikey hadn't located him, Vincent doubted he could. "Seems like the blame could be placed at yer door fer the lad realizing someone was after him."

"One of me boys got a bit too eager. But we'll

find him. How about payment fer his name?"

Vincent realized he was going to have to give him something. Besides, having Mikey watch for the boy was helpful. Vincent couldn't do it himself while aiding his uncle with the experiments. "All right then, but it's not worth much."

They agreed on a price and Vincent withdrew it from his pocket. "The name?"

"Patrick Grisby."

Vincent froze, his chest tightening with shock. "Yer sure?"

"I didn't stutter, did I?" Mikey held out his hand. "Pay up."

"Here." He tossed him the money. "Tell me if the lad returns." Vincent turned away, still stunned by the news.

"Wait!" Mikey stepped closer. "I have something else ye might find helpful."

Vincent waited, wondering what more the man might have to say.

"Someone is planting rumors, hoping one of my bunch will take the bait."

"Why would that concern me?"

"They're sayin' some scientist is in need of meteorites and will pay well for them. Ye wouldn't know anything about that, would ye?"

"Who did ye hear that from?"

Mikey shrugged. "Around. Some lord that goes by the name of Weston is said to have one. I'm not goin' to bother meself with it unless someone is truly willin' to pay fer it."

Vincent closed his eyes, not pleased with this new development. It didn't matter if the information was bait or not. The fact was they needed the damned meteorite. At least now he knew Weston had it rather than Ashbury.

But what was he to do about Patrick Grisby? Christ!

"No, I don't know anyone lookin' for a

meteorite. I'll be in touch if I come across anything." He had no intention of paying Mikey to obtain it for him when he could do so himself.

"I'll keep watch fer the lad and nab him if I have the chance."

Mikey and his shadows disappeared, leaving Vincent alone. Deciding it wouldn't hurt to stop by the pub for a pint on his way home, Vincent turned, only to startle as a cloaked figure emerged from the dark.

"Vincent, I'm quite disappointed in you." His uncle's raspy tone echoed in the night air.

Suppressing a shiver of fear, Vincent halted. "Didn't know ye were coming out tonight, Uncle."

"How else was I to determine what you were up to? Sneaking out like a young lad with trouble on his mind." His uncle moved closer, his cane thumping on the dock.

"I had business to attend to."

"So I heard which is why I'm disappointed. Surely you didn't intend to keep this from me."

"No, course not. Just didn't want to worry ye."

"Well, it's too late. I am worried. Not only did you lie to me about someone witnessing the murder of Berkmond, now I discover it was my other nephew." His uncle shook his head as he heaved a sigh. "I told you to make it look like an accident."

"I tried. 'Tis as I told ye. The bloody lord would have none of it. He refused to cooperate and left me no choice."

"Humph. What do you suggest we do about Patrick?"

Vincent pondered their options. He hated to kill his own flesh and blood unless it was absolutely necessary. The boy had been in the wrong place at the wrong time. Could he possibly be convinced to join them? "Mayhap ye could speak with him."

"How do you mean? What purpose would that serve? The boy probably doesn't remember me."

"Assumin' ye don't want him killed to guarantee his silence, then ye'd better ask him to join us. Perhaps he'd like to be part of yer grand plan."

Silence greeted his suggestion for a long moment. "Your idea may have merit. I will give it further consideration. Let us be on our way home. I want you to tell me why you refused that man's offer to fetch the meteorite for us. That could've been quite helpful."

The dream of a pint faded as Vincent kept pace with his uncle. "The less we involve Mikey the better. The man's got a temper, and I don't want to have to pay him any more than we have to. We should handle this ourselves."

"Very well then. I suppose I must acquiesce to your suggestion. For now, at any rate."

Vincent frowned at the foreign sounding word. Damned if he'd ask what it meant though. He did not care to hear another lecture on his lack of education.

Emma, her mother, Viscountess Weston, and Tessa sat in the gardens the next afternoon, enjoying the sunshine and each other's company. Emma sighed with pleasure, both at the weather and her companions. How lovely that more and more of her time was filled with moments like this that she enjoyed. She refused to worry about tomorrow or the day after that. She would simply allow the peace and joy of the moment to infuse her.

Tessa tipped her head back in the chair, facing the sun, her hat dangling from her fingers. "This is marvelous."

The viscountess, hat firmly in place to block the sun, smiled. "I fear the sunshine won't last, so it's good that we're enjoying it while we can."

Emma noted her mother's fingers tapping the arm of the chair in which she sat. Every so often, her feet would shift as well, billowing out the skirt of her new gown. Idle hands had her practically squirming in her seat. Her mother had yet to learn the art of relaxation. But when she caught Emma's gaze, she winked. That expression, free of worry, lifted Emma's heart. To have her family together and happy was a true gift.

A footman appeared at Emma's elbow with a silver tray. "A message has arrived for Miss Grisby."

Her heartbeat sped. Might it be from Michael? With a glance at the viscountess, she retrieved the sealed message. "Thank you."

The footman took his leave. Emma turned the missive over in her hand. The wax seal bore a fleur-de-lis but nothing more hinted as to who'd sent it.

"Open it, my dear. Perhaps one of your suitors has contacted you."

"Oh!" Tessa sat up straighter. "Hurry and see who."

With a smile at her sister's enthusiasm, Emma broke the seal. The words penned in a shaky scrawl sent her heart pounding with worry.

Dearest Emma,

This may be difficult to believe, but it's true. I live. I have much to tell you, to explain to you. Please meet me in the garden at the ball this eve when the clock strikes midnight. Tell no one of our meeting, especially not Lord Weston. Your safety depends upon it.

Yours,

U.G.

Uncle Grisby? She read the missive again, all too conscious of her companions' eyes upon her.

"Who sent it?" Tessa asked. "What does he say?"

Emma's thoughts scattered. She couldn't tell the truth. How dare he force her into the position of lying to her loved ones? That was apparently what he was good at, not her. She glanced up at her mother, but bit back the words. How could she possibly tell her until she saw him with her own eyes? She needed to hear for herself why he'd allowed them all to believe him dead for so long.

"Dear, are you all right?" The viscountess's voice sounded as though it came from the other side of the garden.

Emma blinked, trying to pull herself together, to think of what she could possibly say. "Lord Tagart is inquiring as to whether I will be attending the Sampson's ball this evening."

"How kind of him," her mother said. "He sounds quite nice from how you've described him."

"Why don't you come with us, Jane?" the viscountess asked. "You'll be able to meet him yourself."

"Oh, I couldn't." She glanced first at the viscountess, then at Emma, then Tessa. "I couldn't possibly."

"Of course you could." The viscountess waved her hand. "You already have a gown that would suffice. Why not come?"

Emma wanted to say, *No, please don't come. Not tonight of all nights.* But instead, she smiled. "You should join us, Mother. It would be lovely to have you there."

"I wouldn't want to leave Tessa alone."

"I will be fine," Tessa protested. "I'll be resting anyway. You should attend. Then I'll have a description other than Emma's of the ball."

Emma held her breath, hoping her mother

would decide against it. How could she step away to meet her uncle if her mother was at her side? As if she wouldn't be nervous enough without the worry that her mother would discover the entire situation.

"Well, if you're certain it would be appropriate."

"Absolutely. It will be fun. Perhaps one day soon, Tessa will join us as well. Won't that be a delight?"

Emma's heart squeezed. The viscountess was so kind. Already she'd done so much for Emma's family. Her generosity knew no bounds and yet here Emma was, lying to her.

Tessa grinned. "A delight indeed. It will be my new goal to do so."

"That is a worthy endeavor. One which will be here before you know it," Emma added as she rose. "Please excuse me. I'm going to send a reply."

She left the ladies visiting while she went inside to the foyer to question the footman who'd delivered the message. Unfortunately, he was unable to share anything other than the messenger had been a lad.

Obviously, her uncle knew where she was staying. She couldn't help but wonder what else he knew. Michael had warned her that her uncle was now a dangerous man, but she still couldn't reconcile that with the man she'd known and loved. Though tempted to share the message with Michael, she decided against it. This was something she had to do herself.

Perhaps she could convince him to stop if he truly was harming others. She had to try.

CHAPTER TWENTY-ONE

Michael glanced again at Emma as they entered the ballroom at Lord and Lady Sampson's that evening. She smiled up at him, but something was awry. Her aura was murky at best. Even more, he could feel it. Somehow, she'd withdrawn from him emotionally. He'd sensed it the moment her eyes had met his in his grandmother's drawing room when he'd arrived to escort them to the ball.

Of course he'd asked what was wrong, and Emma had denied that anything bothered her. That worried him the most. Did she not trust him to aid her if a problem had surfaced? Had she had a change of heart and decided Lord Tagart was better suited to her?

The latter thought had him clenching his teeth. He'd be damned before he'd let her go. He was the better man for her. Not Tagart. If he needed to find some way to prove that to her he would.

But he couldn't quite release the vice that squeezed his chest at the idea of her even considering another man.

"You're certain nothing is amiss?" he asked as he patted her gloved hand that held on to his arm.

"I told you earlier all is well. I'm only worried

this might be too much for Mother." She glanced
behind to where her mother walked with his
grandmother.

Mrs. Grisby seemed quite in her element to
him. She carried herself with confidence in her
burgundy gown. Her hair was swept up in a loose
chignon that took years off her previous
appearance, or perhaps it was the release of so
much stress and worry that made her look so
youthful. Her brown eyes, so much like Emma's,
gleamed with excitement as she looked around the
ballroom.

Michael couldn't shake his unease, but
apparently he'd have to wait and watch to see
what transpired. He hoped Ashbury decided to
attend the ball this evening. Michael would
appreciate another person keeping watch.

After seeing the ladies to a position in the room
which his grandmother deemed appropriate, he
left them to obtain refreshments.

"Glad to hear you're free of that engagement."
An earl with whom he'd attended Cambridge
slapped him on the shoulder. "Narrow escape,
eh?"

"Good to see you, Wiltford." Michael refrained
from responding directly to his comment. No need
to fan the flames of any gossip that continued to
circulate regarding Catherine.

"Looks as if you've already replaced her."
Wiltford's gaze was fixed across the room. "But
you've got some competition, I believe."

Michael looked to where Wiltford stared,
realizing he referred to Emma. Lord Tagart stood
at her side. Even as he watched, Emma gestured
toward her mother, obviously making the
introduction. Tagart bowed over Mrs. Grisby's
hand and had both her and Emma smiling.
Apparently he was laying on the charm. *Damn
him.*

Anger filled Michael at the sight. He wanted to march across the room and interrupt their conversation. To demand the lord keep his distance. Instead, he forced himself to watch and attempted to examine the emotion the scene brought forth. Was he jealous? Absolutely. No doubt. But he realized he also trusted Emma. He didn't expect her to use Tagart to hurt him. Nor did he want to hurt her by acting like an ass simply because she was speaking with another man. Perhaps he wasn't as much like his father as he feared.

If he wanted to be more certain of his relationship with Emma, then he needed to take the next step. He needed to tell her how he felt. He needed to ask her to marry him. The very idea of doing either of those tightened his chest, bringing forth an uncertainty he hadn't experienced in a very long time. He'd been engaged before, but with Emma, the stakes would be so much higher. His emotions would be involved this time. She already knew most of his secrets. But this evening, he couldn't help but wonder what secrets *she* was keeping.

"Are you unwell, Weston? You look a bit off."

"I'm fine." As he watched, Emma looked again at the large ornate clock that stood against the wall. Why was she so concerned with the time? "Nice to see you, Wiltford. I must return to the ladies."

"I'll look forward to hearing of your new engagement soon." Wiltford smiled. "As for me, I intend to avoid the marriage trap for as long as possible."

"Don't wait too long." Michael managed to pick up three glasses of lemonade and prepared to navigate the crowd without spilling. "All the ladies worth having will be gone."

Wiltford's chuckle made him smile.

Emma shivered as the clock struck midnight. She'd left her mother and the viscountess a few minutes earlier with the excuse of the need to adjust her gown. Hopefully that would buy her some time to see if her uncle appeared. Michael was visiting with Lord Ashbury, so he was occupied as well.

She knew her behavior concerned him, but she couldn't help it. This meeting had been all she could think of the entire evening. Though she disliked the thought of deceiving Michael or her family, she had to try to speak to her uncle and convince him to stop whatever crazed scheme in which he was involved.

Her stomach skipping with nerves, she closed the garden door behind her and walked slowly forward, allowing her eyes to adjust to the darkness. The evening air was cool on her bare arms, adding to her shivers as she searched for her uncle. She caught sight of a couple entwined in a passionate embrace and avoided them. It struck her that venturing out here on her own had been foolhardy. Ladies did not wander out in the garden at night by themselves at a ball. Perhaps she should forget this and return to her mother and the viscountess. And Michael. But her curiosity—or was it anger—would not allow her to turn around. Not yet.

As the minutes passed and she saw no one resembling her uncle, she admonished herself. What had she expected? That he'd keep his word and meet her? That he'd actually have a valid reason for abandoning them for ten years? She turned to go.

"Emma."

The gravelly voice was unfamiliar but had her spinning to face the speaker all the same. A cloaked form emerged out of the shadows of the trees and approached her. Wariness filled her. This man could be anyone, could even be someone who intended her harm. He drew nearer still, and she saw that he walked with a cane.

"Emma, 'tis so good to see you." His voice was nothing like her uncle's. His face was hidden by the hood of his cloak. She retreated a step, heart pounding.

"Who are you? Show your face," she demanded.

"I fear my face will not convince you of my identity. It was badly damaged in the accident." He limped closer still, sending her nerves jumping.

"I don't believe you. In fact, I don't believe any of this." She turned to go. If he wouldn't even show her what he looked like, then how could she listen to anything he had to say?

"No! Wait. Emma, I—I am asking you to listen. If I reveal my face, I fear you will refuse to do even that."

"Then prove your identity."

Silence greeted her request for so long that she thought him unable to confirm that he was indeed her uncle.

"When you were a young girl, you used to love my stories of ancient Greece."

Emma's heart squeezed at the memory, but she needed something more specific, more personal to believe him.

The man breathed heavily, as though it was difficult to do so. "One story in particular that you fancied was of Orpheus, the musician who traveled to the underworld to try to bring back his bride from the dead. I never understood why you liked that sad tale, but you said it gave you hope that no matter where you were, someone who loved you would try to find you."

A lump formed in her throat. How would anyone except her uncle know that? "So it is you," she whispered, still hardly able to believe it.

"Indeed, my child. It is."

"Why did you leave us?" Hurt warred with anger as she thought of how many times she'd been frightened because she didn't know where they would live or how she might earn money to feed them. And of how they'd nearly lost Tessa. But she didn't tell him that. He no longer had the right to know those kinds of details.

He shook his head. "I know I hurt you terribly, Emma, for the burden of taking care of our family fell on you. But in my heart, I knew you had the fortitude to prevail. And look at you." He raised a gloved hand to gesture toward her attire. "You've done far more than merely survive."

Tears welled in her eyes. She wanted to rip off her fancy gown so he could see her true essence. One filled with doubt and fear. One who'd been too tired and worried to crawl out of bed some mornings, but had managed it anyway. One who was still uncertain about what the future might bring. "I am nothing more than a fraud. This is all a mask. One more role I've taken on to aid my family. This is not me."

Her uncle tilted his head to the side as though pondering her words. "Truly? Or have you at last found your place in life?"

She shook her head. She didn't know who she was. The only time she'd felt right was when she was with Michael. But how could she allow that to be the case when he couldn't even tell her he loved her? Even that part of her life wasn't real.

"That is what I am trying to do, Emma. To find my place. I believe my life was saved to fulfill a higher purpose."

"What purpose? To aid strangers rather than

your own family?"

"If need be." He drew closer still, but she stepped back.

"Start at the beginning. What happened? Where did you go?"

He sighed heavily. "'Tis too long a story for the limited time we have. I can only say that your cousin, Vincent, retrieved my body from the coffin before the authorities hauled it away. My injuries were severe. It took weeks for me to become coherent enough to realize what was happening. By then, you'd thought you'd buried me and—"

"Who is in your grave?"

"Vincent replaced my body with another so no one would question an empty coffin."

Emma shook her head. "Again, I must ask why?"

"Because of the danger of the experiments I was conducting, we had discussed the chance of an accident happening. We had an agreement in place that allowed for various contingencies. If certain events occurred, I knew it would be best if I took on a new persona."

None of what he'd told her made any sense. Nor had he gained her sympathy. But then, perhaps that had not been his goal.

"It took me some time to regain the ability to function, then even longer to collect my research on electromagnetism. Luckily, Vincent saved some of it. As I studied it, I began to see where I had gone wrong, what I could do better."

"What do you intend to do with this electromagnetism?" While she'd read some information on the use of it, she had no idea what his purpose for it might be.

The chuckle coming from the hood echoed eerily in the night, reminding her that she had not seen this man for over ten years. She had to remember he was not truly her uncle anymore.

From what Michael had told her, he was a different man now. One capable of killing. That was very difficult to absorb. But she had to try to understand. For if she understood, perhaps she could convince him to stop this madness, to stop hurting others.

"I fear I cannot share the details of my plan with you. Your heart is too soft to see the necessity of the end result."

"In other words, you believe the harm you're causing will be justified in the end." She didn't frame it as a question, for she could tell it was what he thought.

"I prefer to think of it as progress."

"How can you call killing innocent people 'progress'?"

"Please, Emma, you must understand." He stepped closer to reach out and take her arm, squeezing it tight. Painfully so. "This is not simply for my benefit. This is for all of England."

Fear crept down her spine, both from the tightness of his grip and the fervor in his voice.

"Release her." Michael's voice cut through the darkness, causing Emma to catch her breath.

"Weston. Delighted you could join us. I wondered when you might follow her out here. Do you have a *tendre* for my niece?"

"Release her." Michael stepped forward, anger in every line of his body, his voice quiet but deadly.

Her uncle continued to hold her tight. Michael did not even look at her. Pain seared through her. *Oh, dear Lord.* Had this been Michael's intent all along? To use her to capture her uncle? Her heart twisted at the thought.

Michael glanced at Emma to make certain she was unharmed. The sight of the professor holding her chilled him to the bone. While not completely surprised she had met her uncle without his knowledge, he was still disappointed. Obviously, she did not trust him enough to share this. That wounded him straight through his heart.

He desperately wanted to jerk Emma away from her uncle and take her somewhere safe. And never let her go. For the moment, he'd have to be satisfied with trying to put himself between her and Grisby.

"Release her," he demanded again.

Grisby dipped his head and did as he asked.

"I can hardly believe it." Michael shook his head, amazed at the sight of the professor standing before him. "You truly live."

"Indeed, but you already knew that," her uncle admonished. "Do not state the obvious, Michael."

"Forgive me, but I found it rather difficult to believe. You had no pulse when I last saw you. Nor much of a face either."

Michael heard Emma gasp at his words. While he hadn't meant to be cruel, he felt it had to be said.

The professor gestured toward the hood of his cloak. "True enough. I won't burden you with the result, but let us say most people find it less than appealing."

"Your appearance is not my concern. Your activities are." Michael studied him closely but could see no evidence of an aura. Whether the hood somehow obscured it or he simply couldn't read it, he wasn't sure. In this case, an aura wouldn't help. The man had to be stopped based on what they knew thus far.

"I'm pleased you broached that subject, for 'tis one I've wanted to discuss with you."

"Then you're willing to stop your experiments

on people?"

Again, that raspy chuckle sounded. His voice must've been damaged along with his face.

"Collateral damage is sometimes a necessary part of progress. You are forward thinking enough to realize that."

"Oh, my God," Emma exclaimed.

"Perhaps if you'd care to share your plan, we could then discuss whether it's worthy of such a high cost as someone's life."

"I would not only share it but ask for your help. It will be like old times to have us working together again. Is it true? Can you and Stephen see auras?"

Shocked, Michael said nothing. How had he come to know that? Deciding it might provide a method to keep him talking, he nodded. "Can you?"

"No. I fear that was not given to me. At times, it must be quite helpful. Lucas will soon return and then we can form our plan."

Michael stiffened at the mention of his friend. "I have to wonder at the coincidence of Lord Berkmond being murdered."

"Surely you know there are no coincidences in life."

Anger ripped through Michael. "You murdered Lord Berkmond with the sole purpose of forcing Lucas to return to England?"

Emma gasped at this news.

"He wasn't coming back on his own, now was he?" The hooded form shook his head. "You must think ahead, Michael."

"What is it you intend to do?" He couldn't begin to guess.

"I intend to restore power and dignity to the Empire. Our country has become weak over the last decade. We need to reestablish ourselves as the strongest country in the world."

"And how do you propose we do so?" While the professor had always been interested in national events, Michael had no idea the man had been so concerned over how England fared in the global view.

"We must have the most powerful weapon. One that will ensure no one questions us. With England so powerful, no one will dare to wage war against us. In the end, the world will know peace as it has never known before."

"By using electromagnetism as some sort of weapon?" Michael wanted to learn as much about the professor's plans as possible before he captured him.

"Of course. The power of such devices will win any war in which we become involved."

"How many people do you intend to kill at one time?" Emma asked, the derision in her voice clear.

Did the woman not realize the danger she was in? Michael was certain her uncle would not hesitate to hurt her in his quest. He already had by disappearing for the last decade. Michael frowned at her and motioned for her to step back, out of her uncle's reach, hoping she'd understand Michael's wish to keep her safe.

But no. She only glared at him in response.

"I would prefer no one had to die, but that is not always possible. Not in the real world. Sacrifices must be made for the greater good."

"Who are you to decide what the greater good is or who should be sacrificed?" she asked.

Michael wanted to tell Emma they needed to go along with her uncle so he could catch him unawares, but in her anger, she didn't look at Michael.

Again, that raspy chuckle sounded. "I have a vision that I would be happy to share with others, beginning with the two of you. Together, we can do tremendous things."

"Does your machine heal the sick? Does it provide food for those who have none? Will it build shelters that are warm and safe? Why don't you put your abilities to good use? Instead of worrying about England's power, you should assist those who live in this city." Her outrage caused her voice to tremble.

"Emma, you have always been such a practical sort. However, I cannot be burdened with such mundane matters."

Emma leaned forward, making Michael wonder if she intended to strike her uncle, or at least attempt to shake some sense into him. "We were starving. Tessa was sick. We had no safe place to sleep. How dare you call such things mundane!"

Michael's heart squeezed with sadness and guilt. Thank God the woman had been clever enough to survive and provide for her family. Her strength was amazing and currently visible in every line of her body. He gestured again for her to step back, wanting more than ever to keep her safe.

"Each individual sets their own destiny just as you have done," her uncle said. "Times of difficulty make us stronger. Look at you now."

Before Emma could launch herself at her uncle, Michael placed his hand on her arm. "Let us ask Emma to find Ashbury. Then he and I can discuss this with you." More than anything, he wanted Emma away from here and out of danger so he could capture Grisby. The man had to be stopped.

"Emma cannot leave us. She may be my niece, but I don't believe she sees the wisdom of my plan quite yet. Is that right, my dear?"

"No, I can't say that I do."

Michael eased forward, trying to place himself

between Emma and her uncle.

"Come no closer, Michael." The professor stepped back to withdraw a pistol from the depths of his cloak. Michael stilled. "You must earn my trust."

"Uncle, no!" Emma cried out.

"How can I when you haven't yet told me of your plan in full?" The professor wielding a weapon was not something he'd planned on, especially not when its aim switched between him and Emma. The thought of her being hurt stole his breath. He moved in front of her despite her protest. "Let her go, and we'll discuss this."

"No. I—"

Michael lunged forward, needing no further urging to bring this to an end before Emma was hurt. He shifted forward and quickly raised his hand, hoping to jar the professor's grip on the pistol.

Boom! The shot cut through the night air.

"No!" Emma's cry came from beside him.

He glanced toward her, praying she hadn't been struck. Her eyes were wide with horror as she stared at him, and he feared the worst. Then a searing pain tore through his upper arm. He looked down in surprise. The tear in his jacket marked the burning pain. "Christ."

"Michael!" Emma cried. She rushed closer, putting herself in more danger.

"Stay back." He turned to see what the professor was doing, whether he carried another pistol, but where he'd stood was nothing but smoke from the gun. "Where did he go?"

"Weston?" Ashbury's voice rang out. "What in hell is going on out here? I heard a shot."

Unwilling to leave Emma unprotected, he called out, "Come quickly. The professor was here."

Ashbury rushed toward them and caught sight

of Michael's bleeding arm. "He shot you?"

"'Tis only a flesh wound. Let us see if we can find him. He can't have gone far."

Ashbury was out of sight before Michael could say another word.

"Do you have a handkerchief?" she asked. "We need something with which to bind this wound."

He handed her the thin white linen from his pocket, and she quickly bound his arm. "Will you be all right if I assist Ashbury in the search?" he asked.

"Yes, of course."

There was something closed off in her expression. He could see it in the set of her lips, in the way she avoided looking him in the eye. That worried him far more than his wound. He wanted to discover the cause, but first he needed to search for the professor. They couldn't lose him when he'd been so close.

"Wait inside with your mother for me, will you? I want you to stay safe."

"My mother!" Eyes wide with fear, she gave him a brief nod and hurried toward the door to the ballroom.

The moment she left, his arm burned like hell. Ignoring the sensation, he moved into the darkness of the garden, searching for hiding spots as he went. In truth, it was an impossible task. The shadows were deep, the bushes and trees many. The garden held more twists and turns than any garden should.

He heard a muffled sound a short distance away and held still, hoping he'd found their quarry.

"Weston?"

Ashbury's whispered voice had him sighing in frustration. "Aye. No luck?"

"None, but it's impossible to find anything in this place."

"The Sampsons are quite regarded for their extensive gardens."

"Just our luck."

"The man walks with a limp. How far can he have gone?"

The clip clop of hooves and the angry call of a driver had them rushing toward the street to see a hackney fading out of sight.

"Damn," Ashbury said. "What did he say? Was it truly him?"

Michael shared all he'd heard but suggested they speak with Emma. "She may know more. I'm not certain how long she was out here with him by herself."

"Why was she meeting him alone?"

Michael's heart squeezed at the reminder. To think he had yet to win her trust made him doubt whether she truly loved him. "That is an excellent question and one I intend to ask."

CHAPTER TWENTY-TWO

Emma returned to the ballroom, intent on finding her mother and the viscountess. Relief filled her at the sight of them unharmed. Luckily, very few people seemed to have heard the gun shot or if they had, hadn't realized what it was.

"Emma, whatever is the matter?" her mother asked after one look at her.

"What is it?" Abigail hooked her arm though Emma's in a show of support.

She couldn't help the tears that filled her eyes. Her worry over Michael made it difficult to speak. "I'm afraid we must leave. Michael and Lord Ashbury await us outside." At least she hoped they did. "I'll explain everything once we have some privacy."

The viscountess patted her arm then turned to lead the way to the entrance, acting as though nothing was wrong. Emma followed with her mother and Abigail, dreading the news she'd have to share.

As they neared the entrance, a footman stepped forward to show them to their carriage. Michael and Lord Ashbury were there, but not her uncle. She looked in question to Michael who shook his head, indicating they hadn't caught him. The tightness around Michael's eyes told her how much pain he was in, but he waved away her concern.

As the carriage rumbled toward Viscountess Weston's, Emma shared the news of her uncle with her mother. It was a conversation that could not be had quickly. Her mother's shock was understandable. The viscountess knew some of the story, so she offered comfort to Emma's mother as well.

Her mother's tears made Emma want to cry as well. Seeing her uncle had been such a jolt. Thinking he might be alive was one thing but actually seeing him was another. Yet in many ways, he wasn't her uncle at all. His voice hadn't sounded quite right but it had been his words that disturbed her the most. He'd changed so much. Too much.

"You're quite certain?" her mother asked yet again. "There has to be some mistake."

"I thought the same, Mother."

Michael leaned forward to take her mother's hand with his uninjured one. "I'm terribly sorry you had to learn it this way. We had suspicions before but didn't feel we could share them until we confirmed it for ourselves."

Her mother's brown eyes were filled with tears as she stared at Michael. "I'm so sorry he shot you."

"Merely a flesh wound and you have nothing for which to apologize." Michael squeezed her hand. "I can only imagine how you must feel upon hearing all of this."

Emma's mind spun the question toward her own rolling emotions. Somehow, she didn't think Michael understood how she felt. Did he realize that doubt had once again taken hold? She couldn't help but wonder if his affection toward her had only been a part of his plan until he was able to lure out her uncle. Now that he had, would

he tell her the truth? That she was merely a pawn
in this game they played?

She felt him watching her but couldn't bring
herself to return his look, too frightened of what
she might see there. No wonder he hadn't been
able to tell her how he'd felt—because he only
held sympathy for her, nothing more. This would
be one more event in her life that she had to
attempt to survive. She only wished she hadn't
fallen for him so hard, for he'd captured her heart.

They gathered in the drawing room upon their
arrival at the viscountess's home. Lord Ashbury
and Abigail joined them as well. Viscountess
Weston insisted the housekeeper dress Michael's
wound. Soon after, they all took turns sharing
what they knew. Luckily, all the commotion didn't
seem to have woken Tessa or Patrick.

Emma moved to the side table to pour her
mother a glass of sherry and sensed Michael's
presence close beside her, the heat of his body
warming her.

"I don't know what's going on in that beautiful
mind of yours, but I would very much like to
know."

She closed her eyes as a wave of pain surged
through her. Then she berated herself. The man
had been shot while attempting to protect her,
and she couldn't be bothered to look at him? She
owed him her gratitude at the very least. She
would sort out his true purpose later, when she
was stronger. Swallowing hard, she opened her
eyes and turned to face him.

The intense look in his blue eyes was nothing
like she'd anticipated, and certainly nothing like
she'd ever seen before. Her breath caught in her
throat and her eyes filled with more tears at the
love she saw there. The hope that rose inside her
frightened her with its magnitude.

He took her hand in his. "Emma, I feared I

might lose you. When I saw that gun—" He shook his head as his voice trembled. "I don't ever want to feel that way again."

"I can hardly believe he pointed it at either of us." She swallowed hard and tried to gather the courage to ask what was on her mind. Better that she know the truth now. "I must ask, did you—"

He put his finger on her lips before she could say more. "Wait, please. There's something I've been wanting to do all evening." Despite his injury and ignoring the others standing nearby, he drew her into his arms and kissed her deeply, passionately.

The room spun until there was no one but him. Only Michael. Her heart leapt, filling with love and something more than merely hope.

"Michael!" His grandmother's voice cut through the fog surrounding Emma, reminding her of their audience. "You forget yourself."

"Bravo, Weston," Lord Ashbury called out.

Emma pulled back, her cheeks warm with embarrassment.

But Michael didn't release her. Instead, he shifted them to face the others in the room. "Emma?"

Her heart pounded as she looked up at him, uncertain what he intended. Surely he of all people wouldn't make a public display.

"I love you with all my heart. Will you be my wife?"

Shock rooted her to the spot for a brief moment. Then joy took over. "Yes!" She flung herself into his arms, all doubts erased as to whether he cared for her, whether she truly belonged here. Now she knew the truth—she belonged in his arms.

He held her tight and kissed her, ignoring the gasps of the people in the room. Then they were surrounded. Everyone congratulated them between hugs and kisses and pats on the back. Through all of the chaos of the moment, Michael held tight to her hand, refusing to release her.

"Emma." Her mother's soft spoken voice caught Emma's full attention. "I don't have to ask whether this makes you happy."

Emma glanced at Michael, her heart soaring with joy before she looked back at her mother. "I've never been so happy, Mother."

"Then I'm happy too." Her mother hugged her tight and kissed her cheek then did the same to Michael. "So very pleased for both of you."

"Wishes do come true," Viscountess Weston said as she beamed. "I couldn't think of a better match for either of you."

"A toast to the happy couple," Lord Ashbury declared. He assisted in acquiring a drink for everyone and then raised his glass. "To Weston and Miss Grisby! To a life filled with joy."

Everyone raised their glasses high and cheered before drinking.

Still Michael held her hand. That link to him, as simple as it was, strengthened their connection until she felt it in every cell of her body. Again, he pulled her close and kissed her. "I love you," he said softly.

"And I love you." She rose up and kissed him.

Much later, Michael tapped softly at Emma's door, hoping to find her awake. He couldn't stand to leave her until he was certain that doubt no longer lingered in her eyes, until he had one last kiss.

Until he could reassure himself that she was his in truth forever.

"Come in."

With a smile, he opened the door to find her propped up in bed clad in a thin nightgown, her long dark hair unbound, a book on her lap.

After locking the door behind him, he paused, drinking in the delicious sight of her. Joy radiated from her face, reassuring him that all was well. Her aura was bright and made him wonder what was on her mind.

"I was hoping you might stop by." She crooked her finger at him to come forward. Her confidence delighted him.

His body hardened as he moved toward her to sit on the edge of the bed. "I didn't want to leave until we had a moment to ourselves. Until I knew you were truly well." He leaned forward to press a kiss upon her lips. "Until I had one more of those."

She smiled and bit her bottom lip. "I would prefer more than just a kiss, but we can start there. If you're feeling well enough, that is." She glanced in question at his arm.

"I am, thank you." The pain of his injury was the last thing on his mind. With a catch of his breath at the knowledge that soon she would be his forever, he bent to comply, allowing his passion for this woman free rein at last. Her lips were soft and warm and so sweet, her tongue moving with his. How had he ever believed that his desire for her could be anything but beautiful?

"Emma," he drew back to look into her luminous brown eyes, "I love you so very much."

"I love you so very much." His words cast back at him created a golden glow inside him, one he hoped never died. The joy in her eyes heated, lighting an answering flame deep inside him. "It's quite warm in here, don't you think?" She slid his jacket off his shoulders carefully not to jostle his arm, then began to undo his shirt.

"Indeed it is." As quickly as possible, he shed his clothes and joined her in the bed wearing nothing but his bandage. Desire pulsed hot and strong within him, but he held back, wanting to take his time and savor every inch of her soft form.

She slid down onto the bed and looped her arms around him, running those fingers along his shoulders and in his hair, making him growl with pleasure. Her lips met his as her hands danced along his burning flesh.

He wanted to tell her to slow down but couldn't find the will to do so. Instead, he moved his hands along her warm body, lingering on her curves, kneading her breasts, then easing up her nightgown so he could caress the length of her.

"Oh, Michael!" Her soft cry pulsed through him, making him heavy with need.

Then she sat up and knelt before him to remove her nightgown. Her naked body took his breath. He couldn't wait to explore every inch of her. Her gaze caught his and the feminine power he saw there made him tremble. She bent over him, kissing his cheek, his brow, his neck. Her hand trailed a path down his body that her lips followed, first to his rock hard nipple, then lower still to his belly button. He couldn't breathe, couldn't think. When she went lower still, pressing her lips to his manhood, he nearly came off the bed. "Christ, Emma. No more."

Unable to withstand her caresses, he reached for her hands to draw her up and over him as he kissed her deeply. She continued to move as though she liked the feel of his body against hers. The motion made him clench his teeth as he tried to hold on.

She shifted to sit astride him. "Oh, my." Her eyes widened with wonder at the position.

"I need you. Now," he demanded, prepared to beg if need be.

"Yes, now." She swayed her hips, caressing him

as if she were some exotic dancer from the Far East. After only a few moments of that torture, he knew his time was limited. There was only one position he wanted to be in when that happened. He lifted her and moved his erection to her very center. Again, she took over, allowing him to touch her soft moist folds as she eased down over him.

"Oh, Michael!"

"Yes, my sweet. Tell me."

"So good," she murmured as she resumed her dance, moving and swaying her hips, pulling and tugging at his body until he could bear it no more. Her soft cries followed his as she arched back with her release.

The warm glow wrapped around his heart as Emma collapsed over him, sliding her legs down to tangle with his. Her quick kisses over his chest brought a lump in his throat. Never would he doubt her love for him. Never would he allow her to doubt his love for her. He cupped her chin to kiss her deeply, fervently, before at last drawing back to look at her. "You are such a gift to me. One I don't deserve. But I will be the best husband you could ever have. I love you, Emma."

She smiled as she shook her head. "I don't understand why you would care for me, let alone love me. But I will be the best wife you could ever have." She placed a chaste kiss on each of his cheeks, then one last one on his lips. "I love you, Michael. I think love this glorious, this right, will bring us joy our entire lives. Forever and always."

"I cannot wait to have you with me always. I would like to apply for a special license so we might be married as soon as possible."

"Yes!" Joy swept over her expression again.

"Your family will live with us unless you'd rather I find them a home nearby?"

"You are the most perfect man on the face of

this earth. I'm certain of it." Tears filled her eyes. "It means so much to me that you care for them as well. Shall we ask Mother what she would prefer?"

"Yes, of course. Perhaps she and Tessa should journey to Switzerland? I've gathered information on a sanatorium there that specializes in patients with consumption. A few weeks spent there might improve your sister's recovery."

"Your generosity is apparently endless," she said with a laugh. "Tessa would love to travel and Mother as well."

"Excellent. Patrick will have the option of accompanying them if he'd like."

"That might be the perfect way to keep him safe until all of this..." Her expression darkened at the mention of all that still remained unsettled. "This situation is resolved, and my uncle is stopped."

He tucked a strand of hair behind her ear. "We will find him and stop him before he hurts anyone else. But you must promise me to never take such a risk as you did by meeting alone with him. No more secrets between us."

She kissed the palm of his hand. "No secrets. I promise not to take risks if you promise to do the same." She gently touched his bandaged arm as she held his gaze.

"I will do my utmost to stay alive. You see, I have much to live for."

Emma smiled. "We both have so much to live for. Forever and always." Then she kissed him again. And again.

Vincent eyed his uncle's scarred face as he tipped back his drink. "I take it the evening did not go according to plan."

Uncle Grisby shook his head as he held out his glass to Vincent for a refill of the nasty green absinthe he preferred. "No, it did not."

Vincent had been waiting with the carriage on the street closest to the garden. His uncle hadn't wanted Vincent to accompany him so as to keep his survival a secret. Vincent had agreed, for he had no desire to return to prison. Being dead was the best way to accomplish that. His uncle had limped toward him after exiting a side gate they'd found earlier in the day. It had been a simple matter for Vincent to break the lock that had sealed it shut so his uncle could have a quick escape route should the need arise.

And obviously, the need had arisen. Vincent had barely shoved his uncle inside the hackney and clamored atop the thing to flick the reins when shouts could be heard down the street. The horses had jolted forward which had probably sent his uncle to the floor, but that couldn't be helped. Vincent hadn't felt the least bit guilty when his uncle had alighted from the carriage with his limp much more pronounced.

"Ye didn't kill Weston?"

"Nay, nothing life threatening. But now he will take me seriously. He needed to understand what I am willing to risk to see this through."

Vincent frowned. He already knew his own life would be forfeit if his uncle thought it would aid him. If he wanted to live, he needed to leave soon, but not before he got his hands on some of the money his uncle had squirreled away. He just needed to figure out where the blasted man had stashed it. He refilled his own glass as he watched his uncle drain his again. "So now what?"

His uncle closed his eyes for a brief moment. "I fear I have yet to convince either Emma or Weston of my plan. Somehow, I must try again. I need Weston, Ashbury and Berkmond together on my side as we progress. Their talents will be invaluable."

"Ye mean the aura bit?" The very idea of such an ability made Vincent shudder.

"Yes. If they can advise me who to trust and who still needs convincing, I will truly be invincible."

"If Ashbury sees good and evil, and Weston sees success and failure, what does Berkmond see?"

"I have no idea. But I look forward to finding out. My sources tell me he's already en route to England. I will not allow this evening's minor setback to sway me from my plan. Soon, all of England will realize my brilliance and thank me for my bold plan."

Vincent shivered. Funny how the terms brilliance and genius often mingled with crazed. God only knew what the coming weeks would bring.

THE END

OTHER BOOKS BY
LANA WILLIAMS

Unraveling Secrets

Book I of The Secret Trilogy

A Vow To Keep
Book I of The Vengeance Trilogy

Trust In Me
Book II of The Vengeance Trilogy

Believe In Me
Book III of The Vengeance Trilogy

If you liked this book, sign up to find out when
the next one is available:
www.lanawilliams.net/contactlana

If you enjoyed this story, please consider
writing a review!

ACKNOWLEDGEMENTS

For me, writing is not a solitary endeavor. I'm very blessed to have so many people on my team.

Brad, Brandon, and Jordan: love you always and forever.

Thank you with much gratitude to my amazing, talented critique partners: Michelle Major, Lani Joramo, and Robin Nolet, and to my beta readers, Linda Benning, Lauren Billing and Sarah Billing. I couldn't do it without your help!

THANK YOU

Thank you for reading Passionate Secrets! I hope you enjoyed Michael and Emma's story! If you'd like to know when my next book will be available, you're welcome to sign up for my email newsletter at:
www.lanawilliams.net/contactlana.html

Follow me on Facebook at **www.facebook.com/LanaWilliamsBooks** or on Twitter at **@LanaWilliams28**.

Reviews help authors tremendously and also help other readers find books, so please consider leaving a review.

The next book in this trilogy, **Shattered Secrets**, will be coming in 2015. The first book, **Unraveling Secrets**, is available now.

More historical romances are in the works! Stay tuned, and thanks again!